THE SUM OF

ONE MAN'S PLEASURE

The

Sum

of

One
Man's
Pleasure

a novel

Danial Neil

NEWEST PRESS

Library and Archives Canada Cataloguing in Publication
Title: The sum of one man's pleasure / Danial Neil.
Names: Neil, Danial, 1954- author.
Identifiers: Canadiana (print) 20230150985 | Canadiana (ebook) 20230150993 | ISBN 9781774390788 (softcover) | ISBN 9781774390795 (EPUB)
Classification: LCC PS8627.E48 S86 2023 | DDC C813/.6—dc23

NeWest Press acknowledges that the land on which we operate is Treaty 6 territory and a traditional meeting ground and home for many Indigenous Peoples, including Cree, Saulteaux, Niitsitapi (Blackfoot), Métis, and Nakota Sioux.

Editor for the Press: Leslie Vermeer
Cover and interior design: Michel Vrana
Cover image: Man and Woman Embracing, Günther Krampf, getty.edu;
    Electropsychometer, Model E-AR-40, Mark Mauno, flickr.com; Flowers,
    MarinaVorontsova, iStockphoto.com
Author photo: Danial Neil

NeWest Press acknowledges the support of the Canada Council for the Arts, the Alberta Foundation for the Arts, and the Edmonton Arts Council for support of our publishing program. We acknowledge the financial support of the Government of Canada through the Canada Book Fund for our publishing activities.

NeWest Press
#201, 8540-109 Street
Edmonton, Alberta T6G 1E6
NeWEST PRESS   www.newestpress.com

No bison were harmed in the making of this book.

Printed and bound in Canada

1 2 3 4 5   23 22 21

for my wife, Kathy Jameson-Neil

I came to the conclusion that there is an existential moment in your life when you must decide to speak for yourself; nobody else can speak for you.

— Martin Luther King, Jr.

1

They told me that they had been watching me. An odd thing to say to an employee of the federal government of Canada. I thought perhaps it was part of a performance review. It was not unheard of in Ottawa in 1958. But there were rumours, chilling accounts of similar revelations. I was working on foreign trade, lumber exports to the United States and overseas. I was highly educated with a degree in forest management and silviculture. I was told that two men were waiting to see me in the lobby of our office block. They didn't say who or why, but that it was a serious matter, that I should attend at once, and that there was nothing to fear. Perhaps, I thought, it was one of the Americans that I had met with over softwood lumber. Meetings had been going on all week. Or perhaps it was the businessman from B.C. who was looking for new markets, new opportunities. I got on quite well with him. But I was afraid. It was a feeling I had. There was something malicious on the wind that was rushing down the city streets. And it had the face of the trusted.

I stood at the back as the early November snow fell heavily over the mourners. They huddled in their woollen coats and hats, solemn with their leaking noses and red-rimmed eyes. Some wore poppies pinned to their chests. They remained stoic, statue-like in the cold, and in good numbers considering the weather. There were immediate family and local people, of course, and there were business types, a few government representatives, and others who didn't seem to fit my assumptions. The snow settled over the casket and the shovelled earth and clung to the branches and limbs of the oaks and maples that stood in their perfect cemetery rows. Out on Fawn Hill Road, it fastened to the telephone lines, their sagging bellies dipping dangerously between poles until the snow, loosened by its own weight, fell in long lines to the ground. Nothing moved other than the relentless snow. Even the jaunty crows were absent in their numbers and taunts. There was no sound. Not even Reverend Le Fleur could offer an encouraging word against the muted pall of it as he held aloft an umbrella to shelter a selected few like mice under a toadstool. I had gained certain powers of observation, a keen eye that comes when you lose trust in the world.

Some would have said that the snow was beautiful, the lattice-work in the trees and shrubbery, a blessing for Fawn Hill's favourite son. Theodore Spencer—Teddy to his devout friends—would have quite liked such a day. And I was certain that the gods, if there were such a thing, and he had believed so, had a fitting part in all the loveliness of snow. Not so Katherine, the Lady of Spencerwood. Her misery was understandable, of course. She began to sway ever so slightly, a tall woman standing ahead of everyone else where she quite liked to be, up front for the world to take notice. Her two daughters stood just behind her as if in servitude. I considered that perhaps she was merely impatient to get it over with, only wanting to get out of the cold. I couldn't blame her for that. I was soaked to the skin in my knobby tweed, my only real suit of clothes fitting for the occasion.

But I would endure it for Ted, what I had called him in order to separate myself from the others. We had become good friends over the years, so much in common between the estate forester and the Lumber King of Vancouver Island. And truth be known, I had felt Lady Spencer's resentment over our relationship. It had always troubled me, put me on edge. I knew that one day soon she would summon me and confirm my musings. She wouldn't tolerate my sentiments, my very personal grief. I was the estate *gardener* to her, after all, only recently elevated to driver and everything else she thought fitting for the hired help. But I should rephrase my perceptions, to be fair to her. I didn't know her that well, only what she showed the world. She was a lake's stormy surface, and I had no desire to understand her or what went on in her cold depths. It was a most frightening prospect.

When the service concluded there was only a brief show of condolences to the grieving Lady Spencer and the girls, quick smiles and a few comforting words, and always a hand on the shoulder, or the arm, as if to help them brace against life's darkest hour. Excuse my cynicism. I don't mean to be uncaring, unsympathetic, but I suppose I found myself on insecure ground for the first time since I came to Spencerwood five years before. And besides, there was a reception at the manor. There would be plenty of time to receive the affections of Fawn Hill and those who came from around the country to show their respects to Teddy.

As the crowd dispersed and the men hurried to clear their snow-humped cars, she pointed to my momentary neglect, all the while shaking her head in disappointment. It seemed to me like the rebuke between a mother and her naughty child. And how strange her glower with the snow in her eyes, as if I had orchestrated such an inconvenience out of meanness.

"Mr. Kenny," she said with a certain emphasis, "you hadn't thought to bring an umbrella. So now you'll have me wait in this dreadful snow?"

How foolish I felt. I was so convinced that I needed to personally escort her that I didn't think to ready the car. Broom off the snow. Warm it for her and her daughters. As the snowflakes melted on her cheeks, I struggled to look at her, into her pitiless green eyes. I was a tall man, and to meet her at the same altitude, as it were, was demoralizing in a way. She made me feel quite small, if that was even possible. "So sorry, Lady Spencer," I said. "I'll clear it right away. I was waiting for you. I thought ..."

"I am not lame, Mr. Kenny. The car!" She pointed indignantly now.

Luckily for me, by the time we reached the parking lot, some considerate other had cleared her car of snow. I opened the door for her. The front door on the passenger side. Another error, it seemed. She stood and looked at me, the snow matting her flaxen hair like beaten grass. It seemed an egregious mistake, but more an insult. I had no intention to offend her. I had forgotten. I opened the rear door for her. She got in and then the daughters behind her. I felt hot in my drenched coat, so miserably damp. My face burned as well, scorched a bright pink, I was sure. I wondered how unlikely it was that I would remain at Spencerwood. I was an arborist. I knew nothing of protocols. Everything in my life had changed the moment Ted's heart gave out.

The leaves had been falling over Spencerwood that day. Sudden yellow and crimson releases, perhaps urged by the gusts of autumn, or it was just their time to let go. The sun was bright, and the colours were vivid and breathtaking. I watched from my cabin. He was walking with her along one of the many paths criss-crossing the twenty-acre estate, which housed the manor and two cabins as well as a woodlot. As always, I could see and even feel her animation from my window. She stopped often and made great dramatic gesticulations with her arms. She was an accomplished painter and well known. I had to give her that. So perhaps she was painting a scene for him. But that would have been much too generous. Because it was during one of those theatrical moments that he suddenly faltered and crumpled to the ground like so many leaves. Something she had said? One more demand that he could not meet, perhaps. One more accusation. Oh, it all was so recent, so fresh in my mind. I played it over and over because he was far too young to die in such a way, clutching his chest as if his heart had shattered like glass.

Lady Spencer's car was a 1963 Cadillac Coupe de Ville. She had to have a new car every year, and yes, it seemed rather extravagant and pointless. I would overhear them at the post office, in the general store, Van Koll's Bakery, the Bramble Café, and even outside the Anglican church on those rare occasions when I attended Sunday service. It had become an expected event in Fawn Hill, the talk of the village. *What would the car be this year? What colour?* I was certain bets were made, cash exchanged, and all unbeknownst to her, and to Ted, of course. Oh, the carnival that she was, that they made of her behind her back.

It was a golden beast of a car, the front seat wide enough for the four of us. And it slid through the slush of Fawn Hill Road now with both my hands gripping the steering wheel like death. I drove slowly through the village with Lady Spencer chortling to her daughters behind me, telling them the virtues of dying in the summer.

"He did it to spite me," she said. "Look, I'm just a mess. What will *they* think?"

"Oh, Mother," Phillipa said, "don't be so melodramatic." She was the elder of the daughters and mildly reasonable.

"It's an awful day," Tiffany said in defence of her mother. "It would have been better on a sunny day. It really would have. You shouldn't be allowed to have a funeral on such a day. It's not right."

"You die when you die," Phillipa pointed out. "Isn't that right, Finn?"

I wasn't prepared to be a part of their conversation. I had no desire to engage them, so I settled for neutral ground. "I suppose there's some truth in that."

"But in the winter, Phill?"

"It's early November, Tiff," Phillipa said. "Good God!"

"Well," their mother said, "your father truly died, and it's *truly* snowing. I hope that's winter enough for you, Phillipa. Look at it. And your father *was* spiteful at times, I want you to know. I can say that much."

I looked in the rear-view mirror. I wanted to see the looks on their faces. How seemingly intelligent people could have such a conversation after leaving the graveside of a husband, a father. It made it all feel more tragic, and astonishing really. They lit their cigarettes and the smoke swirled about their soggy heads. The girls had been away at university. Phillipa was studying law, and Tiffany was in her first year of English literature. They would be staying at Spencerwood for the weekend. I wanted to retreat to my cabin. I didn't want to have to listen to them anymore. And then I wondered what Ted would have said if he could have heard them. Of, course, he had heard it all before but never so brazenly. Where was his good influence now? He had a way to bring out the best in people. Even Lady Spencer with her incessant self-absorption knew the reach of his benevolence. It brought people to Spencerwood, and yes, to her.

It was just a short drive from the village, down Fawn Lily Lane, and soon we passed through the black-iron gates with the word *Spencerwood* spanned and parting, and then down the curving driveway. The snow had let up and the sky brightened. The manor rooftop was covered in snow. It was a handsome Tudor design, and it glistened splendidly in the sun like a three-storey gingerbread house. There were cars parked out front and cars coming from behind. Then Lady Spencer leaned forward to speak to me. I knew what she was about to say. I had seen it, too.

"There's no smoke in the chimneys, Mr. Kenny," she said. "You will help Mr. Bishop with the fires. The oil furnace won't be enough. I don't want a chill in the house. It all should have been done before the service. The reception will be ruined if there's a chill. This is for Teddy, you know. He liked a good fire. The fires should have been lit. Mr. Bishop tries his best, but you know him. Mrs. Bishop is the worker. *He's* a bit of a know-it-all, and getting old, you know." She paused before continuing. "They're an odd couple really. I wonder, sometimes, if they should be with their own people."

"They've been with Spencerwood for a long time," I said, always surprised by her comments. "Ted adored them both."

"Don't start with me, Mr. Kenny!" She rapped her hand on the back of my seat and then sat back. "And for goodness' sake," she went on, "I was speaking of their age. Perhaps they would be better off with their daughter. That's what I meant. Don't put words in my mouth. Spencerwood is not the same now, is it?"

"Yes, Lady Spencer," I said. Her words were like an abrasion, a kind of grinding down of one's sensibilities. I had seen her pistol-whip some good people, all who occupied a low position on her self-made pyramid of life. In the rear-view mirror, I caught something cruel in her eyes. I wondered what would be unleashed at Spencerwood now.

"And I think I will drive myself from now on," she said. "I think it might be too much car for you, Mr. Kenny."

That suited me just fine as I parked the car in the garage behind the manor. They vacated the car as if it were on fire. The doors flung open. It was a strange sight to be sure, to witness the raw side of them, the running mascara and wilted hair and how they fought to be first through the back door. There would be another dash to the bathroom to make themselves presentable. There was nothing low key about the family. Ted had offered a certain balance, his steadiness of bearing. It was his integrity that always shone through. When the light of it touched you, you became more for a brief moment. It was not a tangible thing, only that you wanted to be around him. You wanted a piece of whatever it was that he possessed. And now it dawned on me like an epiphany. What would Lady Spencer do without him? I had overheard it said that she would take over the business. I could not imagine such an abrupt change in the affairs of Spencer Industries. She had no business sense. In fact, she had no sense at all. She knew only her own grandiosity. I realized that I was stalling.

I got out of the car and closed the rear doors. I hesitated once again. I knew that going through the back door would mean that I would be imprisoned by the will and wants of Spencerwood until late into the evening. I looked beyond the gardens and snowy lawn to the cabins. They were separated by a stand of cedar and shore pines, the Bishops' cabin being closer to the manor. It was referred to as the Cottage. My cabin would be cold, I knew, the fire long extinguished. But perhaps the coals would still be hot. I could slip away and add a few small pieces of pitchy spruce. Just to keep it alive. But then all at once I was startled by the sound of someone clearing their throat. I turned. It was Bishop. He found me idle as a cat.

"Finn," he said, "I need you in here, sir. I surely do. Birdie is way behind. She can't keep up while I'm tending the fires!"

"All right, Bishop," I said, "don't panic. I'm coming."

"I'm beyond panic, dear sir. There are sandwiches and baking to put out. And the tea in that big pot. Now the big fireplace is fine. But the fireplace in Mr. Spencer's study, that's the one. Lady Spencer was barking at me to get it lit. Rushing by me like the E&N train. You'll dry out that swampy jacket soon enough. Oh, there some very important people in there, Finn. Not many of the locals at all. Reverend Le Fleur, of course. Come on, get in here. Don't make me throw you over my shoulder!"

"You worry too much, Bishop," I said. A big man with a frosted cap of hair and a rather blunt sense of humour, he could have easily carried out his threat. A former schoolteacher, he always wore suits, black on that day, of course, and a black bow tie. I wouldn't say that he looked like a butler. That word had a certain stigma that I knew he detested. Manor Custodian was the formal title given to him by Ted, one Bishop took great pride in.

"I want to keep my job," he said, holding the door for me. "This is all we have. You're the one who should be worried."

"How so, Bishop?"

"For one, she doesn't like you much."

"Yeah, I think you're right about that. The way she looks at me at times."

"And I think you know why," Birdie said. She looked up from the counter of sandwiches as I walked into the kitchen.

"Hello, Birdie," I said. "I know you don't miss a thing, but ..."

"'But' nothing."

There was a certain look between us all, and the ground beneath my feet felt a bit more unsteady just then. Something they knew. I had seen it in their dark eyes. There was a part of me that wanted to quit right there, spare Lady Spencer the trouble of my dismissal, and my humiliation. But where would I go? I thought I had found sanctuary at last at Spencerwood, something, someone to shelter me from the world. Oh, the shifting sand of me. And it seemed that the Bishops, dependable and loyal servants of Spencerwood, were in jeopardy of losing their jobs as well.

"The fire in the study, Finn," Bishop lamented.

"All right, Bishop." I saw the worry in his eyes. It felt truly different, all of Spencerwood, as if it had changed names, or years, or had even shifted its location on the earth. Something was amiss, and it wasn't just a death.

2

They were standing in the lobby with their hands folded before them, dressed in black suits and fedoras pulled down low so there was only shadow. Tall and lean-looking men, square jawed, without kindness or eyes. They moved toward me at once. I needed no introduction. They seemed to know me by appearance and addressed me formally.

"Mr. Kenny, come with us," one said.

He opened the lobby door, and the other man took my arm and guided me out rather brusquely. His hand was firm and implied that I had no choice in the matter, that I best go willingly. Out in the street, all seemed normal. It was spring and people rushed here and there, guided by their own urgency, their own volition. But I felt an acute loss of my will. It was stolen from me the moment they pushed me into the back seat of their waiting car.

I lit the fire in the study and felt the warmth return slowly to my damp body. The nut-brown leather chairs and Ted's oak desk, and the rich wainscoting along the walls, racks of books and mementos. It all was so like him, the warm tones of hardwood and the sporting guns above the mantle. It had a country club sort of feel, even the stale smell of his occasional cigar. A place for a man's sturdy reflection of what he wanted to show the world. I could hear the conversations from the living room. I wasn't eager to go in there, among the mourners and their polite acknowledgements. But I would, of course, out of respect, duty, and even with a little curiosity. There would surely be talk about Spencer Industries. How could she possibly fill Ted's shoes?

I tended to the fireplace in the living room and then retreated to the periphery. It was a rare moment to be there at all, among the well-heeled. I had heard, of course, Bishop speak of the extravagance. There was a formal richness to the room with its tapestries and fine furniture crafted in eastern Canada. A French country rustic décor. The ornate collection of pottery and china was certainly impressive. Paintings in antique gilt frames on a grand scale adorned the walls like lofty guests. Prime Minister Diefenbaker, the government-commissioned portrait that he didn't like. His scowl. Lady Spencer was to paint another, a more appealing statesman, although he had lost the recent election to the Liberals.

Her accomplishments could not be denied even by the most disproving of her critics. I suppose that would include me and not the distinguished men who stood around the Lady of the manor with their drinks and cigarettes, no doubt expressing their tributes with anecdotes of Ted, and all for her sole benefit, I was sure. She had changed into a more formal dress. A firm-fitting plum affair that made the men flatter her shamelessly and drew ambiguous looks from Reverend Le Fleur. No mourning black for her. She had fixed her hair and makeup and seemed to be enjoying herself—a bit too much for my liking. I could hear her gay laughter now and then, like small eruptions.

Phillipa and Tiffany sat on a couch. The manor cat sat between them. Darby O'Gill, yes, a peculiar name they each had thought fitting for an orange cat that had arrived a week after they saw the movie at the Fawn Hill Theatre. And beside them, the unwed twin Willett sisters who owned the Bramble Café in the village. There was not a word among them all, as if they spoke different languages, which may have been the case—generationally at least. There were few other notable mourners from Fawn Hill. Many who did come to the manor left quickly after offering condolences to the family. But Postmaster Mullins and his wife remained. They had always benefitted from the brisk business that Spencerwood brought to Fawn Hill, as had the proprietor of the general store, the glum but helpful Mr. Schmidt. And Mayor Greenacre, of course, always eager to hobnob, must have recognized that there would be no glad-handing on that day. They all looked on like bored spectators of some hackneyed play. I observed all of that as a man unnoticed until Bishop thrust a tray of drinks into my hands.

"Now don't take offence, Finn," he said, "but that's one shabby jacket you're wearing. I wouldn't let my dog lay on it."

"You don't have a dog, Bishop," I reminded him.

"That fact will not revive a worn-out garment."

"I'm not used to this, Bishop. This is not my area of expertise. I think I need a drink myself."

"Well, do as I do. I keep a glass in the kitchen. I'll put one there for you. On the windowsill that looks out over the garden. There's a bottle of Scotch in the cupboard below. That's the kind of friend I am. Go on, those fancy men know how to drink. No chit chat now."

"Thanks, Bishop," I said, "I appreciate the gesture. And I am offended, by the way."

"Go, on, Finn." He waved me away with his hand.

I tried desperately not to spill the drinks. Luckily Bishop had not overfilled the glasses, and when I approached, they all turned to me as if *I* mattered—Ted's good friend Finn Kenny. But they made no eye contact with me, no acknowledgement at all. They simply deposited their empty glasses and took a full one. Not even Lady Spencer seemed be aware of me. I felt so shut out of it all, as if I had no feelings, had no right to them. Only *they* mattered, men of standing, men of influence. And one I recognized from a photograph I had seen in Ted's study. A barrel-chested man with oil-slicked hair and a fine moustache. He had a certain Hollywood appeal in person, a tycoon-look about him. But I quickly felt ambivalence toward him. Did he truly know Ted?

He was the director of operations, Leopold Fitz, Ted's right-hand man, so to speak. He ran the head office in Victoria where Ted visited once a week to attend the meeting of his managers. Ted had entrusted to him all aspects of his businesses, gave him a certain latitude—as long as he adhered to the basic principles of Ted's success, of course. It was Ted's credo. *Good people create good institutions.* It was a rather democratic approach to business. He had adopted that same principle from his father, a successful distiller in Vancouver.

Before the war Ted had received an inheritance from his father's estate. He wasn't interested in spirits, so took a chance on a dream. He had always been impressed with the forested mountains that posed an enduring backdrop to Vancouver. How trees seemed to be of infinite supply over the entire province. He bought a small sawmill on Vancouver Island. Business boomed, much to his surprise, so he acquired timber licences, logged his allotted tracts of forest, and then processed the timber. It wasn't long before he had made a name for himself.

For a time, he lived alone in a modest apartment in Nanaimo, but he soon began to feel a certain societal pressure. An unmarried businessman just wouldn't do in his ever-expanding social circle. So it was in that city where he met a local portrait artist at a function hosted by the Chamber of Commerce. As he once confessed to me, he was intrigued by her personality, how she seemed to capture the room, seized the attention of everyone in it. Katherine was so different from other women, he continued, so very alive, and possessed an intoxicating energy. She was someone who could share his own dreams, someone to fit the bill, as it were. And soon after a brief courtship, they were married. It wasn't long before the arrival of Phillipa, and then Tiffany.

During the war, he bought sawmills from operators who hadn't been able to keep up production due to labour shortages. He banked on an urgent demand for plywood and lumber once the war ended. And when it arrived, he invested in expansion and quickly made the business prosper. He was an effective government lobbyist, federally and provincially, and not so by guile or pretence but by his good nature. He went on to purchase property in Fawn Hill. He was drawn to the pastoral woods, the rolling landscape, its proximity to Victoria. He built Spencerwood modelled after the same Tudor design of his childhood home in the Point Grey neighbourhood of Vancouver. He raised a family, and Spencerwood became the heart and soul of the community, the pride of Fawn Hill. In twenty-five-years he had made his fortune only to be struck down by the very heart that carried his vision of fellowship and prosperity.

I doubted Leopold Fitz knew Ted the way I had known him. In fact, I was certain. But how could I know of this man—Leo, Lady Spencer called him—and he not know of me? Did Ted not speak of me? And yet I understood who I was and what I was to him. I understood it fully, but still it hurt me deeply, standing before the fervent gushing of affectations while I served up drinks—and my pride. And then at last, he looked at me directly, but it wasn't out of recognition of some reputed quality that I possessed.

"Good fellow," he said, "a match?" He held his cigarette aloft between his fingers.

The provincial Minister of Forests pulled out a book of matches, but I wanted something just then. I wanted the honour, so to speak, to show them who I was. I overcame a certain fear of mingling, of people. I managed to hold the tray of empty glasses with one hand and reached into my mouldy coat pocket with the other for my lighter. I took it out and raised it to him. It was a beautiful gold lighter with abalone inlays. A gift from Ted. I wanted Mr. Fitz to see it. I wanted him to wonder about me.

He leaned down to the flame and lit his cigarette. And then he seemed to pause and admire my lighter. And then he looked at my rather strangely, in a deep sort of way. It seemed that he was about to say something to me. So I took a chance.

"How are you, Mr. Fitz?" I said in a voice somewhat deeper than it actually was. "I'm sorry for your loss. Ted was a good man."

"Oh, yes," he said. Then he leaned toward me and whispered. "That lighter, I have one just like it back at the office. Was that a gift from ...?"

Then the tray just slipped from my hand. My whole body seemed to give way suddenly. The tray crashed onto the hardwood floor and glass shattered across the perfectly placed rugs in the perfect room. The sudden gasp rose up like an agreement at my clumsiness, my inelegance. Mortified, I got down on my hands and knees and began to pick up the glass. There is no feeling quite like it, when you have disrupted the honouring of a man you had admired. And now I was the focus of attention, not the kind I had wanted, but a spotlight of displeasure beaming down upon me. Then what I knew was coming loomed over me. Her displeasure, as it turned out, I had grossly underestimated.

"Mr. Kenny," she said, "what have you done? Get this mess cleaned up. This won't do at all!"

I dared not look up to her unforgiving face. Then she went on to amplify my error.

"Oh, please forgive me," she said to the gathering. "That is the last thing that I expected. I feel awful. You all have been so kind."

Her inflection dripped over them with sweetness, and then the sympathetic gestures, and how she lapped it all up so greedily. It didn't occur to me that I may have been jealous, that I was desperate for a different kind of attention, the kind I once had with Ted. It was all a mess. And it seemed my time at Spencerwood would truly come to a swift end, hard-hearted and abrupt. Then good old Bishop came to my rescue. He joined me on the floor with a broom and dustpan. Her nervous tittering once again.

"Hurry, the both of you," she said. "Good Lord, what a day!"

"It was my fault, Lady Spencer," Bishop said, out of turn, but for my benefit.

"Oh, it certainly was not, Mr. Bishop!"

It was a harsh reproach. She had dismissed me so easily. I didn't have to wonder whose reputation she was protecting. I bravely looked up at her. I wanted to see it on her face. I didn't know why, but I felt that I needed to see what her resentment looked like one more time. Perhaps it would make things easier when she let me go. Surely I would want to go, then. But it was not that at all, truth be told. I wanted her to see my regret, my contrition. You see, I had too much to lose. I wasn't a courageous man at all. And how tall she was standing there as our eyes met, but she turned away quickly, as if she had been waiting for it. Oh, her chilling calculation.

"We can continue our conversation in Teddy's study, gentlemen," she said to the others.

She moved them like a herder out of the living room. And as Reverend Le Fleur followed, he stopped and leaned into my ear.

"I haven't seen you at Sunday service in a while, Mr. Kenny," he said. "I hope you can regain your sense of balance. I know God can be a man's compass. Don't you agree?"

"You think that I am lost, then?" I said to him. But he walked away with his self-righteous smile and his hands clasped behind his back.

"He wants the best for you," Bishop said.

"How could he possibly know what's best for me?"

We cleaned up all the broken glass and retreated from the living room. I didn't want to go back into the study with her grieving spectacle. There were crustless sandwiches and tea to serve, but luckily Birdie had placed them on a sideboard in the dining room. There was only one thing that I wanted, and I found it waiting on the windowsill in the kitchen. I nearly drank it right down—and would have if the Scotch had not burned my throat terribly.

"Not so fast, Finn," Bishop said. "That's not the way one stills his rages. You need a certain recipe that lasts you all day long. Trust me. You will be no help at all. Now go and sit at the table. Just a little bit at a time. Sipping liquor is just that. You need to survive this, and not give her further cause. Do you understand?"

"Yeah, I think I do." I went to the table that was nestled in a nook in the bay window. Outside, the snow began to fall once again. Amid all that beauty, a dark mood had settled over Spencerwood.

"All right, then," Bishop said.

"How are *you* going to survive, Bishop?" I wanted to know.

"As we always have," Birdie said.

"That's the truth," Bishop said. He walked over to the table and sat with me. I offered him a cigarette and he took it.

"We no longer have Mr. Spencer as moderator," he went on, "but we know this place. We know what keeps it going, what keeps it functional. We will do our damn best for Spencerwood." I held up my lighter and he leaned over the table to light his cigarette, then whispered as he concluded. "Lady Spencer may think she can do it all on her own, but I believe she will soon see our worth. That's what I believe."

"Why did you give up teaching, Bishop? That was an honourable profession. Why Spencerwood?"

He seemed surprised by the question and looked to the window. The darkening day. We could see our own reflections in the window glass now.

"I suppose," he said finally, "for the same reason that brought you here, Finn."

I caught the look in his eyes, the knowing depth of them. And then I wondered about what he had said. *She will soon see our worth.* I had great doubts just then. There was no guarantee of that, no certainty in life. I'd heard it said that only the good die young.

And I knew that awful truth. We sat quietly and listened to the murmur of conversation down the hall. The party had moved to the dining room, and her voice climbed steadily above all others. And then I grew weary of it and couldn't listen any longer.

I looked around the kitchen. It was where Bishop and Birdie spent most of their time. It wasn't a bad place to be. It certainly was lovely when the morning light flooded the manor. It had all the modern conveniences, lemon-yellow fridge, stove and wall-mounted oven, forest-green Arborite counters and linoleum flooring, and copper pots in all sizes hanging from a rack in the ceiling like gleaming gamebirds. There were electric mixers of every description and use. A red wall-mounted telephone. It seemed to me that the Bishops rarely had a moment's rest, rarely a day off for themselves, so devoted they were to Spencerwood. I couldn't imagine losing them. I had become an astute observer, a keen witness to everything around me. Yes, I noticed things, always on guard, always looking over my shoulder. It had become my default position, my second nature, and it seemed that it would never change.

The afternoon wore on and I attended to my glass and poured the sanctuary that it offered down my throat. I filled my glass more than I should have. The mourners left one by one. Reverend Le Fleur was the last to leave, and then all was quiet. Birdie stood at the sink soaking dishes. We all looked toward the hallway, toward the silence. Not even the unmistakable pitch of Lady Spencer's voice.

"It seems they're all gone," I said.

"It's about time," Bishop lamented.

"Now you two can get to work," Birdie said. She dried her hands on her apron. "There are ashtrays to be emptied and dishes to be brought in. Percival, go on now."

"Please, call him Bishop," I implored.

"Go on, the both of you!"

"I think I might be a little drunk," I said. "Terribly sorry, Bishop."

"Well, isn't that convenient?" he said. "Glory be, I should have said something. You pour a terrible drink. What was your hurry? Didn't I tell you to take your time with your liquor?"

"It was good advice. I won't argue with you. But you must understand ..."

Phillipa came into the kitchen just then. She stopped and leaned against the door frame rather miserably. She folded her arms. "Mother's drunk," she said, "and she's asking for you, Finn. She's sitting at the dining room table."

"Are you sure she asked for me?"

"Well, let me just say, she's not asking," she said gravely. "She's not in a very good mood. You'd best go." Phillipa shook her head, then turned and left the kitchen.

Bishop reached across the table and took hold of my arm. "Now this is no time to vent your grievances, Finn," he warned. "The both of you drinking away the day. It's not what I would call optimal."

"Drinking can give me a rare temper, Bishop. It truly can."

"That's what I'm afraid of, Finn. Just listen to Lady Spencer. Give her your good ear and keep that Irish mouth of yours shut."

"I'm not feeling so good."

"Birdie will pour you some black coffee. It'll straighten out that head of yours. Now keep it simple, Finn. Do whatever Lady Spencer wants. I'm fearful of a man with a loose tongue. I'm fearful you'll make it easier for her to let you go. Be smart about it, and we'll *all* get through this rough patch."

I looked at him. His head nodded slightly, as if in agreement with some wiser entity that looked down benevolently over the kitchen. I didn't seem to have access to it, but Bishop had a way that could pick a man up off the mat no matter how many times he'd been knocked down. I often wished I had his courage, his sober courage. I had it once, but it was stripped from me as one guts a fish.

3

The car pulled out onto the street. I was alone in the back. I didn't know where they were taking me. I didn't know what I had done. I had heard rumours, that was all. And then I began to realize that perhaps it was all true. My throat was dry. I wanted to speak, but I couldn't. My heart was beating much too fast now. I had to know. They said nothing, no conversation between them. I could no longer stand it.

"What do you want from me?" I managed to say. I leaned forward. There was a thick folder on the seat between them. I got a brief look at it before the one in the passenger seat in front of me picked it up and hid it from my view. I recognized the insignia on the cover. A bolt of fear shoved me back in the seat. They were RCMP. *And then a swift look between them. The driver turned slightly to me.*

"Cooperation," he said.

"I don't understand. I don't ..."

"That's all," the other said.

I drank coffee until I thought I was going to gag. It didn't make me feel any better. Birdie was about to pour me another cup, but I put my hand up. "No more."

"You better go then, Finn," she said. "She doesn't like to be kept waiting."

"Pray for me, will you, Bishop?"

"It might not work for an atheist."

"I'm Catholic, I want you to know, at least until the burning of Cork in 1920 during the Irish War of Independence. My mother lost all faith in God after that. I don't know what I am now."

"I know what you are, and it's no excuse."

"Fine," I said.

Bishop took my arm and helped me to my feet. He guided me to the hallway, and then stopped and gathered my jacket lapels in his thick hands. He tried ineffectively to straighten my rumpled appearance. And then he looked earnestly into my bleary eyes, but he could only shake his head. His bottom lip came up rather ruefully.

"You are on your own, Finn," he said. "I hope you realize that fact. My prayers have no such powers to divert a man from his fate. You are blessed or you are damned. Now go."

I moved down the hallway on unsteady legs, shuffling my feet to remove the clap of them, but I was certain there was nothing I could do to conceal my approach. I didn't want to enter a room with her eyes immediately upon me. I would lose my faint courage or, God help me, even my restraint. There's was no telling what would happen. Such dread could sober a man or drive him to storm and seethe. I could hardly contain myself. I was surely about to be fired. And then the muted voice of Robert Goulet drifted up from the stereo console in the living room. I stopped, waited.

After a few minutes I crept up to the dining room. I leaned in slightly and was surprised to see her looking up at a portrait of Ted hanging on the rose-patterned wall. She sat at the splendid table on a blue velvet chair, one of five on each side. She wore a pink bathrobe, and her mascara and lipstick were still in place. There was something different about her. It wasn't the flamboyant contrast of colours. She was so uncharacteristically still, understated like something in repose, or perhaps simmering. I found it difficult to interrupt her. I dared not even clear my throat. I looked at her from the side, the profile seemingly of a stranger. Not a shrill of protest. It was if her personality had collapsed, had withdrawn from the world. Perhaps out of sheer fatigue. How easily I had forgotten that she had lost her husband. She had a drink in her hand and her fingers stroked it gently. And with her other hand, she held a cigarette aloft at her ear, her elbow resting on the table. The smoke swirled about her hair. I thought that I should back away, perhaps, leave it well enough alone. Leave it for the following day. She might reconsider my fortune after a night's rest. I would clean myself up, of course, and put my best foot forward. But I got momentarily carried away with my speculations and suddenly realized she had turned and was staring directly at me. The penetrating eyes of the she-wolf. The jolt of it nearly toppled me.

"Mr. Kenny. Please sit," she said in a rather listless way. She made a gesture to the chair opposite her.

I just stared at her for a moment, my feet unable to move. I didn't want to be that close to her. But then she frowned oddly, perhaps to encourage me to do something other than to stand like a mute fool. I had no choice but to sit across from her. In unnerving full view. Oh, the shocking power the woman had over me. I folded my hands on the table and waited. She wouldn't look at me now, so close we were. She butted out her cigarette in a crystal ashtray and then opened her pack of du Maurier cigarettes—a strange celebrity association. She removed a cigarette while the other was still smouldering from crumpled black ash. Some ritualistic device to gain my compliance, I was sure. There was a slight bend to the room when my eyes made their furtive foray. I closed them briefly, hoping the world had stabilized.

"Leo thinks I can do it, Mr. Kenny. Me, the president of Spencer Industries. It sounds kind of grand, don't you think?"

I nodded in absence of an intelligent answer. It seemed too absurd to warrant one.

"Can I have a light from your lighter, Mr. Kenny?" she asked.

She had placed her cigarette between her lips. Her eyes seemed to say *I know you have one.* I knew what she was up to now. There was a pack of matches on the table beside the ashtray. I reached into my coat pocket and felt the lighter with my fingers. I realized just then that I needn't remove it at all. In fact, I may have misplaced it. But the game she seemed to be playing made me curious. And yes, as Bishop had so frankly assured me, I was blessed or damned. If I was to be canned, as they say, I thought that I might as well go out with what remained of my self-respect, and with a certain mischief. I removed the lighter and struck the flint and held it out to her. She drew on the flame and then sat back with her arms crossed at her chest.

"Let me see that," she said.

"Oh, it's nothing," I said.

"Are you hiding it from me, Mr. Kenny?" She shot out her hand, the long fingers slender and as pale as candles.

"Not at all," I said. I grudgingly handed it to her and at once she began to study it, turning it over with some familiarity.

"Teddy bought two lighters just like this one when we were in San Francisco. Last spring, it was. One went to Leo Fitz. It was a birthday gift. So how is it that you have the other one, Mr. Kenny?"

There were several answers that I could have given her, some perhaps she would not have believed or accepted. So I gave her the one she could manage. "I too had a birthday, Lady Spencer."

"Why would Teddy buy you a gift?"

"Why would he not?"

"Don't get cute with me, Mr. Kenny."

"I am not trying to be, Lady Spencer. I was his friend. It was a thoughtful gesture. I will treasure it always. He sought my advice on a broad range of matters. I had some knowledge of the forests. At times one needs another point of view, or perspective, as it were."

"You seem to be inflating your contribution, don't you think?"

"No, I don't believe that I am, Lady Spencer."

"You were the Spencerwood gardener, Mr. Kenny, and yet you claim friendship."

She spoke in the past tense. She had made up her hand, it seemed, and was intent on making it all as unpleasant as possible. She took great pleasure in demeaning me, reducing me to nothing at all. And then all at once, I could feel *it* rising. Always frightening. And then it just came out.

"I don't need to defend my friendship with Ted, Lady Spencer," I said. "I really don't!"

"What could you have possibly offered him that I could not, Mr. Kenny? *I* was his friend, and confidante, I might add. If all this is true, then surely he would have told me. He never once mentioned *your* alleged friendship. And he never told me that the other lighter was for you, the gardener. What game are you playing at, Mr. Kenny?"

She was clearly upset that Ted had not told her about the gift. She didn't like to be left out. I knew that much. But she seemed to be implying that I stole it, that it wasn't a gift at all, that I wasn't worthy enough to have earned it.

"I have no desire to defend what I know to be true," I said, my voice thickening with animosity. It was time to leave.

"You are on very thin ice, as they say, Mr. Kenny," she said. And then she scolded, "You don't seem to comprehend the position you are in. I find your tone offensive. I don't really know you. Gardeners should be seen and not heard. Yes, like children. I don't accept your explanation. I do not!"

The rising turned into the risen. My face suddenly felt afire, and I leaned forward to scorch her. "You can do whatever the hell you want," I asserted. "I don't bloody well care anymore. But there's one thing you cannot have, and that's my friendship with Ted. That memory belongs to me. You can go to hell!"

"You're a bloody hot-headed Irishman, now, aren't you? Just like that actor I was reading about in a magazine. Yes, Richard

Harris. There is a likeness, the same indignant blue eyes. I see it now, all red-faced with anger and liquor. That strawberry boy's hair. I always thought you a passive, meek sort of man. Look at you now. All gangly legs under the table having fits. You're nothing but a loudmouth when you drink—your true colours, I'm sure, Mr. Kenny. You are not fit even to be a gardener!"

She glared at me. She hadn't changed her posture. There was a cool confidence about her. She seemed to possess a newfound power, and a willfulness that I could not counter. I wanted to get away from her. I pushed back angrily from the table and the chair fell over with a crash. Bishop and Birdie came running into the room. They hadn't been far, listening, I was certain, to the culmination of a horrible day.

"Finn," Bishop said. "Enough now."

He grabbed my arm lest I lose my mind completely. He began to usher me away, Birdie with her hand covering her mouth. And then the daughters arrived. Tiffany was hysterical.

"What is going on, Mother?" she bawled.

"This man," she said. "He is hiding something!"

"That is awful, Mother. It shouldn't be like this. Not today. Mr. Kenny, shame on you!"

There was nothing that I could say or do. There was not a defensive bone left in my body just then. All was lost. I could hardly look at them with their mean eyes upon me. My head slumped, half-ashamed, half-mad with bitterness. I could feel the pull of Bishop's hand. Then Phillipa stepped forward. It seemed that she would thrust the final dagger into my fading life at Spencerwood.

"Look at you," she said, "the both of you. It was a hard day. Now, please, put it all to rest. Father would be truly aggrieved."

The mood in the room seemed to shift. All was still. Phillipa helped her mother up from the table. Lady Spencer did not object and seemed to yield to the decency in her elder daughter. Phillipa was most like Ted and had inserted his temperament, so to speak, into the foray of wills. It was an act of mercy, and I was glad for it. The dining room emptied, and Robert Goulet faltered in mid-chorus. The kitchen was cleaned, and one by one the lights dimmed at Spencerwood.

It was dark when we went out the back door. I pulled up the collar on my inadequate jacket and lit a cigarette as if it could fend off the cold. A narrow road ran to the Cottage and then to my cabin. It ran past the greenhouse and workshop. The wet snow clung to our hair. We said little, perhaps a grumble or two. Then Birdie stopped under the yard light mounted on a pole attached to the workshop. The snow seemed to gush from it, as if the bright lightbulb were a spout. She held out her arms and twirled playfully, her face lifted to catch the falling snowflakes. Bishop continued on. I felt no inclination to join her and walked on with Bishop. And at the Cottage Birdie caught up to us. I was about to bid them goodnight, but Birdie took my arm.

"You won't win a fight with her, Finn," she said. "You know that now. Come in and I'll make you a cup of cocoa. It'll help you sleep."

I turned to Bishop in the dim light. He nodded.

There was a stone fireplace in the cabin and soon Bishop had a fire going. It took no time at all to warm the small space. I sat in silence with Bishop in front of the fire, both having withdrawn into ourselves. Soon Birdie brought the hot drinks and sat with us. The crackle of wood was succour for the wounds of the day. We sipped our cocoa and smoked and gazed into the flames. There was a primal feel to it, a kind of retreating back to the cave.

"It's not the same," Birdie said finally.

"No, it's not," Bishop said.

"The girls are off to school. They've grown up. They don't need us anymore. I suppose Lady Spencer will make changes."

"I expect she will."

"There's only her now. I think she will ..."

"Now, don't worry, Birdie," Bishop said. He placed his hand on her arm. "We just don't know what she will do. Whatever happens, we'll get by."

"I thought we were family," Birdie went on. "I truly did. Mr. Spencer said so himself on more than one occasion. You know he did. And his two girls ..."

"I know. I know."

"She's unpredictable. That's what she is."

"I think I would like to go fishing," Bishop said. "On the Cowichan River. It's been a while. I'll take you, Finn. One day. You can be a moody son of a bitch, and it'll do you good."

I sat listening. The fire pulled me into a dark mood, for sure. I saw no future in Spencerwood. It was a sad moment. I noticed that Bishop's hand still rested on Birdie's arm. They had each other, and they had a daughter up island in Campbell River. She was a teacher. They could stay with her if they had to. That was something. It was something that I didn't have. I had no one. Outside in the cold dark, a wind came up and branches rattled against the windowpane. It all seemed so terrifying.

I had come to know that silence in some was not merely a mark of their reflective nature, or even the result of a personal dilemma that rendered them withdrawn and uncommunicative. The two men, with their terrible silence, had a sinister quality. They drove, and said nothing, as if I didn't matter, as if my fear was groundless, inconsequential. Nothing at all. They drove along the Ottawa River, away from public view, past the idle machinery of failed industry, past old shops and abandoned cars where weeds sprouted up from under flattened tires. They stopped under a bridge abutment, stopped in its shadow. The driver turned off the ignition. The dark skin of the river moved slowly as if it had nowhere to go. We just sat.

After an hour, I realized that they were working on my nerves. My hand slowly crept to the door handle. I had the impulse to jump out, to run. What had I done to be made to feel so criminal, so worthless? The door wouldn't open. In a way it saved me, because a part of me sought refuge in the cold murk of the river. Would they have cared if I had drowned?

"Say something," I said. The jarring trill of my own voice. "What have I done?"

"Shut up, Mr. Kenny!" the one in front of me said.

I awoke with a start. There was a loud knock at my cabin door. Someone seemed to be breaking it down, or attempting to. It had to be the meat-fisted Bishop. I got out of my bed and looked out the window. It was raining and the snow was all but gone. The doubtful world looked tilted, fuzzy, and yet I was certain of the look on his face. He was as grave as a man could be. It wasn't good news. I had taken on the habit of locking my door, something that had arrived at Spencerwood with me. I went to the door and let him in.

"The girls have returned to university," he said, "and we've been called to a meeting with Lady Spencer. This seems to be the day, my friend, when we will learn our fate."

"This is a hell of a time for a meeting, Bishop. I'm not feeling very well. Surely not this morning."

"It's past noon," he said. "And I'm afraid, Finn, your excuse will only inflame her already aggrieved mood. We have to face this. It's not the end of the world."

"You don't think so?"

"No."

"Don't give up so easily, Bishop. We can negotiate."

"And what is your leverage?"

"We serve the estate. That's our leverage. That's what we do. That's what we can continue to do. Don't quit on me, Bishop."

"Quit on you?"

I saw the hurt in him, his subtle withdrawal. I felt worse just then. "Sorry," I said. "You would never quit on me, Bishop. It's just ..."

"It's all you have," he said.

"Yes."

Bishop looked around my cramped cabin, my every possession in a sad orderliness, the typewriter on the table the only thing of value. It seemed to pull his mouth down, my trivial life.

"Get dressed," he said. "Birdie's got coffee on in the kitchen." Then he looked out the window. "Take your truck. It will start?"

"Not without a battery, I'm afraid."

"Well ..." He shook his head.

"I've been planning to get one sent over from the garage in town. But she ..."

"You've been busy. I know."

"She's a vile woman, Bishop."

"Don't let it turn to hate, Finn. I'm warning you. The day that happens, it will turn against you. You will become what you despise."

"You don't hate anything, do you, Bishop?"

He let out a long restless breath. "She lost a baby," he said soberly. "They called it crib death. That was a long time ago." Then he turned and went out the door.

That was the first time I had heard about it. I suppose it was too sad to talk about. Some things are best left alone. I couldn't say that it changed how I felt about her. It made me feel worse in a way, as if we existed at the opposite ends of bitterness. Bishop wanted me to know, perhaps to steer me away from my fears. And it didn't change my circumstance. She was still a difficult woman with her fistful of resentments waving in my face. Oh, I wasn't cold-hearted. At least I hoped I wasn't. Bishop, on the other hand, was a pragmatic man, and I suppose he was close enough to retirement that he wasn't as bothered about his future as much as I was. And there was more, things that I would have to face, the world beyond the iron gates of Spencerwood. So I did the only thing that I could. I cleaned myself up, put on my best sweater, a smart argyle in mauve and grey. Put a shine on my shoes. I would find in myself the most hospitable, the most pleasing and affable of manner. I would grace her with my clear sobriety and above all a dependable and faithful temperament. However distasteful it was to imagine my fawning desperation, I decided that I would do it to save my job.

I trudged across the soggy lawn and mud sprayed up from the sods. I should have stuck to the road, but I wanted to get it over with, whatever the day would bring. I couldn't take much more fretting over my future. And there I was, dressed so nicely with my shins awash with muck. My shoes, as if unearthed by Bishop's make-believe dog. I felt all at once the full misery of failure, the return of the collapse that had once nearly killed me. The sky was unkind, the grounds without mercy. And then at the back door of the manor, Bishop stood shaking his head. How I had let him down.

"Finn, for the life of me, I do not understand you," he said. "You could have taken your truck if you had the damn thing fixed. Stay right there, and I'll get you a towel." He regarded me rather pathetically.

I waited for him, discomposed. He returned with a towel, and I wiped away the mud and cleaned my shoes. And when I went in, I realized why he met me at the door. Lady Spencer was standing in the kitchen. She had one hand on her hip and a cigarette in the other. She wore a navy-blue suit, the kind a modern businesswoman might wear. She looked confident, prepared, and displayed nothing of a widow's dark plumage. And we didn't seem to share the same effects from drinking. I was disadvantaged in the worst way.

"Sit," she said. She motioned with her head to the nook where Birdie sat, where coffee had been poured for me.

I sat down and Bishop joined us. He had a folded newspaper in his hand and set it down on the table in front of him. I added cream to my cup of coffee and stirred, the clanking like tiny assaults to my brain. She was still standing, and it seemed she would address us on her feet. I sipped my coffee, then lit a cigarette. I needed such comforts. An executioner grants such last requests. There was no mistaking her posture, the way she stood before us. She had all the power, and we had nothing. We sat silently, waiting for her to speak. The lull was uncomfortable, as if awaiting a verdict. I turned to her slightly and recognized with some certainty a smirk on her lips. How she seemed to exploit the silence, seemed to enjoy the tension that it created. She leaned against the counter now, watching us. I thought I heard Birdie moan, as if it was the leaking of her will. Then Lady Spencer stood away from the counter.

"You are all so quiet," she said.

We said nothing and looked to our folded hands on the table for solace.

"Well, I'll just say it," she went on. "Spencerwood is not the same anymore. How could it be, really? Teddy is gone. Everything has changed. You all can see that. It is all so big and empty now with Phillipa and Tiffany away at university. Much too big for one person. Oh, I do love it dearly. I surely do. My studio is just divine. Teddy built it all for me, you know." She paused and looked around the kitchen, then behind her to the hallway.

Something seemed to distract her, perhaps a memory, or even real emotion. I thought of the child she had lost. I don't know why, but I did. And then I wondered if we had been relieved of our duties. I wasn't sure. We turned to one another in some doubt. And then it seemed that Bishop required clarification. He leaned back from the table, straightened himself, and then lifted his big hands palms up like a faith healer.

"Are you sure that Mr. Spencer would agree?" he asked thoughtfully.

"Agree with what, Mr. Bishop?"

"It seems to me that you are no longer certain of our place at Spencerwood. Are we finished?"

"Did I say that, Mr. Bishop?"

"Not in so many words."

"And, Mr. Bishop, Mr. Spencer hasn't much say in the matter now, does he?"

"I suppose not, Lady Spencer."

"What an odd thing to say, Mr. Bishop."

"Well, then, I do believe you should give proper notice to your employees."

"Do you wish to leave, Mr. Bishop? I won't stop you. And if that is the case, then you would need to give me notice."

"I must say this is quite a shock, Lady Spencer."

"Is it now, Mr. Bishop? Do I need to remind you that I have lost my husband?"

"No, of course not."

Then Birdie spoke up. "You see, Lady Spencer," she said, "we have nowhere else to go. We've been here nearly twenty years. We think of it as our home."

"I fail to see why I should be responsible for your home. Don't you have family somewhere?"

"Yes, we have a daughter in Campbell River. You know her, Lady Spencer. Isabel. She looked after your girls. They were ..."

"Yes, yes." She swiped at the air dismissively.

"They were good friends."

"What is all this carrying on?"

"Lady Spencer, please ..."

"Now, now, Birdie," Bishop interjected. He patted her hand.

"One would think that you would be grateful for Spencerwood," Lady Spencer said. "God knows your people were a poor lot. You came to a strange country. I suppose for your freedom. Well, you have had a fine time here, haven't you?" She reached for an ashtray on the counter and knocked the ash off her cigarette.

It was all quite unsettling. The tenor of the conversation seemed to be deteriorating further, if that were even possible. Her change of heart seemed unattainable now. There were no grounds for negotiations. There never was, really. And then I heard what sounded like a deep rumble, as if from the belly of a just world. I turned to Bishop. Lady Spencer had touched the nerve of a good man, and it seemed he was about to address it.

"I have been in your service for a long while, Lady Spencer," Bishop said. "And still, I believe that you do not know me. You don't seem to know much about my family. I want you to understand ..."

"Percival, not now," Birdie said. She knew where he was about to go.

"No," Bishop said, raising his hand. "This must be said."

"Then speak up, Mr. Bishop," Lady Spencer said impatiently. "Tell me *who* you are."

"Very well, Lady Spencer," Bishop said.

I watched him. There was something terribly personal now. I couldn't say that I knew what it might be. I had an idea, perhaps an assumption. He never talked about it in any detail, his past, his view of the world. I never thought it my place to ask. And because I never shared my past, my own history with him, I respected his privacy. And then Bishop drew a deep breath, and when he exhaled, out it came.

"This is still a new country, Lady Spencer," he began eloquently, "but the Coast Salish people lived here long before Captain Cook sailed the coastal waters of British Columbia. And as time went on, it wasn't long before people began to come to this land. The gold rush of 1858 on the Fraser River offered the promise of prosperity, and my people ..."

"That's enough, Mr. Bishop," Lady Spencer said. "I get your point. But it's not *my* history, now, is it?"

"Whose history is it, then?" Bishop asked her.

"Why do you think that I need to care?" she answered coolly.

"Perhaps you are better off with your own ..." Bishop didn't let her finish.

He lifted from his seat. It was certain that common decency made no impression on her, could not sway her. "Segregation is only in *your* mind," he said bitterly. "It is all of *our* history. That's all I want in my life, to see the day when society no longer divides the world by the colour of a man's skin, as if there is another world for him in which to live!"

"Please, Mr. Bishop, you're boring me with your melodrama. Now, I need get on with my day. There's the important matter of

Spencer Industries. It seems I will soon have more than enough on my plate. Can't you just be thankful?"

"Thankful?"

"Gratitude, Mr. Bishop."

Just then I recognized that something was amiss. The subject of the conversation was divergent, moved in opposite directions. Poor Bishop was beyond consoling. But had we been given our notice? I wasn't so sure anymore. And then Bishop picked up his newspaper all at once. He opened it and slapped the page with the back of his hand and held it up to her. The headline: *Martin Luther King Wire-Tapped.*

"I do not have freedom until every man, woman, and child are free," he said, his voice quavering. "You've done nothing for me, if you don't know that!"

Lady Spencer stood a moment. The air around her was thick with bewilderment. "I have upset you, Mr. Bishop," she said. "But you see, you have made assumptions. You have worked yourself into a tizzy, and it is all your own doing. You stole the conversation. I'm not to blame for your grievances. If Spencerwood no longer suits you, then by all means you can go. I only wished you to recognize that things have changed. I will have a new role to play, and I will need your help. I will need Mrs. Bishop's help. I only suggested that, perhaps, at your age, you would prefer to be with your daughter."

"At my age?"

"Yes, at your age."

"I don't understand," Bishop said. "You don't want us to leave Spencerwood?"

"No, I do not. But this discussion has me troubled. There seems to have been some discussion amongst you all. Conjecture, I'm sure. Well, that can stop."

"I'm deeply sorry, Lady Spencer," Bishop said. He was clearly contrite. He slumped in his seat as did Birdie beside him.

Lady Spencer reached down and picked up Darby O'Gill. She stroked the fur along his back and spoke to him as if to a baby. She hadn't addressed me. In fact, she hadn't acknowledged me at all. Then before she left the kitchen, she turned to Birdie.

"I would like a devilled egg sandwich for lunch, Mrs. Bishop," she said.

We sat in a kind of muted hell for a few minutes. Birdie held her head with her hands. She was sobbing. I was afraid to speak. I was afraid to look at Bishop. There were things that I didn't know about him. And *I* didn't know the history of our very own province. I felt guilty, as if I were culpable, as if he had spoken to me. Oh, the things I didn't know could be excused. I had hardly left the confines of Spencerwood since I had arrived. I didn't want to know, truth be told, lest my own history be dragged out into the light of day. Still, I admired Bishop's courage and attempts at self-disclosure. I had to say something.

"I didn't get a chance to say anything," I said. "It was all on you, Bishop."

"What does it matter now?"

"I could have said something."

"But you didn't, did you?"

"I'm sorry." More silence like another death.

"She didn't look at you, Finn. That was a most troubling meeting. The invisible man. Yet she picks up an orange cat with an Irishman's name. Coos to it like an infant. That was about as close as she got to you, Finn. Now that's a curious thing, indeed. It wasn't exactly a dismissal, now, was it?"

"I'm not sure what it was," I said. I sat with my coffee and smoked. Bishop did the same.

"Mr. Spencer would take his coffee here in the morning," Birdie said after a time. "He liked to read the newspaper. He was always curious about the world, what was going on. Even worried. He would talk to you."

"I miss our conversations," Bishop said.

"But Lady Spencer took her coffee in her studio," Birdie continued, "never with Mr. Spencer." She cradled her cup of coffee in her hand now, as if it was the source of such mysteries. "She never seemed to want to know us at all. We were just hired help to her. It's truly not the same. I wonder if she has changed. Perhaps she'll take coffee with us in the morning."

"I don't know," Bishop said, "I assumed too much. And I was a bit aggressive."

"*Defensive*, Percival. Nothing wrong with defending yourself."

I listened to them, to their cheerlessness. They should have been relieved. I suppose they were deep down. Yet, a death has its effects, its ripples that touch, that transform circumstance. We had all been touched by it. I turned to the window, to the rain streaking on the panes of glass, inching down, merging, dripping, and the dismal world beyond like a bruise. All hope and reason seemed to have abandoned me, all meaning and purpose gone with Ted. I looked down at my nice sweater, its pleasing colours, to the sense that I had of myself. I had wanted her to notice it, as if it had the power to petition her admiration. But it had only mirrored my own shallowness. It was rather pathetic, and I speculated just then why hadn't she asked me to leave.

5

I lost track of time. I leaned my head against the door window and watched the crows picking at bits of bread the driver had tossed in the gravel. How strange to think that they had packed a lunch, as if it was just another day of police work. What was their police work? What were their instructions for the day? I was afraid. I was angry. And I was hungry, but they offered me nothing. At times they mumbled to each other, some mundane language. Perhaps a code. They seemed to be talking about a hockey game, the Toronto Maple Leafs.

The day wore on and the light began to shift. I feared the coming dark. And then I felt something inside me give up a little, yield to what they wanted to know.

"Say something," I said. "Please. I'll tell you anything. Just let me go."

Then the one in front of me turned to speak to me. "We want names," he said.

"Names of what?"

"You know."

"I'm sorry, I don't know."

"He's not ready to talk," the driver said.

"Too bad," the other said. "We're having roast beef tonight."

"That is too bad," the driver said.

"Why are you doing this to me?" Just then, I felt it deep inside me, the cracking of my spine, like ice under pressure.

I sat by the fire pondering whether I should leave. Frank Sinatra's imperturbable voice lifted from my record player, "I've Got You Under My Skin." I nursed a glass of whiskey. It was too early in the day to drink, perhaps, but a certain mood had settled over the estate. I was dressed in old tan slacks and a white undershirt, as I liked to when not working. It was a warm and cozy cabin when the fire was lit and the wood crackled. It gave a nice amber light. I had always felt safe sitting by the fire. It took you to a place of long ago, before time was even considered something to track in a linear way, when people shared their existence, counted on one another, and never judged one for his differences. The fire would soon be extinguished. The town garage had replaced the battery in my truck, and soon I could leave if I wanted to. I was close. I was feeling low. It wasn't like the blues in winter, or the normal cycles and rhythms of life. That time, it was different. It reminded me of another time, when the world seemed to turn against me for no reason at all. Some would say that there was a good reason for it. Some would put the blame squarely on my shoulders.

There were cardboard boxes sitting on the floor. I was in the middle of sorting through my things, but I felt in no hurry, even resisting the circumstance I had found myself in. I didn't know why, but I suppose I just couldn't accept this unsettling limbo. Perhaps because for the first time I was answering to her. It didn't seem real. But Ted's death didn't seem real. Yes, I was in some kind of denial, and I was intelligent enough to recognize that fact. Still, it didn't change how I felt.

I went to the window with my drink and looked out. I had no reason to go out now. The estate was covered with the wreckage from the snowstorm. Douglas fir rarely tolerated the weight of wet snow in the high limbs, snapping even thick branches at the trunk. Pinecones and needles were scattered over the grass. But I could leave them now. Cedars tolerated such upheavals of weather, and I listened to the drip of rain from their great skirts, which shrouded the cabin. Then a car came up the driveway toward the manor. It was a long black Chrysler, a rather flashy car on a drab day. I lit a cigarette and stood at the window smoking and wondered who it was. I would miss Spencerwood. Part of me knew that it was over. I would drive away into a frightening world. Lady Spencer would never know the truth. The truth belonged to me. She would never have it.

My thoughts were rambling, one chasing another in bitter circles. Some random, some dark and brooding. I wasn't finished my cigarette when all at once Lady Spencer's car started down the road toward Bishop's cottage. But she didn't stop there. She carried on. It seemed that she was coming to my cabin.

I finished my drink and moved away from the window as she approached. I didn't want her to see me. She wouldn't know that I watched with a certain dread, that I feared what she was about to say to me. Perhaps she had brought my final paycheque and had come to say goodbye. But I was far too cynical to believe that. Likely she wanted the key to the cabin, and to the manor, but more bitterly, she wanted to hasten my departure. I heard her at the door and opened it. I stood at the threshold to dissuade her from coming in.

"Lady Spencer," I said, "how can I ...?"

"Move away from the door, Mr. Kenny," she said irritably, nearly pushing me inside. "It's terribly cold outside."

I flicked my cigarette butt out onto the wet ground as she came inside. Lady Spencer stood in the middle of the room wearing a green knee-length wool coat with a fur collar. She was dressed as if she was going out, perhaps to a lunch for some charity. She was always busy with lunch engagements of various kinds or hosting lunches at the manor. I watched her remove her gloves one finger at a time, all the while surveying what had been my home. She turned to the record player but showed no appreciation, oblivious to the irony of the song. Then she looked at the empty glass on the table, and then unfortunately her eyes fell upon my typewriter. I hurried over to it and made a rather weak attempt to block it from her sight. I had been writing that very morning, but the rest of the manuscript was kept in a cupboard in a shallow wooden box.

"What is this, Mr. Kenny?" she said, trying to look around me.

"Oh, nothing really," I said. "I like to tinker with words." My faced burned with trepidation. It was not meant for her eyes.

"What are you writing about, Mr. Kenny?"

"Stories, I suppose."

"What kind of stories, Mr. Kenny? Don't be shy, for goodness' sake."

"Well, I suppose you could call it my memoirs," I said nearly choking on my words. "That's all, Lady Spencer. Nothing you would be interested in."

"What could you possibly write about, Mr. Kenny? You were a simple Irishman in service. What grand things could you concoct? I suppose it could be a work of fiction. Yes, of course. That's it, isn't it?"

It was the perfect answer for her. "Yes, a work of fiction," I agreed. "I'm just using my imagination and all that. It's like a hobby, really, and poorly written, I am sure."

"Yes, and you surely drink like a writer. I've seen that, now, haven't I?"

"We both had too much to drink that day. I apologize. It's not like me."

"It's not like you to drink, or not like you to have fits?"

"It was a difficult day for all of us. It won't happen again."

"You're right about that, aren't you, Mr. Kenny?" She snickered rather callously. "And I suppose that's the reason you haven't taken a wife. She wouldn't stand for it."

"Yes, that's it," I said unremarkably.

"Of course, you know that better than anybody."

It seemed that there was nothing I could do to neutralize her dislike of me. I attempted a weak smile and nodded agreeably, but it was all in vain. She exposed a vulnerability that cut me to the bone. I realized then that I could hate her, that it could find its way inside me, just as Bishop had warned. I could hate her, even knowing that she had suffered the loss of a child and a husband. Hate could unseat empathy, and the power of it, unleashed, was of the most terrifying kind. I had nothing more to say.

"Well then, Mr. Kenny," she said, "it seems you are wanted in the study."

"And what am I wanted for exactly, Lady Spencer?" I was taken by surprise by the request. Did she want me to serve drinks, one more task before I was to leave?

"Teddy's lawyer is opening *his* will. And your presence has been requested. I suppose as a witness of some sort. You know, legal ... things and such. Just a formality, I'm sure. Then you can finish doing whatever you are doing."

She removed an envelope from her pocket and handed it to me. "What's this?" I asked, pretending to be coy as I fought for civility.

"It is your pay, Mr. Kenny. You have been paid in full. I have included extra cash in recognition of your recent efforts."

"That's most generous, Lady Spencer," I said. I opened it. There was a cheque, as well as a ten-dollar bill for my "recent efforts." It felt like a cruel joke. It was contemptuous, but at the same time consistent with her low opinion of estate staff. She seemed to tempt me as if by design, and affirm what I had thought, that her very nature needed to clash with the world. Even in her grief for Ted, she seemed to oppose those who served her, who could offer comfort. Her grief seemed estranged from her, as if she had no time for it, or perhaps simply wouldn't allow it.

And as her eyes continued to look around my cabin, I managed to study her in that confined space. I saw the measure of her rummage, her scrutiny. She was looking for something. Her eyes pried and searched. And then I knew what had really brought her to my cabin. I held the ten-dollar admission fee. She was looking for an answer to the very thing that she resented me for. And, I'll admit, it provoked me.

I put the money and envelope down and removed a cigarette from my pack of Players on the table. I placed it between my lips. She watched me. I made sure. I left it there for a few seconds, then reached into my pocket for the lighter. I held it to my cigarette, took my time. I wanted her to see it once again. I wanted it to drive her mad. I finally lit it, drawing the smoke deeply into my lungs. And as I exhaled, I opened the door for her to leave. She made a sound like a hurt animal, a throaty whimper. It seemed that she had no words to counter my own wickedness. Oh, the rare triumph. But alas, it was short-lived. She waved at the smoke, then looked me up and down, offended.

"Put on a clean shirt, Mr. Kenny," she said, "and shave for goodness' sake. You are truly a mess."

My Chevy pickup truck started right away. I let it run for a few minutes as it didn't get driven now as much as it used to. I had driven it, after all, all the way from Ottawa. It once had a bright red shine, back in 1955 when I drove it off the lot, a time when my job was secure, and I had money in the bank. It wasn't a lot to show for a career in government. And I hadn't a lot to show for five years at Spencerwood. I suppose it had kept me sober, more or less, and allowed me to offer what I could to my small world. Ted was a friend, a certain kind of friend that I would dearly miss, a friendship uncommon to most men. I would miss Bishop too, and Birdie. But Bishop seemed more like a father to me than a friend. But I was certain that a man needs both in his life.

I parked at the back of the manor and went in through the kitchen. Birdie was making coffee, and Bishop had his head down over a newspaper open on the nook table. He briefly looked up at me.

"Forget to shave, Finn?" he asked.

"No, as a matter of fact," I said.

"I wouldn't talk to him, Finn," Birdie warned. "He's in a bad mood."

"I'm looking at the Help Wanted ads," Bishop said.

"Logging camps," Birdie said. "So don't be telling Finn how well they pay."

"I'm only seeing what's available," Bishop said, "just in case." He looked at me with his head shaking slightly. He clearly had his doubts about me, but he seemed truly saddened. I believed that he would miss me.

"Lady Spencer told me to send you right into the study to sign some papers," Birdie said. "Witness, I think she said. I'll bring in the coffee in a few minutes. It seems we'll soon know what she'll be up against. It will be all new for her. So go on."

Bishop looked up from his newspaper as I went through the kitchen. He had that knowing look that I had come to value. I always paid heed when he took on such an aspect, as if he was privy to things outside the awareness of common men. I wanted to ask him what was wrong, what was on his mind, but he just returned to his newspaper.

I went right into the study, no knocking on the door, no announcement, just a kind of a surrendered walk to fulfill what may have been my final act of service for Spencerwood, for Ted. It was rather formal with Leopold Fitz present, and the lawyer, I assumed, along with a middle-aged woman. Lady Spencer took a seat on one side of the room and Mr. Fitz on the other. The lawyer sat at Ted's desk, his assistant in a chair beside him. She held a pad of paper. It seemed she was there to take notes. It was a strange gathering, and I felt absolutely like a fish out of water. I couldn't understand why I was needed at all. I stood in the middle of the room. They were all looking at me. Lady Spencer's mouth hung open slightly as she regarded me. It was my appearance, I was sure, my rumpled exterior. It was rather uncomfortable for me. I didn't like it at all, the examination of how I looked, the raised eyebrows, as if something so offensive and outrageous had suddenly appeared before them. I wanted to do my part and leave.

"Where do I sign?" I said abruptly. I turned to Lady Spencer, then to the lawyer.

"Mr. Kenny?" the man behind the desk said.

"Yes."

"Oh, well then, my name is Charles Buckley. I represent the estate of Theodore Spencer and Spencer Industries." He stood up from the desk and reached out with his hand. I took it and he shook it rather tentatively. He had a surprised look on his face—bewildered, really.

"So, Mr. Buckley, what is it that you need me to do?"

"I think my first order of business should provide a context before the opening of the documents." He spoke with his hands, gestures of order. "If that is satisfactory to you, Katherine, Leo, I will proceed?" He looked at them in turn.

"By all means, Charles," Lady Spencer said in a chummy way.

"Of course, Charles," Leopold Fitz said.

It was clear that they were all quite familiar with one another. It made the need for my presence all the more mysterious. I began to worry. Perhaps the proceedings involved something else entirely, some bad advice that I had given Ted, something that caused Spencer Industries to lose a large sum of money. And then I began to sweat. A trickle of fear ran down my temples. It suddenly occurred to me that Lady Spencer may have discovered the truth. They wanted answers, the assistant's pencil at the ready to record my confession, my admission. And then I could feel it coming. It was like the sudden collapse of the sun and the rise of the predatory dark. A shadow descended over me like an executioner's shroud and spilled down my throat with questions grave and thick. The questions. The relentless questions until I could no longer breathe.

6

It was dark when the one in front of me suddenly got out of the car with the folder that had been on the seat. He opened the rear door and got in beside me. He put the folder down between us. I stared at it. That's what he wanted me to do. Everything that they did was designed, it seemed, to make me afraid, to break me. Even the silence was used against me, against my nerves. It was their job, it seemed, to intimidate, to pressure, to get the information that they believed I had. They did it so casually. Another hour passed before the man beside me said something. It absolutely shocked me. I thought for a moment that he had hit me on the side of the head.

"We know you are a homosexual, Mr. Kenny," he said. "How do you answer to this charge?"

He was staring right at me, but I wouldn't look at him. My heart drummed insanely in my chest. "You are wrong," I said, my voice strangled. "I have someone I want to marry. She's my fiancée. You are wrong."

"It is a sickness, Mr. Kenny."

"Sexual deviancy is a crime, Mr. Kenny," the driver said. He had turned in his seat. "We can get help for you. Therapy."

"I am not sick. I want you to take me back. I am a Canadian citizen. I work for the Canadian government. This is not right. You can't do this to me. I have done nothing. Please!"

46

"We know who you are, Mr. Kenny. We know all about the work you do. You are a homosexual, Mr. Kenny. Give us names!"

"No. No!"

The one beside me opened the folder that wasn't a folder at all. It was a photo album. Photographs of men. There must have been hundreds of them. He turned several pages and stopped at one particular page. He stabbed his finger at a photograph and then glared at me.

"This is you, Mr. Kenny. How do you explain yourself?"

I looked down at it. I wouldn't cry in front of the bastards. I couldn't because I was overwhelmed with such hate for them. The world faltered. The sun would never rise again.

"Are you all right, Mr. Kenny?" Mr. Buckley asked.

I looked at him, then to the others. Lady Spencer's mouth pursed in confusion, but more annoyance, I was sure. It seemed that I had been away, perhaps several minutes, to another place and time. I wanted to leave once again, go back to my cabin. "What do you want from me?" I asked him. My distrust was all too evident, I'm afraid.

"You seem a little upset, Mr. Kenny. Is there something I can get you?"

"Just don't offer him a drink," Lady Spencer quipped.

"I'll be fine, Mr. Buckley." The sting of her contempt.

"Please take a seat, Mr. Kenny," he said. "If you allow me, I will explain."

Mr. Buckley seemed to be a reasonable man. It would have been just like Ted to appoint an even-handed man to do his bidding. I took a seat and lit a cigarette, and soon I felt somewhat composed. I was beginning to feel that I was part of something. I wasn't sure what that was, but one thing was certain. Lady Spencer didn't look well. Her thoughts must have been spinning in her head. She didn't really understand why I was there. Yes, that was it, and it galled her to no end.

"Katherine, please bear with me as we proceed," Mr. Buckley began. "This is the last will and testament of Theodore George Spencer. It is dated September nineteenth, 1963, and ..."

"That can't possibly be his will, Charles," Lady Spencer interrupted.

"I can assure you that it is, Katherine. Two months ago, at Ted's request, a new will was drawn."

"I was not informed of this, Charles. What is going on here?" Lady Spencer stood abruptly and marched up to his desk, hands planted on her hips.

"I will explain. Please sit, Katherine."

"I will not!"

"Then it will be read and recorded, and you will be notified of its contents forthwith. Please, hear me out. You will understand once I explain. I will then allow you to peruse the contents of the will."

She grudgingly returned to her seat, plainly aggrieved. "Why would he do such a thing?" she muttered to herself.

Mr. Buckley paused to collect himself, and then began to read from what appeared to be a prepared statement. "Last summer, Mr. Spencer experienced several disturbing physical sensations relating to his heart. Examination confirmed abnormalities that would be best described as a congenital heart defect, one shared by his late father, which ultimately took *his* life. It was this condition that kept Mr. Spencer out of the war. It was at this point that Mr. Spencer thought it prudent to look after his assets, namely Spencer Industries and Spencerwood Estate. He did this upon advice of his doctor. I had met Dr. Reed myself and supported Ted the best that I could. I know that all this comes as a shock to you, Katherine, but I can ensure you that Ted thought heavily on this matter. He dearly loved his family."

"Charles, this is an outrage. He kept this from me. *You* kept this from me!"

"Katherine, it's what he wanted. I was in no position to argue with him. It was his wish. He was facing his mortality. There's nothing more a man fears than his own death. He didn't want it to interfere with whatever time he had left. He wanted my word, and I gave it to him."

"I will never forgive you for this, Charles!"

"I'm sorry, Katherine. I'm only carrying out his wishes. Now, may I continue?"

"Well, you don't need my approval now, do you?"

Mr. Buckley took a great draught of air into his lungs and then continued. "As he understood that his life would be cut short, he laboured mightily on the consequences of his untimely death. He was determined that Spencer Industries and Spencerwood be sustainable in their operations and enduring in their legacy. He put forth a business plan toward that end. Mr. Leopold Fitz will remain as director of operations for Spencer Industries. He will oversee all holdings of Spencer Industries and assist in all transitions that will be necessary as part of the restructuring of assets and duties. He will be given the utmost cooperation.

"The following instructions are contained in the will, and both will be made available for your examination. On the matter of Spencer Industries, ownership will be transferred to Katherine Jane Spencer, who will succeed Theodore Spencer as company president." Mr. Buckley paused to let the announcement settle with her before continuing.

I managed a glimpse at Lady Spencer. She was clearly upset with the proceedings. If there was a hint of pride on her lips, then I couldn't detect it. If she was pleased, it would have been simply the sound of the title that she was about to inherit. She had little grasp of the business world, none of forestry. I wondered what Ted could have been thinking, leaving her with the burden of work in which she had no experience. Then I realized why Mr. Buckley had taken a moment.

"Finn Thomas Kenny," he went on, unhurried now and deliberate, "will serve as advisor to the president." And then her gasp matched my own like the blowing of a whale. "This has been approved by the Spencer Industries board. Mr. Kenny will only be required to accept this appointment in writing. Secondly, as ownership of Spencerwood Estate is currently in the name of Theodore Spencer, ownership shall be transferred to Katherine Spencer. It is the last will and testament ..."

"Stop!" Lady Spencer demanded, once again on her feet and bearing down on Mr. Buckley. "He did this?" She pointed to me now. "How dare you bring this man into our business! I will not accept this. I will not have it! Get him out!"

Charles Buckley ignored her and hastened to finish. "It is the last will and testament of Theodore Spencer that Spencerwood remain in perpetuity as a family endowment. The contents of the will serve that end. The parties shall realize the need for conciliation and cooperation, and above all else, determination and commitment to carry out the enterprise of business in a spirit of good will and integrity." Charles Buckley put down the paper and sat back to cool his inflamed cheeks and weeping neck.

I buried my head. The shock of Mr. Buckley's words. The sound of pencil on paper. The scribbled notes. And then the ruffling of fabric, shoes dragging, and then all at once a blast that seemed to strike me across the back. It was Lady Spencer and the heat of her rage. I turned to face her. She loomed over me, screamed like a wounded thing. Her twisted face a deformity of fury and indictment. I was clearly to blame for something that I had known nothing about, no knowledge whatsoever. In her mind, I was responsible for all things wrong in her world.

"What have you done?" she screamed. "What have you done?"

Mr. Buckley came to my rescue, and so did Leopold Fitz. It wasn't a matter of taking sides, of right and wrong. It was a matter of duty.

"Now, Katherine," Mr. Buckley assuaged, "Mr. Kenny had no knowledge of this. It was Ted's wish. He was well within his right to do so."

"And reasonable," Mr. Fitz added. They stood around me as if they had come upon some wreckage on the street.

"You knew all about this, Leo!" Lady Spencer charged. "Why didn't he tell me? Why didn't *you* tell me?"

"I suppose he knew you wouldn't take it well."

"Cowards, the both of you!"

I had always been the object of her irritation, her objections, and now her wrath, that I somehow managed to wiggle my way into the affairs of Spencerwood, making claims of friendship with her husband, and now a greater insertion into *her* life—as her advisor. I couldn't blame her, really, and felt reluctant, even terrified, of such a proposition. The fact that I needed to approve the appointment in writing seemed a way out of it all. I could simply decline.

"I think it's best, Katherine," Leopold Fitz said, "to have a recess from what you have learned today. Take time to digest it all. I know it's a very emotional time for you. In a few days you can come into Victoria and get reacquainted with the staff. I think you will find that the company is in fine shape. How does that sound?"

"I can do that, Leo. That is not my problem. My problem is sitting before us. Can you explain why Mr. Kenny has been granted such an appointment? A simple answer will do!"

"I can say only that Mr. Kenny had been advising Ted for nearly five years on matters ranging from logging practices to forest stewardship. He knew how to find new markets for Spencer Industries. He had a unique perspective that Ted appreciated. I can tell you, and quite honestly, that Mr. Kenny's advice helped avert certain calamities in our forest operations. Ted recognized shortly after receiving the sad news about his health that you would need Mr. Kenny's expertise if you are to succeed. It's no small job to be president of a large company, let me tell you. Saying that, the Spencer Industries managers are a competent group, so not to worry. Still, you will be challenged on matters from mill closures to labour disputes. Mr. Kenny will be your assistant, someone to answer questions that may be beyond your ability to answer. And of course, you will attend the weekly staff meetings in Victoria."

"I don't like it. That's all I can say," Lady Spencer had lost some steam.

They stood around me, speaking as if I were absent, as if I had no say in the matter. My jaw felt welded shut. I dared not say a word, lest it incite her. But I was most impressed with Leo. He had been so discreet at Ted's service, keeping what he knew was coming my way from Lady Spencer, and more importantly protecting my privacy, my need for anonymity. I was sure now that Ted had told him about me, at least enough to give me a certain regard. And I liked that about Leo, how he honoured Ted. I believed that he was a good man. I could trust him.

"And I will be a phone call away, Katherine," Leo concluded.

She couldn't say anything more, it seemed. She was outnumbered. Perhaps, I thought, the shock had settled into her brain, lodged between her anger and loathing. But I knew that she was not done by any means. Momentarily distracted was more like it. She had a dangerous intelligence. I believed that she was capable of unlimited acts of malice against those who stood in her way, or those she simply didn't like. I realized that my greatest asset was silence.

And then at the pause in the proceedings, there came the opportune clearing of a throat at the door. We all turned to Birdie and Bishop with their wide eyes, and of course, coffee and sandwiches. It seemed that they had borne witness to the calamitous and the unexpected as they waited for their chance to serve. I was happy to see them, even though Bishop was telling me something with his eyes. A kind of reproach. *What have you done now, Finn?* But it came at a good time. I always felt safe with Bishop about. I didn't know what I would have done without him. He just had a way.

How could I deny the photograph? It was surely me. In fact, I could remember that day in the bar under the Lord Elgin Hotel where I used to drink at noon. It was a safe place to drink when you didn't want to be found. I hid my drinking, kept it confined to the bar. My job had stresses, demands, and I had the remedy for it. And I knew there were homosexuals there, men who looked much as I did, who didn't want to be found, who just wanted to be left alone. The man behind the newspaper, who was concealed, who never showed his face. I glimpsed something that he did once, secretly taking photographs from behind his screen of newsprint.

I explained to the RCMP officers that I drank there. I wanted the interrogation to end in the worst way. I couldn't go on much longer. I confessed to my drinking problem, my need to stay out of public view. I had much at stake. I had been given the responsibility and privilege of participating in bilateral trade talks with the Americans. I loved that part of my job. I needed to protect the integrity of my position. And, of course, they knew all about that.

"Who is this man, Mr. Kenny? You have sat with him more than once."

He pointed to another photograph. It was Ivanov. We had sat together at the bar. He was an interesting fellow. I quite liked him. "I don't know his name," I lied. "We just talked sometimes. It was not the place to ask questions."

"He's a Communist, Mr. Kenny," the driver said bluntly. "Are you a Communist?"

"No."

"Did he try to bribe you or blackmail you?"

"No!"

"And this man," the one beside me said, "the well-dressed man. What is his name?"

I stared at the photograph. I was stunned to see it. "I don't know. I've never seen him before."

"That is strange indeed, Mr. Kenny," he said. He turned the page.

There was another photograph. We were sitting together at a table. It was recent, a few days old. We had worked all week together. I had been assisting him in opening foreign trade markets for his lumber. I was shocked at the time to see him at the bar. He was terrified. But I had reassured him that I was hiding as well. I never judged him. His name was Ted Spencer. I had felt a strong connection with him from the very beginning. And I wasn't afraid to like him, to be his friend.

"I don't know that man," I said, my voice desperate to sound truthful. "It's just like I told you; no one asked questions." Then more photographs of men I didn't know. My life seemed to be leaking from me, draining away.

Finally, he closed the album of photographs. I was relieved. They drove me downtown. I thought they were returning me to my work, or at least letting me go. But they stopped at a building I didn't know. They got out of the car.

"Where are we going?" I asked frantically.

They said nothing and led me up the stairs to an office. It was tiny, strange. A desk with a machine of some kind, dials with a meter. There was a camera and a screen and a bare light bulb above. A clinician in a white smock. I knew what they were doing now, what they wanted from me. Ivanov had warned me about it. It was called the fruit machine. They sat me on a chair before the screen. It was awful. The imagery, naked men, the camera measuring my responses. I thought that I would go mad, run screaming out …!

At times when the rain had stopped and the skies were clear, I would walk out onto the lawn in the early morning. The stars shone brightly, but it was the stillness of the estate at such times that I liked. The Bishops' light would be on, of course, but the estate would be dark, asleep, peaceful. I would listen to the firs, unseen in the dark, but I could hear the slow dance in their high crowns as the winds began to stir just before sunrise. I was a moody son of a bitch that way, as Bishop liked to remind me. It was the only time that I could feel my world, when it was asleep, before I had to be someone that I had to be. A servant to the whims of others.

I never begrudged Ted for my station in life. I could only thank him for the opportunity. You see, I had warned him about the RCMP, the purge they were on. I didn't want a good sort of fellow to be trapped like I had been, interrogated until I pissed myself. And he was eternally grateful that I had spared him that humiliation, and undoubtedly the ruination of all that he had created for himself. And so, after I was fired from my job, lost my career, and was then smeared for my Communist affiliation, he offered me a position at Spencerwood. The estate forester, a million miles away. My engagement with my fiancée was over. Her name was Susan; she refused to see me. Heartbroken, I accepted Ted's offer, and we kept our knowledge of each other a secret.

On that morning I waited for Bishop. I left my truck idling outside his cabin and walked out onto the lawn. I lit a smoke. It was cold and damp, and I gathered in my shoulders and stood stooped with a slight shiver down my back, although I had dressed for a day of fishing. A thick sweater and good coat. Bishop was taking me up the Cowichan River. I was driving, of course. His old Rambler was ill suited for back roads. And it was the perfect day for it as Lady Spencer was going to spend the morning in Victoria. There was much for her to do, to learn, and it left me with a day to decide my future. Would I accept the position that Ted, and the board, had so graciously offered me, and yes, the exposure that may come with it? I had so much trepidation thinking about working with her. The hostility ran between us like an acrimonious fuse. I didn't want to use the word *hate*, for I had experienced the cost that comes with it, the way it seeps into your bones. Perhaps she would leave me alone and sort things out for herself. That was possible, but highly unlikely.

There were no stars and a slight drizzle as Bishop came out. He lifted his hand as he saw me standing in the beams of the headlights. He carried two fishing rods, hip waders, and a knapsack. He placed them in the back of the truck. Then he went back to the Cottage where Birdie stood at the door under the porch light. She handed him a straw basket of what I was certain was our lunch. She wouldn't let her precious Percival go without lunch even for a day. And I knew that I would be a happy benefactor. I headed back to my truck as she hugged him and kissed his cheek. I stepped beyond the light beams and didn't look away from their tender moment. It was so life affirming, the way they treated each other. It was when I first felt the pull of them, each with an arm wanting me to stay. One cannot truly know the value of friendship until it is threatened with being taken away. And the mood of it began to rise in me.

We drove away into the morning with daylight more than an hour away and the streets empty and wet. When we drove through the village, the deserted streets seemed lifeless and grim. The big sign at Charlie Sales's B/A gas station was unlit, and the Red Ensign flag at the town hall was limp on its cords. All was dark and shadow save for the yard light at the hardware store. The marquee at the theatre was nameless. But we came upon the milkman as we were leaving Fawn Hill. He carried a crate of milk from his truck to a front porch and waved as we went by, as if he needed his own reaffirmation, his own reminder that the world still existed.

"Frank's an early riser," Bishop said. "Fishermen are the only other fools up at this hour." He chuckled to himself, then pulled out two cigarettes from his pack of Sportsman and lit them. He handed one to me. "Might bring you luck."

I simply nodded, not being a talker so early in the morning. I smoked and watched the weakening dark as I turned off Fawn Hill Road and headed down to the highway at Mill Bay.

"You're quiet," Bishop said.

"I suppose it's been a while since I've been away from Spencerwood. It feels strange."

"You need a day on the river, my friend."

"And it's been a while since I've been on a river."

"You never talk about your past, Finn. Do you mean to tell me that you actually fished at one goddamn time?"

"That's what I'm telling you, Bishop."

"I never knew."

"You never asked me to go fishing with you before. Did you know that?"

"I suppose I haven't."

"Why now?"

"Everything's different. You know what I'm talking about. Ted's gone. He was a friend to both of us. Now here we are. And it's Friday. We'll have the river to ourselves. I don't like a crowd."

As we neared Duncan, I was thinking of the last time I held a fishing rod. It wasn't a happy time, but I remembered how it felt to be along a river. I remembered its soothing nature. "I fished the River Lee near Cork," I said.

"Is that a fact?"

"My father died in 1918—in the war. I was born in the year he died. It was my grandfather who took me fishing. He was a fly fisherman, just like you, Bishop. There were sea trout, and brown trout, and what we called grilse. A long time ago."

57

Bishop just looked at me. Beyond him the eastern sky was paling. "You're a hard man to know," he said.

"I don't mean to be."

"I suppose not."

"I've never felt settled. It's just the way I am, I guess."

"Well, there're brown trout in the Cowichan River. Catching a good fish can settle a man. You'll see."

We drove west from Duncan, past the land of the Cowichan Tribes, and soon followed the twist and turn of Riverbottom road. It incited no further talk, as if human language could not account for it. Bishop pointed the way. He knew a good spot along the river. Now and then we got a glimpse of it in the headlights. And now and then black-tailed deer ran in front of the truck, as if they waited for just the right moment to startle us. The road was slick from the rain and the rear tires slid to miss them. After a few miles Bishop shot out his arm. "Pull in here."

A narrow track broke off from the main road and we followed it until it stopped at a small clearing above the river under the arch of trees. All around us the woods had withdrawn into their deep wells of darkness. I turned off the engine and we sat a minute listening to the drip of raindrops from the reaching limbs. The drumbeats of autumn. I knew that sound, its tonic, its comfort. I turned to Bishop. He liked it, too.

"Let's have a smoke while we wait for the good fishing light," he said.

We lit our cigarettes, and Bishop rolled down his window. The sound of the river rushed into the cab. We didn't say a thing, just listening, as if we were expecting a message, something essential for men. It was if we waited for the primal voice of the world, that transformative moment when fishermen leave all their troubles behind. Soon colour seeped into the clearing. Fallen maple leaves were scattered about like great golden hands. And then the white riffles of the fast water. The long green pools. It was time.

Bishop went to work on his rod, threading the fly line through the eyes. He had brought along one for me, a nine-foot steel rod. He never told me what to do, but I noticed he kept an eye on me to make sure I hadn't forgotten the basics of fishing. And I hadn't forgotten, as it turned out, preparing my rod and reel with a certain confidence. It felt good, the way I seemed to impress Bishop. And he was a fisherman. I watched him, the way he looked in his hip waders, tweed fishing cap, and vest studded with ready-made flies of feathers and dyed wool. I wore a black toque pulled down low over my eyes and a yellow raincoat. The hip waders Bishop had brought for me barely covered my knees.

"You look like a damn bumblebee," he commented.

"Are sure these waders will keep the river out?"

"I will leave that to your fine sense of judgement."

"Which means?"

"If your feet start getting wet, Finn, then you're too deep."

"You are so wise, Bishop."

"We'll see how wise I am. I'm going to work the pool. The browns have finished spawning and will be down deep. They might be a little spooky for both of us. You try the tail below the pool. There's some good holding water. You never know."

We tied our flies onto our leaders and soon slipped through the brush and onto the river's edge. There was a narrow gravel bar to work from. The water had been high the past weeks, but now it had lost some of its urgency. It moved darkly, but not too much colour to conceal the bottom. There was a heaviness to the Cowichan River, a brooding character that would seem a man-made attribute. The cedars and the alders that still held onto their leaves remained dark beyond the bright water, and there were several sweepers dragging in the current. The smell of dead fish. Gulls began to drift over the gravel bar. Mergansers floated past us. From the top of dead snag, a bald eagle looked on, as if sworn to supervise the folly of men.

Bishop moved up toward the pool. I could plainly see his smoking breath in the morning chill. He stepped into the river and waded out several feet. The water surged up against his legs. There was a rock face along the river's far edge and the current had slowed. The water was a dark bottle-green, and eddies boiled at the surface now and then. I watched him steady his footing, then withdraw fly line with his left hand. It looped in the current. And then he shot the tip of his fly rod upstream sending the coiled line to the far side of the pool. He watched the loop stretch out and the fly sink. He didn't seem to like his delivery and drew in his line and repeated his cast. He did this several times until he was pleased with the drift.

I was in no hurry. All at once I was so aware of our surroundings, the river and the rank smells, as if I had forgotten my life, if only for an instant. Leaves floated on the current, vine maple gushing red, cottonwood as yellow as daffodils. There was cascara, alder and birch, a progression of leaves, of autumn. And waving in the current the last days of chum salmon, grey in their ruined skins. But the mind will not grant you such respite from despair, not for long, at least. Pleasure, it seemed to me, was a fleeting affair. Still, there was pleasure on the river. Oh, the freedom of it. I remembered now. I wouldn't squander it for the mind's sake. Yes, I remembered, it was the fishing, the very activity of it, the concentration, the attention, that delivered a boy, or a man, from his woes. And there was Bishop, so single-minded. The man and his river.

8

The tail water was fast. It churned white and spilled around several boulders, dropped a few feet, and then flowed into a long section where it lost its momentum. It was the water Bishop wanted me to fish. It didn't look that promising. I quite liked the pool where he stood and mended his line. The pools on the River Lee were long and dark. They had intrigued me as a boy, the great fish of the imagination lurking in their depths. You could see them when the light was just right, in the early morning when the snipe would explode from your feet and wheel overhead for the fields. The dark backs of trout holding on the bottom, side by side like chunks of firewood. But now, before I cast my fly into the river, I turned to see how Bishop was getting on. As it turned out, he had been watching *me*. I raised my hand and wondered what he had been thinking. And then, after he seemed satisfied that I was where he wanted me to be, or perhaps it was something else, his arm came up.

It was then that his rod suddenly bent double. He turned back to the pool and seemed to stumble, but he steadied himself as a fish broke through the water. I heard him shout, an affirmation perhaps, a kind of primal reconnection with the river and the fish that ran through it. I was excited myself and hurried up to him. I splashed through the shallows watching Bishop work the fish. He followed it downstream and when it neared the end of the pool, he wouldn't give it another foot and held the rod up against his chest. The fish strained against the line, thrashed at the surface, and then went down again, trying to make another run. But Bishop held him. The fish eventually began to tire, and he reeled it in a bit at a time, holding the tension of the rod. Soon he backed out of the pool and landed the fish on the water's edge.

"It's a brown," he called out to me, as excited as a boy, "a good one."

He reached down, pulled the fish up on the rocks, and dispatched it with a wooden club he kept on his belt. And then he gripped the fish by the gills and held it up to me. A crimson trail ran down its length and dripped onto the rocks. It was a beautiful fish, golden belly, dark spots and halos. It brought back so many memories. How a fish could give a man a gift like that.

"That's a nice fish, Bishop," I said.

"That's an eight-pound fish, Mr. Kenny," he said. "A good brown trout. Birdie knows just how cook a brown. She truly does."

I'd never seen Bishop so full of something, perhaps it was life itself, something we lose along the way. Well, he found it there in the green pool. And I was studying that same water as he carried the fish a short distance to a puddle of trapped water in the gravel bar. He set it down to keep it cool and then turned to me.

"Go on, try your luck, Finn," his voice raised against the sound of the river.

"I think I will," I called back.

"Get your fly down deep. If you don't, it'll tail out in the fast water. There's more fish down there. Browns like company. They surely do."

Bishop lit a cigarette and stood by his catch admiring it as I moved into the pool. I watched the water pushing up against my waders. I couldn't go deep, not as a deep as Bishop, but far enough that I could get a good cast. I liked the water near the end of the pool. The water was quicker, a paler green. I thought I had seen a flash of silver. Perhaps it was only the light, the reflection of the sky. I didn't know why I liked that water. Bishop wanted me to catch a fish, just what a father would want for his son. But a son, a boy, would want to catch a fish on his own terms. He would want to impress his father, make him proud, show him that he could be someone, perhaps just like him. So I fished the tail.

I was conscious of Bishop watching me. I made every cast a perfect cast. I had tied on a Royal Coachman on a number six hook. Perhaps too big for browns. It had good colour and travelled well along the rock wall, sinking before it came to the tail end of the pool. Bishop was coaching me.

"Move upstream, Finn," he said. "You have to get down deep in the pool. You're too far downstream. There's nothing down there. Browns don't like the fast water."

On my third cast I watched the fly move through the surface tension and then slowly sink. I lost sight of it in the faster water. And soon as I did, something hit hard. It nearly pulled the rod out of my hands. Bishop was frantic and hurried to assist me.

"Get it up into the pool, Finn. You'll lose it if it goes downstream. Turn that big bugger. Damn, it's a good one. Come on, turn it. Don't let him go!"

I had no choice with that fish. It seemed to have wedged itself down on the bottom. I hadn't been able to have a good look at it. But I knew it wasn't a dark fish. I held it, but it wanted to move. I backed out of the water and moved along the gravel bar. It made a run downstream and I followed it. Everything came back to me now. I tried to slow it by palming the reel. It helped. I began to bring in the line. I had him on the reel now. All the while I could hear Bishop shouting at me, "Keep your tip up. Keep your tip up, Finn!"

I looked downstream. The river narrowed, and then another emerald-green pool, but somewhat smaller than Bishop's. I led the fish down into it, and then it went down deep to the bottom. I could feel it through the rod. The vibration ran up my arm alive and electric. Then it broke the surface and thrashed its head side to side, then made several leaps, one clear of the water, landing on its side with a great splash. It was a bright and silver fish. Bishop was hopping on the rocks like a man far removed from his vocation, a man undone.

"It's steelhead, Finn," he shouted. "Holy Mother of God!"

I suppose it was a religious experience after all. And when I finally landed that beautiful fish and it lay on its side, it glorified me, I was certain, in Bishop's eyes, at least. That's what mattered to me. He said it had to be twelve pounds, a fish just in from the sea. It was an early fish for the December run. There were sea lice on its back. The world was made right for just a little while. We studied that fish, admired the green back and nickel-bright belly, and smoked until the retelling of *our* fish filled us with pleasure. We felt no further need to fish that day. It was time to light a fire. It was time for lunch and the retelling all over again.

We gutted the fish and left the entrails for the mink and ravens. And then I took an axe from behind the seat in my truck and we went to work collecting firewood. I broke the dry sticks from under the boughs of a spruce tree and Bishop gathered cedar bark from stump in the woods. Everything was soaking wet, but we managed enough dry wood to get a good fire going. We pulled up blocks of wood and sat around the fire. We lit our smokes and warmed our hands over the flames. Wet hands can turn a fisherman's fingers ice cold in the late fall, but Bishop had a constant smile on his face, even through the woodsmoke. We were quiet. The river had an eternal sound, never ceasing, never failing to comfort. After our smokes, Bishop retrieved our lunch from the truck. He opened the basket and brought out two cups and a large thermos. Red and black tartan. He handed me a cup and then poured steaming coffee, but only half full. I watched him curiously as he pulled out a mickey of rum and topped up my cup and then his own. He raised his cup for a toast.

"Here's to your splendid fish, Finn," he said. "I must say that you surprised me."

I raised my cup to return the gesture. "And here's to your brown trout, Bishop, a beautiful fish indeed."

"Oh, I share a history with those fine fish. We both found our way to British Columbia. The world is a strange place, so full of mysteries. I think rivers can teach a man about life. I really do. I have a book by Roderick Haig-Brown, a fisherman who thinks so. I think you would like it. He speaks a kind poetry. Yes, it's all here in the dark water."

"And I am equally surprised by you."

"And why is that?"

"I guess because I only see you one way at Spencerwood."

He nodded thoughtfully and took a sip of coffee. "Why is it that you rarely leave the estate? Tell me that, Finn Kenny."

"I don't know," I said simply. I wasn't expecting such a question from Bishop. But I was sure just then that it wasn't the first time the thought had crossed his mind.

"You're a hard man to figure at times. I suppose you have your reasons. But I must say you're a fine companion along the river. I want to tell you that."

I sipped my coffee. The rum warmed my insides. "I want to hear the rest of your story, Bishop," I said without thinking. It just came out, perhaps to deflect his curiosity. The freedom that I felt that morning made me careless. Had I said too much?

"My story?"

I felt obliged to continue. "The history you talked about that day, that you didn't get to finish. I didn't know. I had never asked you."

"And you feel bad about it?"

I lit a cigarette, fully aware of what I was asking of him now. I wanted to know, even if it took me to a frightening place. I felt brave, but I didn't know why. "I want to hear it."

Bishop reached into the lunch basket and removed two sandwiches wrapped in waxed paper. He handed me one, homemade

65

bread with bologna cut thick and mustard. He claimed it was the best thing to satiate a fisherman's hunger. He was right about that. And I knew what he was doing. He was preparing himself. I waited for him.

"I will tell you a story about fish," Bishop said finally, "and how they have a right to exist." He was serious now, and I was beginning to regret my attempt at honouring him. Something in what he said touched a nerve. He gazed into the fire as he began a strange tale.

"The Fish and Game Department brought the brown trout from Montana in 1932. Yes, they transplanted those fish in this very river, where none existed before. There were some opposed to the idea, claiming that it would be detrimental to the native fish. Maligned they were. But the fish didn't have a choice in the matter. They came and they thrived, and still thrive. They do what fish do. They want to live. They want to exist on their own terms. People are no different. Do you know what I'm saying, Finn?"

He looked at me through the smoke with a kind of look that sought permission. I knew he wasn't finished. I wondered just then if I had a right to exist. Was he talking about me, too? "Go on."

"Well, it was a strange time in America," he continued. "It was a long time ago now. Black people had been granted their freedom, only to face oppressive laws that threatened their freedom once again. My grandfather fled Missouri in 1859 for a better life for his family. He brought them to California, where he joined with six hundred fellow Black people. The governor of the colony of British Columbia, James Douglas, who sought skilled people to assist in the Fraser River gold boom, who wished to bolster his population against American expansion, invited them to settle in what is now the province of British Columbia. My grandfather and his family arrived in Victoria in 1860 and soon settled on Salt Spring Island. They helped build a thriving Black community. That's what I wanted to say to Lady Spencer. I wanted her to know. I wanted her to know that we have a right to exist in the way of our choosing and that we don't need her permission. Sometimes she only sees that we're the help. And that ...!"

"Bishop ..."

"Sorry, I get rattled thinking about that day," he said. "But *this* is a good day."

"This is a *grand* day." I held my cup out to him and he topped it with rum. He did the same for himself.

"That is where I was born," Bishop continued, "on Salt Spring Island. My father was a schoolteacher, and I after him. Now, I see Isabel doing the very same thing. It makes me proud to think how it all began. If you go to the Ganges Community Cemetery, you will find the grave of Sylvia Estes Stark. She came to Salt Spring Island that same year as my family. She lived to be one hundred and five years old. Think of that."

"I feel humbled," I said. "The things I didn't know, and the things I assumed."

"We can't know everything about someone," Bishop said.

I nodded in agreement. We finished our sandwiches, and then I noticed that Bishop had that look, a certain narrowing of his eyes.

"Tell me about your life before Spencerwood, Finn," he said. "You never speak about it. I know nothing about you really."

Our eyes met across the fire, through the smoke that might have concealed his burning curiosity, but I know it burned. I was a mystery to him. And then I realized that there was only one person on earth I could talk to, who perhaps would understand why I did things, and why didn't, and why I rarely left Spencerwood. And I was looking right at him. If there ever was a time, it was along the Cowichan River on that November morning. And the rum loosened my tongue, my fears, and I truly felt that I could tell him about an Irish boy who had a dream. But I would begin with a question. And he would answer it according to his good nature or he would answer the way most people would. Out of fear.

9

The question was stuck on the end of my tongue, a question that would challenge most in a profound way, that would arouse a loathing they never knew they possessed. I had seen the worst of men, their insidious agendas. Just the thought of the question was enough to terrify me, enough to bring the two RCMP officers back to haunt me. And now it was the fear of not truly knowing a man that you admired. I couldn't look at him, not while I asked it. I poked a stick into the fire.

"Bishop, do you think homosexuals have a right to exist?" I asked, my throat squeezing the words out of my mouth, my heart drumming its fearful tattoo. I regretted it at once.

"What did you just ask me?" His jaw dropped, unhinged from his gaping mouth.

I had to ask it again. I couldn't just leave it now. "Can a man, or even a woman, have a right to live their lives according to their true natures? It's a question. I would like your good opinion."

"That's one strange question to ask a fisherman on the banks of the Cowichan River. Glory be, Finn. Wait a minute. Are you telling me that you ...?

"No, I'm not telling you anything."

"Why are you asking me such a thing, then?"

"I'm asking it for someone else."

"Oh, I see."

"No, Bishop, I don't think you do."

"This is one peculiar discussion, my friend. Perhaps you should enlighten me on who it's for."

"He might be listening at this very minute. It could be that he's not too far away."

"Now you're worrying me."

"I don't mean to."

"Tell me who the hell you're talking about. I'm a big man. I think I can handle it."

"Ted."

"Are you serious?"

"As serious as I've ever been in my life."

"That doesn't make any sense at all, Finn. Are you talking about Theodore Spencer? Are you talking about *our* Ted?"

"Yes, I am."

"Ted was a homosexual, Ted, with a wife, and the father of two children, and one child deceased? Ted, the president of Spencer Industries?"

"That's what I'm telling you, Bishop."

"Let's just hold on for a minute."

"It was just a question."

"It was more than a question, Finn. Surely you can see that. What you're saying changes everything."

"What does it change?" I watched him. It seemed he needed time to think on the matter. He took the bottle of rum and poured what was left into his cup. And then he shook a cigarette from his pack, reached into the fire, pulled out a burning piece of wood, and lit it.

"How could you come up with such a thing?" he said. "It's an outrageous idea. I believe you are quite wrong about this, Finn. It's not possible. The implications."

"I knew him before I came here."

"And?"

"I know certain things."

"Really? Then maybe now you can tell me why you don't leave the estate," he said. "And tell me why Ted paid you those visits? Now *there's* a question for you." He paused, then shook his head. "Forget it. I don't want you to answer."

"It wasn't like that at all. He was a friend, pure and simple. I liked him the first time I met him. It was in Ottawa. Someone's sexual orientation doesn't change him as a person. He was the kindest man I'd ever met. A decent man. He got himself in a jam when he was lobbying the government for new market opportunities. I was on the government team." I paused and looked away. The river moved darkly. The trees dripped. Then I looked up at Bishop. I felt bad that I had told him, perhaps ruined his memory of Ted. But I had a story that few would want to hear. I prayed I hadn't lost Bishop.

"You can go on and tell me more, Finn. The rabbit's out of the hole now, isn't it?"

"Will you answer my question?"

"I'll answer your question, but what if you don't like the answer?"

"I guess I trust you, Bishop, or I wouldn't be telling you."

"Maybe you should trust that I will answer. You don't know what I think."

"I don't."

"But you're taking a chance."

"I am."

"If what you're saying is true, Finn, and I don't know if it is or not, why not just keep all to yourself, the way you have been? Your secret."

"I suppose it festers inside me. All the things that happened back then. I don't know that I can keep it all stuffed inside myself for much longer. I get these rages sometimes."

"I've seen them."

"Lady Spencer, she brings out the worst in me."

"You don't have to stay at Spencerwood. You have a decision to make, my friend. Just walk away. You can do that. Take your story with you. Get on with your life."

"It's not so simple."

"It's up to you, Finn."

"Yeah, it's up to me," I said ruefully. I felt dejected. I wanted him to ask me to stay on at Spencerwood, but he didn't.

Bishop watched me from across the fire, and then he shook his head slightly, perhaps reproaching himself. He was a curious man who understood that life was not so simple. He knew that more than anyone.

"Tell me about Ottawa," he said, "but first tell me about the young Irishman who fished the River Lee."

I hadn't lost him after all. Bishop listened as I had hoped he would. I never thought it was possible that I could share the story of my life. It would invite certain judgement, and I realized that Bishop was just a man, susceptible to the insecurities and sentiments of the day. But I believed he was different. You see, I gave him all the pieces of the puzzle, the puzzle of me. I saw it in his face that he enjoyed hearing about the rivers of Ireland, the civilized approach to fishing, the riparian ownership and responsibility, a kinship with the rivers and streams that he shared himself. And I went on to tell him that when I reached my teens, my mother wanted to get me away from Ireland's violent uprisings against the British forces and took me to Canada, to New Brunswick, to stay with her sister. And in my new country, I grew a keen fondness for the forests, the endless forests that seemed so impossible to an Irish boy born to field and sky. And later I joined the merchant marines, served on a ship of service and support for the war effort. I was witness to the demise of ships lost to the German U-boats, pulled the dead and wounded from an oily sea afire. My own ship took a torpedo in the Gulf of St. Lawrence and was lost like so many others of the merchant navy.

I told Bishop that after the war I graduated from New Brunswick University in Fredericton with a degree in forestry and land management. As a graduate, I was offered a position in Ottawa. It was a dream come true. So he soon knew how the good civil service could turn on you. He came to know how a democratic country, one that so despised the Communists and fascists and all they stood for, could deploy the police force of Canada, the highly respected red tunics of the RCMP, to purge its own citizens from government jobs, to harass and interrogate homosexuals, and those whom they suspected, and use all manner of fear and threats to do so. And the fruit machine and its vile purpose. I told him about Ted, and Ivanov, and how unimaginable it was to have fought a war against such oppressive regimes only to face such tyranny on your home soil, and by the government to which you had sworn unconditional loyalty. You had trusted. And then you trusted nothing at all. I told him about my fiancée who walked away, who could no longer look at me. I told him what I had lost.

He had listened without interruption. And after I had finished, and it had all settled inside him, perhaps even rearranged his ideas, perceptions, and assumptions, he raised a finger to me.

"We fear what we don't understand," he said.

There was no judgement. "I think you're right, Bishop."

"The Americans had their own purge of Communists and such. I suppose that's where we got the idea. McCarthyism drew suspicion to anyone the government thought was a Communist. Actor, writer, homosexual. That fruit machine, another device of government, like a lie detector, I suppose. And the Cold War. Such suspicion and distrust. And now with the North Vietnamese war underway and the threat of Communist expansion south. It is fear, and the Americans have it in a big way. Human nature has the potential for such good, but rarely allows the good to exist, the good that someone has decided is not good. Who decides what is good or bad?"

"Governments."

"Yes, governments. And the reserve we passed this morning. You know the one."

"I remember."

"They take their children, Finn. They place young boys and girls in an institution on an island. Kuper Island. It is a residential school. The children, the families, have no choice in the matter. Many have died trying to escape. Two girls tried to swim back to the mainland and didn't make it. They drowned. Who decides? Sometimes I am dismayed at what a democracy can do, what a democracy is capable of under the guise of democracy. That is the danger. Governments fear what they don't understand. There's no telling what a few men with bad ideas can do. That's my answer."

We sat a moment. And then I shared one more thing with him. "I'm writing about my life," I said, "what I just told you."

"I knew you were writing something, Finn. But that's a brave thing to do, to be honest like that. I don't know if I could."

"I think it's more out of desperation. I want to make sense of it all."

"Well, I suppose it would be helpful."

"It's not easy to go back, but yes, I think it helps."

"Is it something you want to publish?"

"Who would want to read such a book?"

"I don't know, but it would sure as hell get you noticed."

"No, I'm not doing it for that. When I die, perhaps ..."

Bishop got up all at once and went down along the river. I suppose he wanted to see it one more time before we returned to the manor. And I think he wanted to *feel* it one more time, too, let the river run through him. The dark and moody river would sweep away the injustices and the personal affronts, the things I told him. He didn't like any kind of oppression or subjugation. I knew that much about Bishop. The natural rhythms of the river would set right what was good in his world.

10

We drove back in protracted silence. I was a little regretful for the things I had told him. How could a man be prepared to hear such things? The rain had persisted all day, but only a thin drizzle. It made everything look drab. We smoked and kept our thoughts to ourselves. I was worried that I had somehow distanced myself from him. And Bishop would have been considering the plausibility of my story, I suppose. And then along the highway he turned to me, as if he finally had the proper answer to my question.

"You really think that someone is watching you?"

"Well, that's what they told me."

"It's been a while, Finn. You can't keep hiding."

"I don't want to hide."

"Then don't."

"When two policemen push you up against a wall and tell you that they'll be watching you every minute of every day, and that you will never work again, and that they will expose you wherever you go so you can't prey on children or spread Communist ideas, you believe it."

"That's not our country."

"But it is."

Bishop returned to his quietude for a few minutes. He seemed to get that way when troubled, or perhaps in rumination. Then after a few more miles, all at once, he lifted those hands of his, his storytelling hands.

"There was a boy when I was growing up," he said, "a neighbour's child who kept to himself. He never seemed to have many friends. He was different. He got teased at school for his mannerisms. He wasn't a physical boy. His name was Cornelius Harper. They called him Corny for short. I would see him now and then on the weekends when I went fishing on the Ganges dock. He wouldn't be fishing, but he would be there, out of the way, reading a book he always seemed to have with him. When I was with one of my brothers, we would ignore him. He wanted to be left alone. One day I was by myself and got curious. I wanted to know what he was reading. Well, as it turned out, he was reading a book of poetry. I wasn't interested in poetry. I was only interested in fishing. I saw him a lot after that, down on the water. I think he liked the idea that I was interested in him and treated him well. We became odd friends in a way. Sadly, he hanged himself in 1920. Something that poetry couldn't help him with.

"And many years later when I had come to know literature and poetry, I came across a W.H. Auden poem. It was in one my own poetry collections. It seemed to speak to me, as if to resolve something I'd been carrying unconsciously. Some unresolved circumstance. I memorized a stanza. It reminded me of a time, of people who are different. I thought of Corny.

'O stand, stand at the window
As the tears scald and start;
You shall love your crooked neighbour
With your crooked heart.'

"Yes, he taught me something without even knowing it. And how we can forget. Damn it, Finn, I want you to stay. Birdie wants you to stay. And I'm sorry as hell that your girl left you. You deserve a good life. Glory be, don't let all that keep you a prisoner. Don't make your past a life sentence."

I drove with tears welling in my eyes until I couldn't see the road. I swiped at my cheeks with the back of my hand. I so wanted to hear him say that. I didn't know exactly what Bishop possessed, but it was a certain wisdom, a way to repair anything, a predicament or even a crisis. He couldn't just come out with it, answer a difficult question without putting his mind and heart to work.

The day brightened as we neared Fawn Hill. There was the possibility of something that I could manage. I could be something. I could be what Ted had wanted me to be. It seemed that all was not lost after all.

And as we passed through the village there were children leaving the school. It was early afternoon, far too soon for dismissal. We slowed as a group of children crossed the street. There was a schoolteacher with them—Mrs. Olsen. She seemed distressed. Something surely had upset her.

"That's a curious sight," Bishop said.

"I wonder what happened."

"Pull over, Finn."

I stopped on the side of the road. There were people coming out into the street now, customers, shop owners. Stores were closing for the day. It had the look of a fire drill. Everyone was leaving with that same look on their faces. Even the bank manager, Mr. Neaves, was out in the street with his money behind him. I had never seen such expressions. It was more like grief than fear.

Bishop rolled his window down and stuck his head out. "What's wrong, Mrs. Olsen?" he called out to her.

"Oh, Mr. Bishop," she said tearfully, but with her lower lip clearly trembling couldn't utter another word.

"Take your time, Mrs. Olsen. Just tell me."

She stood shaking her head, the children looking up at her. "President Kennedy has been shot," she finally blurted out.

"Shot?"

"He'd dead. Someone assassinated him. He was in his car. It's just terrible!"

"Good God!"

"It's terrible, just terrible," Mrs. Olsen moaned. The children stood around her. They appeared frightened and confused, and she gathered them and continued down the street.

"I can't believe that, Bishop," I said. The shock of such news was just that. It made little sense, did not quite resonate as true.

"The world is truly a mad place," Bishop said, holding his head in his hands. "He was a man I thought would make a difference. This is a sad day. We better hurry back, Finn. It'll be on the news. We need to find out more. And by the look of everyone in the street, it's true enough."

I turned to him as I pulled back onto the street and headed for Spencerwood. He had a grave pallor, a bloodless complexion even with his dark skin, a man so full of life along the river just a short time before. It seemed that pleasure could only be doled out in meagre amounts, a ration that kept a man wanting more. It had come that morning, it truly did, but it was countered with an unimaginable event, as if we had relished our gladness and satisfaction more than we deserved. And though we felt the personal loss, we would soon know the scope of sadness that swept across borders like a desolate wind.

Birdie was waiting outside the kitchen door as we pulled up behind the manor. Her wide eyes and the dam of her pressed lips surely contained the news for us. As soon as we got out the truck, she stepped out to greet Bishop.

"A dreadful thing has happened, Percival."

"We've heard," Bishop said. He took her into his arms and comforted her. "Now, now, let's see if we can find out what happened."

"Lady Spencer is in her studio," Birdie said. "The television is on now. She can't leave it. She's in a bit of a state. You both smell of woodsmoke and stink of fish. Go and wash up in the kitchen sink. I'll clean it all up later."

We left everything in the truck, went right in, took our turns at the sink. After we towelled off, we followed Birdie to the studio. Birdie went in, Bishop behind her, but I hesitated. I wasn't so sure of myself anymore, there in *her* presence, and in her studio where I had never set foot. How the Spencerwood constellation had quickly reasserted itself, and I was on the outside. Bishop turned back to me and waved me in. I hesitated, then went in.

Lady Spencer was sitting in a chair, her back to me. I was aware of paintings on easels, tubes of paint and brushes in jars on tables. The big bay window and Walter Cronkite's voice like grave punches, describing and repeating sequences, moments, seconds. The whole world perhaps hanging onto his words, and his calm appraisal embodying horrific facts.

I wanted to see and crept forward. Birdie sat beside Lady Spencer, and Bishop pulled up a chair. I looked around the studio. There was only a stool at a table. I quietly picked it up and set it down behind Bishop, a kind of timidity that assured that she wouldn't see me, that I wouldn't have to look at her. It seemed far too intimate to share such upsetting news with her. My habitual brain galloped away with my courage. But soon the news, the compelling drama of that day in Dallas, Texas, was replayed for us, and I was transfixed, so attentive, anxious to know why the President of the United States had been shot and killed in such a public way. The motorcade, the waving, the smiles, and the crowd lined along the streets so pleased to see him, and then the incomprehensible.

We watched and listened for two hours, and no one had moved. I needed to leave. I rose from my stool, and one of the legs dragged across the tile floor. It made a rude, guttural sound. Bishop and Birdie didn't flinch, but Lady Spencer turned and looked at me. I was startled by her appearance. It was not like her at all. Her mascara had run down her cheeks, and the wells of her eyes were blackened with grief. And yet there was no malice for me, not in her eyes nor in the curve of her mouth. Then she looked at what I was wearing, her eyes running up and down me like a livestock appraiser. The fish-reeking crust on the knees of my denims that glistened with slime and scales. But oddly, it seemed to be without judgement, as if she were wondering who it was that had joined her in her studio. I backed away, then left. And as I went out through the kitchen, I was stricken with her outpouring of grief, her unbridled emotion, and how she had not a drop for Ted.

I went to the truck, removed the fish, put them in the kitchen sink, and ran cold water over them. Birdie would know what to do with them. And then I got in my truck and stopped at the Cottage and set Bishop's fishing gear by the door. The day had been altered, the brief joy supplanted with the morose realties of a cruel world. The fishing rods were inanimate things now, without lore or romantic affections. It seemed unfair somehow. And how the others reacted to the tragedy. I noticed that I did not feel it in the same way. Oh, it wasn't some callousness that had seeped into me, or insensitivity to the pain that it clearly elicited. But also it was not lost on me that the Americans had brought many of the Canadian purging initiatives to bear. Their government had been the instrument for the witch hunts of collaborators and turncoats. And the innocent caught in the vast net that had been cast were but putative casualties. I had little respect for the heavy hands of biased arbitrators. Pure and simple. Still, the death of President Kennedy, as a man, was a sad indictment of the times. It made one less hopeful, made cynics of the most optimistic. I had seen how it had affected Bishop. There was a civil rights bill that he had hoped for. And what now?

I parked my truck and was looking forward to a hot bath. Perhaps I would reflect on the day—salvage the good and put the bad in its rightful place. An American tragedy. I unlocked the door and went into my cabin, and then the immediate slam of my heart. I smelled her. I had walked into a wall of her lingering presence. I turned on the light. She had a key, and she had been in the cabin while I was away with Bishop. And the smell of her, her signature perfume, quickly faded against the river's fusion of fish and smoke. I stood looking, angry but attentive to what she had seen, what she had been looking for. I studied every corner of the cabin, the placement of things that might inform me. The sheet of paper in the typewriter was blank. I knew better now than to be so careless. But the rest of it?

I went slowly to the cupboard. I hesitated, then opened it. I removed the wooden box that contained my manuscript. I carried it over to the table and sat down. I studied it. It seemed to be all there. And then I leaned over it, and there it was once again, the fragrance left by her fingertips, her curious insistence. Sheet by sheet, the same calling card, the same violation. She knew it all now. And I held the papers, the story that I had wanted to tell the world, if only had the courage. It was a story that many would want kept hidden. Now she had drifted her eyes over it, knew too much about me. It was her reaction that worried me, and her capacity to despise me even more. I wondered what she would do. Perhaps the story could never be told. She would make certain of it. It was then when I remembered what Bishop had said to me that very day. It could not be easily forgotten. It was simple in its message, profound in what it asked of me.

You deserve a good life. Glory be, don't let all that keep you a prisoner. Don't make your past a life sentence.

I poured myself a glass of Irish whiskey. I drank it down, then lit a fire in the fireplace. I waited until the flames licked at the sticks of birch and burned orange and blue. Then I sat in my chair with the manuscript in my hands. My story was complete. It would burn well enough, chapter after chapter, vanish up the chimney and into the sombre sky, all ash and gone. Erase all account of the purge. Erase my past. Would I be free then? But I must have had something of value deep down inside me, some nerve, some mettle that had not been extinguished, a part of me that wanted to count for something, that wanted to seize Bishop's words in some outrageous moment of glory. *Stand up, Finn Kenny!* I wouldn't allow her to vanquish me. And then, in some incomprehensible way, I felt a certain relief.

I lit a cigarette and stared into the embers that pulsed with a red heat. The coils of white smoke like snakes. It was a kind of ritual, a primal act of purification. Fire had a way to burn away the impurities of the day, a simple metaphor perhaps, or preparatory therapy for the resurrected. I settled into the calm pools of reflection. I was comforted. I took the last page from my manuscript and re-read it. It wasn't profound as it was a forewarning, a cautionary illustration that I had given myself. Where did it come from? I wondered. Was there a part of ourselves that knew everything? Perhaps it was so.

11

November 23, 1963
Spencerwood Industries
Victoria, B.C.

Dear Mr. Fitz, and the Spencerwood Industries Board:

This letter serves as my acceptance of the position of advisor to the president of Spencer Industries. I am truly grateful for your consideration, and your confidence. I will uphold the integrity of the former President, Ted Spencer, and continue his legacy of good business practices as it relates to my duties. I commit my unwavering support to President Katherine Spencer in all manner of activities as she dictates.

Yours truly,
Finn Kenny
Spencerwood Estate Forester

cc: Katherine Spencer, President of Spencer Industries

And now, a perfect Sunday, and I had been invited to the manor for a special dinner, along with other guests. A hastily planned affair. It was Lady Spencer's idea, Birdie told me, and it would be a celebration of my success. That was curious indeed, I thought, coming from *her*, with her essence still pervading my cabin like affronted vanity. And yes, Bishop was pleased that I had accepted my *new* position. It seemed that she had told him herself.

I had driven to the village the previous day and dropped the letter in a mailbox outside the post office. I hadn't hesitated at all. I had made up my mind. There was no going back. But I did pause to look down the street and take a mental snapshot of the collective mood. People were coming and going as the world still recoiled from the unthinkable events in Dallas. But life goes on, of course, as it must. I felt a certain ambivalence toward Fawn Hill. It had never felt like *my town*, in the way Ottawa once did. I wondered if it ever would, but I was eager for the first time to make it so. And then I thought of something absurd. I could go into every store and reintroduce myself. Shake hands like a shameless politician. But of course I was getting far too ahead of myself. Later that afternoon, I left the copy of the letter with Birdie. She would see that Lady Spencer got it in a timely manner.

I put on a white shirt and my best cardigan sweater, ash-grey and made from fine Irish wool. It went quite well with my black cotton slacks. I combed my ruddy hair. It was getting a bit long, so I added a little hair crème. It glistened. I wanted to look good when I saw her. It would make me feel more confident—pretentious, yes, and her game, but it would be the first time since her trespass. I suspected a set-up, the great revelation of the truth about my past. She would relish the opportunity to shame me in front of the others—or would she, without exposing something about herself? I wasn't so sure what she would do, so I would watch her. I would pay attention to her manner, her language, what her eyes might reveal. Everything had changed, and I was unwilling to tuck my vulnerable head into my shell. I was the advisor to the president of Spencer Industries, after all, more than what Ted could have given me, although he did in the end.

It had been a while since I felt a measure of personal pride. The Irishman in the mirror I once knew, the Irishman stepping out into the world once again. But as I walked into the fading light, up the road to the manor, I was assailed with a litany of thoughts, all telling me otherwise. Perhaps it was the coming dark, or being away from my cabin. There was anger when I thought of her, what she was doing. It came very fast, and I had to stomp it out like a grass fire or it would surely grow. I couldn't let it ruin everything. I had to be strong, stronger than I had ever been. I never sought to be the centre of attention, and certainly not now when all eyes would be on me looking for evidence of my failures, my defects, and yes, some nefarious past. Such aggravation rising in me. I needed a drink in the worst way. But no, I couldn't dare.

I stopped by the greenhouse and lit a cigarette and had a good talk with myself. I could see into the kitchen, Birdie working at the sink. Darby O'Gill on the windowsill gave it a homey appeal, the swish of his tail now and then. And Bishop moved back and forth like a shooting-gallery duck. I wished that he had seen me. I needed him just then. I waved foolishly. But his simple presence rallied me.

I remembered quite fondly our day on the river. It seemed like something truly sublime in contrast to the past few days. There was a quality to a river, and Bishop knew what it was. He sought it for himself, the solitude, the silence, the presence of wild things. Men in history have sought it too, a place to revive a tired heart. Fishing connected one to the eternal rhythm of life. To me, it seemed the sum of one man's pleasure. A place where he could be with the best of himself. I was certain that I would think of that day often when I needed to escape for a moment or two. But life urges you on. It wants your full measure of attention. The consoling currents of the Cowichan River began to ebb in my thoughts, in my imagination. The green pool slowed. The deep water darkened. And then there were only the manor lights.

I flicked my cigarette into the night. The long dying arc of fire and the burst of ash as it hit the ground. I soldiered on to the back door and went in. Bishop greeted me at once.

"Well, don't you look dapper."

"Very nice indeed," Birdie said in agreement.

"Thank you," I said. "And is that fish in the oven?"

"Yes," Birdie said, "your prize catch."

"I was just thinking of the river."

"That's because it's in you," Bishop said.

"Don't start, Mr. Bishop," Birdie said. "I don't know if I can listen to that story one more time. Two *boys* with their fishing poles. Good lord, not only do I have to listen to such tales, but I have to cook the very prize of such laziness." She laughed, of course.

It was good to see the Bishops in such good spirits once again. But I had a more relevant question just then. "Now tell, me, Birdie," I said, "who are the invited guests this evening? I would just like to know. I suppose, I'm curious of who would really care to celebrate me."

"The banker and his wife, Mr. and Mrs. Neaves. The E&N Railway station manager, Mr. Portman and his wife. Reverend Le Fleur, of course, and the mayor and his wife."

"Mayor Greenacre?"

"Yes, Mayor Greenacre, Finn. He'll be here in spite of his bad heart. And he'll like the fish. Why are you so surprised?"

"It doesn't seem to warrant the fuss, that's all."

"It's no fuss," Bishop said. "We've managed many such occasions over the years. Isn't that so, Birdie?"

"I'll say," Birdie agreed. "And Finn, you declined almost all of them since you've been here. I think it's a good thing. So much has happened lately. We need a little celebration. So enjoy yourself."

"And you will be joining us at the table?"

"No, I'm afraid not," Birdie said. She went over to the oven to check on the fish.

"It's not our place," Bishop affirmed. He too moved away from me to attend to the bottles of wine on the counter.

I could plainly see that they wanted to be a part of the celebration. "You are the only two people that I would *choose* to have dinner with," I said. "Do you know that?"

"Finn," Bishop began. He put the wine down and walked over to me, rested his great hand on my shoulder. "We know this is not easy for you. No, don't explain. You don't need to. We're all still here at Spencerwood. It's not the same, granted, but we're all here. I don't particularly want to rub shoulders with the mayor and the reverend. Hell, no. You a have part to play now. You have a new position. Well, perhaps it's not new, but it has been recognized, at least. You'll be coming in here for morning coffee like you do every day. Don't worry, we're not offended. We're just fulfilling our duties."

"I guess I have forgotten how to be with people," I said quite honestly. "I'm not used to it." I hadn't told Bishop about Lady Spencer's intrusion into my private affairs. I wasn't ready to tell him. Perhaps the moment would present itself. Bishop knew my story well enough, but now it was between me and Lady Spencer. It would play out according to her plot, and I would be a participant to the degree of my silent consent. I would know her intentions soon enough.

"You'll be fine," Bishop said.

"Yes, Finn," Birdie said, "and they'll do all the talking. They love to talk." And then she spoke in her discreet voice. "A room full of people who love the sound of their own voice. You'll just need your ears, and a smile now and then. It's all a bit of an act, if you ask me."

"Yes, I suppose it is," I said. "And where is Lady Spencer?"

"She's up in her room getting ready," Birdie said. "She won't appear until the guests arrive."

I lowered my voice. "She was in quite a state the last time I saw her."

"Yes, she took it hard. She was very fond of President Kennedy. One time when I took a copy of *Time* magazine to her studio, she said something quite revealing. His photograph was on the cover. A very handsome man, I will agree. But she said it in a different way. 'Isn't he a dream?' She gushed like a schoolgirl."

"Watch your gossip, Birdie," Bishop reminded her.

"You do your fair share, Percival. Good Lord! Weren't you just telling me about her fantasies?"

"Be quiet, dear woman."

"Tell me, Bishop," I said. I was keenly interested in learning something more about her, even if it was Bishop's opinion.

"Oh, God, you two," he said, then lowered his voice to a mere whisper. "It is only my theory. She imagines herself with such people as the Kennedys. She has visions of her own grandeur. She likes the limelight. You may remember learning of the young Greek, Narcissus, who fell in love with his own image in a pool of water. He turned into a flower that bears his name. That's all I was talking about. Now just pipe down."

It made sense to me. She seemed to be of one dimension, but there had to be more to her. What of *her* past? It was almost if I deserved to know, had earned the right. And then the doorbell sounded.

"The fun's about to begin," Bishop said. He straightened his black coat, and Birdie came up and adjusted his bowtie. He winked at me as he stood tall for her, then left the kitchen to welcome the guests.

I waited in the kitchen as Bishop greeted the local dignitaries. Then I heard the sound of Lady Spencer's voice, the grand elegance of her speech, not in connotation, but in tone, like splendid flourishes of her paint. My whole body listened. I felt rigid all at once. It was if I could not make sense out of her temperamental nature, the willed regulation of her decency. She was so many things, but none of them was certain. How was I to unravel the layers of her and find out who she truly was?

"Bishop will take their coats," Birdie said. "Then you can go in. Drinks will be served by the fireplace. Are you all right, Finn?"

"I'm fine, Birdie," I said as the last page of my manuscript rose up in front of my eyes. The words didn't seem like my own, but from someone else far wiser. I could hear the river and its language. The way water moves over stones, sluices down rocks, speaks like Bishop.

To hide from life, to run away from its complexity, its demands, and its shadow, is an act of courage and of death. The loss of experience was my greatest sacrifice. It was not the loss of my work that haunted me, but the loves I never had, the intimacy of a lover's touch, and the freedom to be myself without question, without the need to defend my good nature. I believed that I was a good man. I have my faults, but that is a truly human quality. We grow into our perfection. But when the running becomes hiding, it becomes your life, what you have done with it. Your evolution ceases. You will die with all the bitterness you have cultivated, and all blame you can muster when your last breath seeps out of you and your heart falls silent for all eternity. And I have surely pointed my finger at the society that I so faithfully served. There is no higher betrayal. I could hate with the best of them. I could hate and never understand that in so doing I became just like them. It is a lesson that I was unwilling to learn. You cannot hear the whispers of your heart when so consumed with hatred. And I feel it still. And the lessons continue, and the student abides by the teaching, but refuses what is most difficult.

So in the end, I sit in a cabin under a great canopy of trees. That is my world. It is small, contained by four walls that keep me safe. I do not want to go outside them. It is dangerous, unpredictable, and unknown. I am safe in my box. I know what it wants from me. I know its secrets. I know what comes next. I will have my cigarettes and my whiskey, and please, if you don't mind, slide my food under the door. And when I die ...

... or I could walk out into the day and face whatever it shall bring, and be pleased to be alive, to be given such a gift. I could lift my face to the sun and feel its love. I will tell the world that I matter, that I have something to give. I am a man who deserves to be loved. I have gifts of my own. I will venture out into the world because I am the world. There is nothing to fear because nothing outside of me has any power to make me afraid. It's my mind that has betrayed me because I allowed it. I gave it permission to do whatever it wished, whatever would keep it safe. I am more than that. I am more than a man's discontents. The day is mine, and you shall tell me what I have chosen.

12

Bishop passed me with an armful of coats. I glimpsed only his white crown of hair but heard his brief advice: "Have fun." I was certain it was cynical, because how could one have fun in such a setting, where personalities grappled for attention? And then I was suddenly aware of how cynical I was, that I was bringing that to bear upon people I scarcely knew. It would be a long night of posturing. I would be better served, as far as celebrations go, by the attendance of Charlie Sales from the garage. He delivered a truck battery to my cabin. A mechanic, at least, would be interesting. And there was Lloyd Koop from the lumberyard. He smelled like a pine tree. What's not to like about such a man? But no, even in Fawn Hill, there was a ladder of importance, and men with grease under their fingernails and slivers piercing their weathered skin never made it to the top rungs. I asked their forgiveness as I entered the living room with my outstretched hand and guile.

"Mayor Greenacre," I said, enthusiastically taking his hand. "Thank you for coming."

"Oh, yes, congratulations on your new appointment, Mr. Kenny. And you remember my wife, Della."

"Yes, how nice to see you again, Mrs. Greenacre," I said. I took her little boneless hand, held it briefly. She seemed so tiny standing beside the heaving chest that contained her husband's tired heart. He wasn't that old, which belied the silver bristles erupting from his head.

And then a crowd gathered around me. Lady Spencer hovered like a dragonfly with her multi-faceted eyes. She wore an impossibly tight skirt, blue like a summer day. I had never seen another woman quite like her in Fawn Hill. I kept my own eyes on her, but only peripherally. I had the feeling she did the same thing with me. And I was struck by the way she corralled the guests, as one conducts an orchestra. She even arranged them in rank, it seemed. Next up was the E&N Railway station manager, Mr. Portman. He looked the part with his suit and vested jacket, complete with a pocket watch on a little gold chain. A tall man, who, I was certain, worried himself thin over schedules. He could manage only a nervous smile. His wife, too, noticeably afflicted. And the banker, Mr. Neaves, a simple head nod, but a sweet smile from his young wife who perhaps didn't know better. How strange that they all lost their ability to speak as we neared the lower rungs of the ladder. I guessed that they didn't want to be there. I couldn't blame them really. But Reverend Le Fleur would not pass on the opportunity. He was last, perhaps not in importance but in otherworldly eminence. So he thought.

As the guests took their seats on the sofas and chairs, the reverend took my hand in both of his. He held it firmly and seemed to be unwilling to let it go without some vital news for me. He looked strangely serious, perhaps even distraught. It was more than a handshake. It was an appeal.

"Finn," he said, whispering into my ear, "someone is looking into your past. You will not find the answer in socialist views. I pray to God for your patriotism and decency."

"What?" I said, not fully comprehending what he had just said. Then he let go of my hand and moved to the fireplace. I watched him. He had his back to me and to the others. I was dumbfounded and momentarily couldn't breathe, couldn't think. It felt like he had punched me in the stomach without my knowing. And then my faculties returned and my face burned with a sudden fury. He had warned me about her. I wanted to grab him, spin him around. I wanted to hear more, but I had to find my resolve, and I had to understand why she had entertained the reverend with the unwarranted allegations from my past only to be betrayed by him. But I wouldn't look at her. Her eyes would be upon me. I couldn't allow her to even consider that I knew about her incursion, her scheme. She was clever, and more than that. Her treacherously, measured mind. I had to find my good sense, my artifice, to get me through. I wouldn't surrender to something that didn't exist. I drew a breath, then another, then took a seat in a chair beside the fireplace where I could watch him. The both of them now.

Bishop came with the drinks, and all hands reached enthusiastically, save the reverend, who declined. And my good friend had a message for me. "Here's your *one* drink, Finn," he said a bit too loudly.

I tried to disguise my dirty look, but of course, the others picked up on that right away.

"One drink, Mr. Kenny?" Mayor Greenacre chortled.

"Quite right, allergies, you know," I said cleverly, but felt foolish for it.

"Allergies indeed," Lady Spencer said.

Well, they had a good laugh at my expense. I suppose my occasional bouts of inebriation had become town fodder and would account for such a brazen outburst. I let my eyes fall aslant, to the floor, to the safety of the Persian rug. I didn't know what else to do just then. It wasn't a celebration at all. It was something mean and vile, perhaps how one with an agenda might build a case against another, to prove a man unfit for Spencerwood Industries. And

I noticed how Bishop lingered as he was leaving. The poor man had heard it all.

The others started conversations among themselves, and Lady Spencer began to speak about the assassination of President Kennedy, and it seemed to distract them all, take them away from me, at least momentarily. I had a brief notion that she had done so purposefully, as if she regretted her unkind comment. But she didn't possess such qualities. I knew that much. She wanted merely to maintain a sense of the ordinary. And I had nothing to add, nothing intelligent to say to people who didn't care one way or the other what I thought. *Oh, by the way, President Kennedy was in Cork, Ireland, this past June.* But no.

I held the drink in my hand. I could see the amber fire in the liquor. I brought it to my lips and sipped, and it ran down my throat warm and kind. That was when I caught a look between Lady Spencer and Reverend Le Fleur. It was one of a certain familiarity, and yet distance. An association, freshly estranged. My discerning qualities were acute, and I could see the danger in my hand, but ignored it. It seemed to push me into the intrigue of it all, as if it were some game. Bishop had a left a drink on a tray and I took it shamelessly.

After our drinks, we made our way to the dining room. I was shown my place at the end of the long table opposite Lady Spencer. It was extremely challenging to be under her plain view knowing what I knew, fighting to maintain my composure like some high-strung hound on a leash, on a trail. The strain of our circumstance was trying to say the least, and so I was relieved to see Bishop and Birdie serve dinner. I watched how they listened with their duty, saw with their unseeing eyes. The Cowichan River steelhead looked magnificent, even on a platter for the greedy mouths of Fawn Hill. And I had noticed that Bishop had poured the wine and had intentionally avoided my glass. I had to wait for the foolish old man to return to the kitchen before I reached for the bottle. Alcohol blurred the lines of my resolve and my weakness the way coffee melts a sugar cube. Oh, so predictable, it was no contest.

I was grudgingly pleased that Lady Spencer carried the conversation, finding bits of information, news, and tossing them like table scraps down the table.

"You did a fine job this term, Mayor Greenacre," she said, "and I think you're on to something with the painting scheme for the village. It will look quite smart with the yellows, blues, and greens. A happy town."

"Oh, yes, well, thank you, Lady Spencer," the mayor said. "I take considerable pride in our town. I want every citizen to share that same pride." His wife patted his arm.

He had used the word *pride* twice. "Oh, you're just proud of yourself, now aren't you, Mayor?" I said. Luckily I laughed, but really was laughing at him. The obnoxious oaf.

"And so he should be," Lady Spencer said vigorously, "just as we are proud of you, Mr. Kenny. Here. Here. I propose a toast to the new advisor to the president of Spencer Industries."

They gave me a resounding toast. I was no match for her. The table was tipped in her favour. She was so clever, so exacting in her speech, her charm, never bringing anything to do with me to the fore unless she gained from it. I supposed that way she controlled the conversation, to suit her, to suit her agenda. I was nothing to her, only someone to get rid of once and for all. I must admit that I felt braver after a few glasses of wine. That is not so astonishing, as a thousand drunks will tell you. But I had depended on it too much. It had such a spell over me that I truly believed at times that I was brave indeed. I deserved my new place in the world. And when Bishop came to the door, damn it, I was fortified by his presence. I stood and told them all.

"I would like to see a new era of prosperity for Fawn Hill," I said, holding onto the table to keep myself steady. Words seemed to spill from my mouth like vomit, words I didn't recognize as my own. "Every man, woman, and child deserve a franchise for good. They deserve every social amenity. Yes, I think we all need to share in the wealth of this country. Away with capitalism. Don't you agree, Mayor Greenacre? That is my vision. I am considering running for office in our fine town. We need new blood. Yes, *red* blood. Thank you. You all have been so gracious." I raised my glass and they cheered momentarily. I felt the power, the false power of my own audacity. Still part of me revelled in it, if only for a moment. And when it quickly subsided, and I realize what I had done, what I had said, I felt hung over all at once, dull and impotent. I had played the fool. I had played right into her hands. I gave her more than she could have hoped for.

After a few moments, one by one, they all turned to look at me. My words had settled into their tiny brains. Meaningless words, words I had heard once. I didn't know what they meant, really. Ivanov spieled such dribble in the basement bar of the Elgin Hotel. I had written about it in my memoir. It had seemed laughable somehow. The reverend's head was bowed over his plate. The men sat back and lit their cigarettes. They cleared their throats uncomfortably. What had I done?

They left one by one after a muted and mortifying dinner. Most of them seemed rather dour. I stood at the door as Bishop handed them their coats. I felt bad for old Bishop. He looked as grave as a father would at a shamed son. But Lady Spencer carried on with the same enthusiasm, the same grace tossed like cheap confetti. The reverend looked at me with such sorrow and disappointment, then went out the door like an eclipsing star. Miserable man. It seemed that he had such hope for me, such promise. And he hadn't offered a parting glance to her.

The living room was tilted rather badly. I was quite drunk. Lady Spencer seemed to vanish. I stood on unsteady legs, feeling that I had committed a most serious offence. And then I felt a firm hand on my arm and Bishop pulled me down the hallway, through the kitchen, and out the door. He literally dragged me back to my cabin. He never said a word; only his disgusted grunts shook the night air. He opened the door to the cabin and shoved me in. He turned on the light and sat me down, then stood looking at me with his hands on his hips and his head shaking side to side like a rancorous bear.

"I'm not going to say a word about what you have done," he said. "You won't remember. But I will tell you in good time. Do you understand, Finn?"

"Bishop, you're my friend," I slurred. "Don't be mad."

"You don't understand. Sleep it off now. I will deal with you tomorrow."

"Bishop ..." I reached out for him, but he turned away and left.

I made my way to the bathroom. I splashed cold water on my face and looked into the mirror. It was difficult to discern in such a state what was said, what I meant, or what I was even aware of doing. I knew only that the reverend was sullen as cement and Bishop was angry with me—but more likely utterly disappointed once again. My thoughts were unhinged, fastened to nothing, but then my mother came up behind me.

When I was not quite a teenage boy and my mother had dreams of Canada, a friend and I got into some spirits one Sunday afternoon. Donny O'Reilly was an older boy who thought it would be great fun to introduce a fatherless boy to what men do in the taverns. Not only was it a stupid thing to do, but it was sacrilegious in the worst way. A constable, who easily spotted two merry lads carolling some elegy of the ages, brought us home. After my mother had met him at the door and apologized for her son, she escorted me into the bathroom and pushed my face up to the mirror.

"Look at yourself, Finn," she said, truly heartbroken. "What is to become of you when we go to our new country? Tell me that. You are no good, Finn. You are no good!"

I went to the table and sat. I lit a cigarette and rested my head on my arm. I felt isolated, derelict as a fallen tree in the forest.

Regret is a terrible thing when you cannot find reason for it, or remedy. But the effect is visceral. It rests in the body entire and follows you wherever you go. My mother, she forgave me. Of course, it was a shock to her, and she was right to be worried. I often wondered if she had seen something in me that day that my father had possessed. She never spoke about him in that way, never spoke poorly of him. But I had eyes. I had seen that drinking was sound medicine for your troubles. It was a way of life. And she had been looking over my shoulder my entire life, wanting me to see at last that it wasn't. After she passed on, she visited me still, with the same hard love.

13

I was a man in a midlife crisis, a crisis of spirit. I would not say that it was the religious kind that Reverend Le Fleur would gladly appease with his incurable faith. No, but a calamity that would surely kill me if I didn't find the means to mitigate the host of demons that stalked me. The only thing to do was to face my shortcomings like the man I truly wanted to be. It seemed such a simple thing on a day that was bright with clouds drifting like soft pillows in the sky. The sun melted the frost on the lawns, but it still gleamed white as snow in the shadows. There was a tree to clean up. A large tree had come down at the far end of the estate. I had an axe and swede saw in the back of my truck. The trunk was too thick for the saw, and it seemed that I would need the chainsaw, but the teeth had dulled from use. I was happy for it as the saw would be too much to bear with its gnawing nasal drone. Like an appalling death.

The tree, a cedar, had been snapped mid-trunk by a gust of wind during the last storm. I chopped the limbs with the axe and stacked them in a pile for burning. As I drew the branches into the pile with a rake, I stopped to look at my surroundings, back to the manor as if to confirm where I was in the world, that I was still in it. It was peaceful in the cool morning. The sweet smell of cedar boughs crushed underfoot. I leaned on the rake and lit a cigarette. There were crows near the manor. They waited for Darby O'Gill to bring whatever he had caught in the night. Sometimes he would leave a blue mole outside the door for them, a piece of chewed, wet suede. Then I saw Bishop coming toward me, his head down in that way of his when he was burdened with troubles not of his own making. I knew that he would be coming. He had said that he would. He couldn't wait, I supposed, the way it would be working on him. As he came up to me, I braced myself. Everything that he would say would be true, more or less. I had no real answer for him, no excuses.

"I forgot my cigarettes," he said. His breath billowed like smoke in the cold.

"No, you haven't," I said. He hadn't forgotten his smokes, not at all. He just liked to ease in on a situation. I shook out a Player's for him. He said nothing and lit his smoke.

"That's a fine tree," he said. "It's a real shame."

"Well, there will be no shortage of kindling for the winter. There's a big one down farther back, but we'll leave it for now." He turned to look at my truck. There was a can of gas sitting on the tailgate.

"Are you planning to have a bonfire?"

"It's a good day for it." He seemed nervous, perhaps from the nature of his visit. He turned completely around trying to avoid the questions that he knew he had to ask. Then he looked right at me. There was a powerful man behind those eyes now.

"How are you feeling, Finn?"

"I'm all right. My head's felt better. How are you, Bishop?"

"How am I?"

"Yeah, just asking."

"You see, I have a problem."

"And what's that?"

"I think I'm losing my mind."

"No, not you."

"Yes, me."

He played a little game that skirted around the matter that was lodged in his throat. He was taking his time. I hoped it all had a point. I would have rather he just come out with it. "What makes you think that you're losing your mind?"

"Well, I woke up in a sweat last night. You see, I had a nightmare. It was the strangest dream."

"Yeah, and what was it about?"

"You."

"Me?"

"I had a dream that you pissed on the mayor."

"Bishop, what ...?"

"I had a dream that Lady Spencer put on this party for you. It was supposed to be a new beginning. Yes, it was your time to shine, Finn. But you ruined it. Damnedest thing I've ever heard. Pissed all over Mayor Greenacre. Pissed on everyone!"

"That's a bad dream, Bishop."

"It was no dream, was it, Finn?"

"I suppose it wasn't."

"Do you remember?"

"It's a little foggy, Bishop, I must say."

"It's that fellow in that bar in Ottawa that you told me about. He planted something in that thick head of yours. Surely he did. What were you thinking?"

"Ivanov talked like that. I never listened to him."

"You listened enough to make Karl Marx proud!"

"What has my country done for me, Bishop? Tell me that."

"So you have a little revolution going on in your head. But you're living pretty good, don't you think?"

"Am I?"

"Can't you see what you've done?"

"Those people last night, Bishop," I said, throwing down the rake, "they don't give one shit about me!" I marched away, and then turned to face him. "I knew it right from the beginning. I played along, put my best foot forward. That's what I did. Lady Spencer's little game. Well, I suppose I wanted to show her that I was no fool. It was all a sham, Bishop. She couldn't give one fat damn about me. She was in my cabin. Yes, the day we went fishing. She read my entire memoir. Everything. She knows it all. She knows the truth about Ted, who he really was, what he hid from her all those years. Don't you understand? She doesn't know that I'm onto her. And the reverend leans into my ear to tell me she's looking into my past. She wants me out, Bishop. She told him what she had learned. But something terrible must have come between them. So I came a little unglued. Sorry to hell for that. I haven't done a damn thing, Bishop. I haven't done anything wrong in my entire life. All of this drama is not my doing. And now, what, I'm to pay the price once again? Oh, I gave it to them, pissed on them, you say, the lot of them with their freedom and titles!"

"All right, Finn, calm down. It's not a fault to be successful. Ted, for crying out loud, was the epitome of success. Spencerwood exists for that very reason. You know that. But you've been burned bad, my friend. Don't let it turn your life into a living hell. And no one, by the way, lives this life without doing something wrong. We're not perfect, and God knows, *you're* not perfect."

"I know."

"Hell, I'm not perfect."

"I want to get out of that prison I built. You're the one that told me that I had a choice. I believe what you said. I truly do. And I thought that's what I was doing. It's her, Bishop. It's Lady Spencer. She has evil in her. I swear she does. I don't know why I bring it out in her. And she's making up things in her mind about me, and even Ted. Who knows what she will do next? I have nothing but this place. I have no where else to go."

"I want you to be honest with me, Finn. All right?"

"Yeah, all right."

"What will she find?"

I didn't answer right away. "Nothing," I said.

"You hesitated. There's something you're not telling me. Let's have it!"

I looked at him, into the full face of Percival Bishop. I couldn't lie to him. He was my only friend in the world now. "I went to a meeting once in Ottawa," I said, "with Ivanov. It was after I was let go and was feeling betrayed by the government. I was in bad shape. I never took it well, but why would I? He talked me into it. He told me that there were alternatives, that I should come and listen. I could make up my own mind."

"Who were they?"

"Socialist Youth League. The meeting was in a basement in an old house downtown. They were young and left of centre, if you know what I mean. Intellectuals. They wanted the abolition of social classes. They spoke of revolution. It was an ideology that I didn't understand."

"So you never went back?"

"No, that was the last time I saw Ivanov. I left Ontario. I just left. I came here."

"Well, the Cold War is somewhat behind us. I say somewhat, because there still exists in this country a fear of Communism and such. It is seen as the biggest threat to our way of life, our democracy. And as much as you dislike our government, and you may have good reason, it's still the best country in the world. I'm not going to try to convince you. She will exploit you, my friend. She will take whatever she can find and use it. It's the board who are your employers. They can remove you. So when the president of Spencerwood Industries informs the board of an employee with Communist connections, you will be summarily removed. That's guaranteed."

"I'm sure it will be just like that."

"So keep your nose clean. Once again. If you are as innocent as you claim to be, then be innocent. Do your job when asked to, when called to, and give that very best part of you. That's all you can do. No more hiding. You cannot control that woman. And goddamn it, Finn, you have to stop drinking. It will be all for nought, if you do otherwise. I'll come down to your cabin and you will hand over every liquor bottle."

"Why do you insist on helping me?"

"Because you're worth it."

"That means a lot to me, you know that?"

"And if you mean that, then you can promise me."

"I'll stop drinking."

"Say it. Look me in the eye."

He was a fierce-looking son of a bitch. I wanted to be on his side. "I promise I'll stop drinking."

"Good."

"I don't want to let you down, Bishop."

"Then don't!"

"I won't."

"I never had a son, you see. I was blessed with a daughter. But don't get me wrong, Finn. You are not the son I never had. You are the friend I never had. Come on, let's do it."

We took my truck back to my cabin. I had an odd feeling. I had made a promise to Bishop, but I wasn't so optimistic that I could do what he asked me to do. I suppose it was a lack of faith, a lack of faith in myself. You see, I knew myself all too well. I knew when the pressure got to me, I would want it. I knew that if I dwelt on a problem, I would convince myself that a drink would calm me, would help me resolve whatever it was that bothered me. I had depended on it for as long as I could remember. And as I was driving that short distance, I could feel Bishop. He was watching me. It would be a defining moment, perhaps short-lived, or perhaps it was a true beginning. How many chances does one get?

Bishop followed me into my cabin. There was a bottle of Jameson Irish whiskey on the table. That was an easy one. "Put them all on the table, Finn," he said. "Every one of them."

I went to the cupboard where I kept my manuscript. It was a fitting place to keep liquor as the story of my life was infused with it, guided by the need for it. It was such an isolating affair, drinking alone, numbing a good man's brain so that he could sleep at night. I handed Bishop the bottle and he placed it on the table. I kept a bottle, just in case, under the sink in the bathroom. There were those times when I would look at myself in the mirror and tempt my good mother to appear over my shoulder. I would never touch that bottle. She would know if I did, of course, so I left it alone. That was the hardest bottle to remove. It was full of symbolism, a mire of temptation and shame. Bishop appeared in the mirror. I reached down for the bottle and gave it to him.

"That's all," I said.

"Are you sure?"

"I'm sure."

Bishop cradled the bottles in his arms as I drove back to the fallen tree. The glass clinked as the bottles jostled. I liked the sound. A strange and familiar kind of music. Once at the tree, he got out of the truck and went directly to the pile of branches. I knew what he was going to do. I just watched him. He poured that good Irish whiskey all around the base of the pile. Then he stepped back and lit a match. He looked at me, another symbolic gesture, as if I was about to be purified. He nodded his head, then tossed the burning match. The cedar limbs flared, a surging ring of fire. The burning of my imperfections, my weakness. We stood back as the cedar boughs crackled and flamed, and soon great clouds of white smoke billowed up into the air, into the sky. And what would rise from the ashes, I didn't know.

14

Clouds had rolled in without interruption all week long. It rained most of the time. It was cold and it crept down your neck as if it had a mind to, a mind to hurry you along. I made my way to the manor at a half-run. I could only think of Birdie's coffee waiting for me. I liked to start the day in the kitchen. We would talk about the events happening around the world. The assassination of President Kennedy, and the murder of his assassin, Lee Harvey Oswald, by nightclub owner Jack Ruby. There was no end to the story and its theories, even conspiracies. And there was the Vietnam War, and the damn weather. Bishop was keenly interested in Martin Luther King, Jr., and would apprise the kitchen of the United States government's outrageous persecution of the man. He held up the newspaper as soon as I walked in, Birdie shaking her head. It was the same every day, but I had grown quite fond of those mornings.

"See, it never stops," Bishop said from the nook table. "Arrested again. For what?"

"The Beatles have a new song, Finn," Birdie said. She was kneading bread dough on the well-floured counter.

"I'm not that taken with them," I said. "They're a shaggy bunch." I went over to the stove and poured my coffee into a cup she left for me. "But maybe I should let my hair grow a bit. What do you think, Bishop?"

"I think there's more important things going on," he said.

"Like what?"

"For instance, see that tray on the counter?"

"What of it?"

"Lady Spencer put it there for you. The top tray is your inbox. The bottom tray is your outbox."

I went over to look at it. There was a file folder in the top tray. A memorandum was paper clipped to it. "What's this?" I asked.

"It's your first assignment, Finn. Your expert opinion on some matter has been duly requested. I'm guessing, of course. You put your response in the bottom tray. That's the outbox."

"I worked in an office, Bishop."

"I know, but this is not a typical office. It should be interesting. This is what you wanted, Finn."

I picked up the file folder and went to the table, but I had to move a sleeping Darby O'Gill before I sat down. I lit a cigarette and glossed over the memorandum without reading it carefully. "There seems to be some kind of production problem," I noted. "What do I know about that?"

"And by the way, you are getting a telephone line to your cabin. Welcome to the twentieth century."

"This is a bit strange." As I stared down at the folder, I felt the weight of what I had undertaken. It had an unsettling quality, perhaps beyond my abilities. And then it occurred to me that was the very reason it was sitting in front of me.

"Labour is what drives production," Bishop said with his ever-ready answers. "What you don't know seems about to change. You're about to learn all about the IWA."

"I suppose I am. I'm just a little short of confidence right now."

"It'll come."

"I should get back to my cabin."

"It's coffee time, Finn. This is the place in the morning where you gather your thoughts for the day. Clear your head. Relax into it."

"Listen to the expert, Finn," Birdie said.

Bishop looked at me over his reading glasses and shook his head. "She's my biggest fan and just won't admit it."

"Well, Percival," Birdie quipped, "reading that paper everyday does seem to keep you informed. I'll say that."

He put his hand up to acknowledge her, but his attention was on me. "I don't know much about labour in the forest industry, Finn," he said. "I won't be of much use to you. But I know fairness, and I know a man named Emmitt Holmes."

I didn't want to ask him who the man was. I had already started to think about the folder in front of me. It was such a distraction. I finished my coffee and excused myself.

"I'd best go read this," I said. I took the folder and went to the door. And as I did, Bishop called out behind me.

"Emmitt Holmes," he said.

I stopped and turned back to him. "Is that your idea of helping me?"

"Just casual manipulation. That's what I like to call it."

"I'll keep that in mind."

So there it was, my first assignment. It seemed that there would be little contact with Lady Spencer. I didn't mind that at all. In fact, as I walked back to my cabin, I felt a certain eagerness, almost purposeful. And once inside my cabin I placed the folder on the table. I had no desk to work from. It was s small space, but the table would do. I had a small library of books, mostly forestry management. *Forests of the Pacific Northwest, Forestry Handbook UBC, Silviculture, Applied Forest Management,* to name a few, and others. But first I had to read the memorandum. It was handwritten in a stylish cursive. It surprised me, the flare of her letters. The careful formation. My mother had written with a fine hand. It was strange that it caught my attention in such a way.

Mr. Kenny, Advisor to the President of Spencer Industries
Re: Production Decline

Please find attached a report on the current standing of
Aldercreek Sawmill in Courtenay. There appears to be a short-
fall in revenues in the second quarter of this year. The mill
was once profitable. The information has been provided by our
accounting firm, Johnson and Associates. You will need to
assess the viability of the sawmill in the short term, and long
term as well. A site visit may be required, but only if absolutely
necessary. You should leave nothing off the table. It may mean
discarding this asset.

Do not confer with the I.W.A. (International Woodworkers of
America) in this matter. This last point is extremely important.
You will adhere to these strict instructions. I will expect your
report by mid-December.

Thank you.

Katherine Spencer
President
Spencer Industries

I sat staring at the memorandum, still feeling the tone of it, the
harsh closing directive. That is what struck me. It was terse,
impersonal, all business. I wondered what she had been thinking
when she wrote it. Was it a part of her scheme? But I would do
whatever was asked of me in spite of it. I was committed. I opened
the folder. There was a letter from the accountant to Leopold Fitz
with a letter from Leo to Lady Spencer. A chain of command,
all orderly and succinct. I understood that well enough. It was
the numbers that I need to look at, the operating costs against
revenues. All of it. I had no real experience with mills and such,

but I generally had a good feel for what Ted had expected from his sawmills. And as I read more background information, revenues over the past five years, monthly expenditures, it seemed that something was amiss. A business goes from black to red in such a short span of time. I spent several hours reading, digesting hard numbers, when it occurred to me that I should go to the Fawn Hill library to see what reference material—periodicals, business journals, newspaper articles—might assist my review of Aldercreek Sawmill. I had once been a skilled researcher for the federal government. That was something, at least, that I could take away from my abridged career. I gathered up the folder and went out the door.

I drove to the library in the light rain and gusts of wind. As I got out of my truck, I couldn't help but notice Lady Spencer's gold Cadillac parked down the street. There was nothing unusual about that. It was more unusual that *I* was in the village. But before I went into the library, I stopped to look up and down the street. I wasn't really thinking but practising an alert surveillance of my surroundings. I was always on guard when she was about, vigilant to know more about her. As I pulled open the door, I glanced to the outskirts of town in the opposite direction. That's where the Anglican Church kept vigil over the town, so to speak. And there she was. She was standing in the cemetery, unmistakable between two trees that partially screened her. She was wearing sunglasses and a plum-coloured scarf over her head. I let go of the door and stood watching. I thought, perhaps, that she was visiting Ted's grave, but it couldn't have been. She was standing nowhere near his plot. She appeared to be holding a bouquet of white flowers. Then the wind blew loose strands of hair across her face, and she quickly swept them away with her free hand.

I went into the library and watched her from a window. The distraction was so intense that I had forgotten why I was there at all. I was spying on her, and I must confess that it made me feel like bit of a scoundrel. But allegedly she was doing the same with me. She knelt down out of sight, then appeared once again a moment later. It seemed she had placed the flowers on a grave. After a few minutes she turned and walked away. I watched her come out through an iron gate and onto the sidewalk. She didn't seem to notice my truck parked at the library and continued down the street toward her car. All at once a gust of wind caught her and pushed her aside, but she turned and fought against it. Then she stopped at Van Koll's Bakery. She went in and came back out holding a small white paper bag. I watched her until she got into her car and drove away.

I didn't know how to interpret what I had witnessed at the cemetery. Perhaps it was nothing but a moment's respect for a lost friend. I just had to let it go and do what I had come to do. I asked Mrs. Cosgrove, the librarian, where I might find information on businesses, specifically anything newsworthy in Courtenay. She showed me a rack of issues from the *Courtenay Herald*. Understandably, out of space concerns, the weekly paper was only for the current year. I placed the rack on a table and began with January 1963, leafing through each edition I was looking for anything that involved Aldercreek Sawmill. It was tedious work, moving from page to page, from Easter celebrations to a May Day parade, local little league scores, sales on beef and pork, Sears fashions, a missing person, a found person, the July First celebration in the town park, and then a death a week later caught my attention. A brief reference to the sawmill. It was a drowning, but it was likely nothing, so I continued my search through the pages, through the months. There was no further reference to the mill for that year, so I went back and wrote down the drowning notice from the newspaper.

BODY IDENTIFIED

The body found in Comox Harbour on Sunday, July 7, by a passing boater has been identified as 45-year-old Roland Lantz of Courtenay. Police believe the death was not the result of foul play. The one-time employee of Aldercreek Sawmill leaves behind a wife and five children.

It seemed that I was about to go on a road trip. I would arrange a meeting with the mill superintendent and perhaps get an idea of what was troubling the mill. The numbers were one thing, but if there was a reason behind it, then perhaps the mill could be saved. The last thing that I wanted to do was recommend to Lady Spencer the closing one of Ted's mills. But I knew that it was a business, and things change. The market changes. Mills need to be upgraded, new equipment to replace aging and outdated machinery. If that's all it was, then perhaps it wouldn't be so bad for my first assignment.

Before I left the library, I asked Mrs. Cosgrove if she could look up a name for me. I wrote it on a piece of paper, and she took it and went into the vaults in the backroom. She said she knew that name and thought she knew where to look for it. I waited, and after about fifteen minutes, she returned with a newspaper article. It was on a rack of *Province* newspapers. She placed it on the table in front of me.

"He's an interesting man," she said. Nothing more.

"Thank you," I said, and read the article. It wasn't long, but it was "interesting." I shook my head, not in total disbelief or surprise. It was Bishop, after all. Still, he never ceased to amaze me.

As an IWA delegate to the Vancouver Labour Council, Emmitt Holmes became a member and chair of the Joint Labour Committee to combat racial discrimination, a role he held for 14 years ...

Outside the library, I was tempted to walk across the street to the church. I was curious about everything she did now. It was in my best interest to know everything about her. And how convenient for her that she gave me nothing. She was a mystery. A puzzle to be solved. I thought that I would come back in the morning, early, just a casual visit to a gravesite. It may have been nothing at all, or perhaps a tiny piece to a puzzle that I was determined to piece together. It felt like a mission, a purpose that grew stronger every day.

The next morning, after I telephoned the Aldercreek mill and arranged to see the mill superintendent, I stood in the kitchen waiting for Birdie. I had on my good tweed jacket and tan slacks and had managed to put on a brown checkered tie.

"And if you smoked a pipe," Bishop said, "you might be mistaken for one of those intellectuals."

"You wouldn't know, dear," Birdie said.

"I believe that Bishop may be one himself," I said.

"I wouldn't be able to live with him if that was the case," Birdie said. "I prefer him to be his most humble self."

"I suppose that's a compliment," Bishop said.

Birdie was making me a ham sandwich for my drive up the Island Highway. And a thermos of coffee. It was Bishop's fine tartan thermos.

"Look after that," he said from the nook table. "I've had that for twenty years. It's helped me ponder on many a topic. And it's my fishing thermos, I want you to know."

"I know it is. Don't worry, Bishop, I'll treat it like gold."

"You surely will."

"And I read about your man at the library, by the way."

"Did you now?"

"... no man is an island, entire of himself ...'"

"That's Emmitt. So keep him in mind on your travels."

"Bishop, I'll be fine. I'm not going to meet with anyone from the union. I've been given clear instructions. In fact, more than clear."

"All right, Finn. I hear you." He lifted his hands, seemingly satisfied that he had made his point.

Birdie handed me my lunch and thermos. "Thanks, Birdie," I said. "I guess I should go."

"That old Percival Bishop," she said. "He's a sneaky one. Did you notice how he always gets his way?"

"Don't listen to her nonsense, Finn."

"And see how he likes the last word."

"Don't worry, Birdie," I said, "I'll be fine."

"Yes, you'll be fine."

Before I went out the door, I found myself looking at something familiar on the counter. It was a white bag. That was not so remarkable, but it was from Van Koll's Bakery.

"You're not having one of those," Birdie said. She shook her head playfully.

I just looked at her, speechless and little bewildered. I left and Bishop's voice rose up behind me, muted, but I understood him plain enough.

"Good luck, Finn," he said.

My truck was parked behind the kitchen. As I got behind the wheel, there was something that I realized. It was the Bishops and how much they meant to me. It was our playful talk, our silliness, and above all, our mutual respect. The way they looked out for me, even at times when I didn't deserve it. Bishop and Birdie were the anchors of my life. I loved them more than I had a week before, more each day, but of course, I could never say so. I suppose it was their way of addressing a harsh world with all its troubles. They seemed to care more about the simple things, things we all take for granted. It was the care they had for one another, for behind the ribs and jabs, there was immutable kindness and grace.

As I pulled away, before I turned down the side of the manor, I turned back to it, more by habit than anything else. I passed her studio and saw her, a dark silhouette by the inside door, an impression. I wasn't overly surprised. And although I could not have been positive, I was damn sure that she had been listening to us.

15

I drove slowly through town as it was waking up to a new day. The sun was peeking through the endless clouds as if to hearten one not to give up hope. Charlie had waved to me as I turned the corner onto Fawn Hill Road. He had been rolling a tire into one of his garage bays. A flatbed truck backed into the lumberyard with a load of dressed lumber. I had the window down and could smell bacon and eggs wafting from the Bramble Café. Children walked to school. It all seemed so ordinary. I hoped that it was, a day without the ache of seeing fear in the eyes of children. That day on the river with Bishop that I would never forget. Such divergent moments.

The cemetery was not a place I would normally visit. I had no relatives, no reason to be there. Reverend Le Fleur lived in a little white house on the far side of the church, and as I drove, I looked for him. I wanted to be discreet. I had a good idea where to look in the cemetery. It wouldn't take long. I decided to pull over and wait along the curb opposite the church. I lit a cigarette. There was no one around. It took a certain calculation. I finished my smoke and got out of the truck. I walked across the street casually and stopped at the gate. I opened it slowly, but it yawned and mauled noisily, and I had to stop. But I managed to squeeze through. I waited before

I continued. I listened. There was the clamour of crows in the tall firs bordering the church property, perhaps harassing a hawk or eagle the way they do. Then the hollow thud of chopping wood. Woodsmoke settled thick over the Fawn Hill neighborhoods in December, the smell of home. And then I saw the flowers.

I felt nervous as I crept along the mossy sidewalk, under the gaping church windows, silent witnesses to my curiosity. But it was more than that as I moved between the rows of graves on the damp grass. You see, I was following her. I came up to where she had stood the day before. The flowers that she had placed on the grave held droplets of rain that shimmered like jewels in the sun. White lilies and stems of salal covered the inscription. And strangely, another bouquet. Tiny pink roses resting beside the other like an accompaniment. Someone else had stopped to pay respect. I knew who rested beneath me, and reached down and gently moved the stems.

MICHAEL SPENCER

JUNE 5, 1955–DECEMBER 2, 1956

REST IN PEACE, HEAVENLY CHILD

I looked down at the gravestone for only a moment before I had to turn away. A sudden mood descended upon me, a sick feeling in my stomach that surprised me. It was sadness and regret. It was anger and sympathy. Poor Ted, I thought. I didn't consider *her* so much. I understood that it would have been the worst of times for her. But I just couldn't go to that place. I couldn't give her *human* emotions. I didn't want to think she had bought Birdie pastries from the bakery out of gratitude for the things she did around the manor. I could manage my feelings only as they related to my good friend. That was all. And how strange that Ted was not buried beside his only son. I hurried across the street to my truck. I wasted no time. I turned around in the middle of the street and headed north out of town.

Once on the open road the mind will have its way. There are things you can't shake, that you can't let go of, even though you tell yourself just that. Or you do, but it doesn't last. I knew that my interest in Lady Spencer was more than curiosity. It was a growing obsession. I knew little about her, only that she had been an artist in Nanaimo, nothing more. And yet she knew all about me. It had been no work at all for her. I had these dead-end thoughts as I drove up the Island, through Duncan, then Ladysmith. Time flew by, as if my mind were occupied with something other than driving. I don't know how I had negotiated curves on the highway, how I slowed for deer. I tried incessantly to figure out her motives, why she despised me so. I couldn't remember one instance where I had fallen from her favour. Perhaps that was it. I had never been in her favour. I was never in her life, for that matter. I was a weak appendage. There was just one common denominator, as it were, and that was Ted. The only possibility that could muster such enmity would be jealousy. Yes, I had something that she did not. She had everything, money, admiration, but not his companionship. That one thing unseated all others.

I pulled off the highway at a rest stop at Fanny Bay, the roiling sea cold and dark. Gulls flung down into the green troughs for the fun of it, it seemed, then wheeled away in sweeping arcs, rising like balloons, only to do it all over again. I got out of the truck and lit a cigarette, sheltering my lighter from the wind. I walked to the edge of the parking lot with waves crashing up against the rocks below me. It was a raw west coast day, the kind that would keep most people close to the fire. I wasn't too far from the mill now. I began to think about what I would say, what questions I would ask.

I ate my sandwich and had a cup of coffee from the thermos. I felt a measure of liberty on my own. It wasn't the same freedom of the river that I had recently felt: it was of a different sort. It was the autonomy of my assignment. It was granted in spite of *her* displeasure, sending me away for a day. There were times when I would have avoided such a venture. There was much to fear in the world. Yet I stood with my legs firmly planted, as if I had thrown down roots deep into the earth. The wind pushed and shoved, and I leaned into the stiff will of it, as adventurous as I had been in a long while. I was about to represent Spencer Industries on my own, without a net, without a place to hide. I finished my lunch and continued on.

I saw the smoke from the beehive burner as I pulled off the highway in Courtenay. The sawmill was situated on the outskirts of town on Fraser Road. As I followed the rural macadam, I noticed that my heart beat a little faster and there were butterflies in my stomach. It was just like exam time at university. Time to perform. Soon I came up to the sawmill and passed the yard with endless stores of cut timber, towering stacks of lumber. There were steel-clad sheds and structures that housed the saws and millwork. Long belts of moving lumber. Sorters along the belts, and forklifts backing, loading. The sawdust burner, a tall metal cone, coughed out thick smoke and sparks. I found the office building, turned in, and parked. I sat a moment. I had the file folder with me and gave it a quick review. I still wasn't sure what I would say. Perhaps the superintendent would help me. His name was Welch.

There were stairs leading up to the office, and as I got the top, I noticed someone watching me from down below. He was standing in the yard that connected the office to the mill. He stared up at me. I waved to him for lack of a better response, and he waved back rather tentatively. I wondered if the word had gotten out that the owner's representative was visiting the mill for the day. What anxiety it might cause, a man with power, a man holding a folder that contained their fate. Oh, I suddenly felt the pull of my sensibilities. Perhaps such proclivities had no place in the halls of management. I would have to watch how I presented myself. As the man turned away, I went into the office.

A middle-aged woman greeted me at the door. "Mr. Kenny?"

"Yes. I'm here to see Mr. Welch." I quickly looked around the office. Three women watched with fingers poised over typewriters, another at a filing cabinet. Their swift assessment.

"Welcome to Aldercreek," the woman said. "My name is Mrs. Bradshaw," and then under her breath, "and boy, are we glad to see you."

"Thank you."

"We are so pleased to have you," she said, refreshing her tone. "We don't get to meet the owners very often. But I do remember Mr. Spencer. He was a nice man. Such a shame ..."

"Yes, he was a good man," I said. I noticed the other women were still looking on. They too seemed keenly interested in my visit.

"Please have a seat, Mr. Kenny," Mrs. Bradshaw said, pointing to a small sitting area. "Mr. Welch will be with you shortly."

I took a seat and picked up a magazine—*National Geographic*, of course—but before thumbing through it, I looked up at the clock on the wall. It said one o'clock. I turned to his office door. A template read *Dennis Welch, Mill Superintendent*. I could hear a voice coming from inside. It seemed that he was on the telephone. I sat patiently looking at photographs of Egyptian treasures, pyramids. At one fifteen, I felt annoyed by his indifference and put the magazine down. At one thirty I got up. Mrs. Bradshaw got up as well. She looked a little nervous, even apologetic. She must have seen my growing displeasure.

"He shouldn't be long," she said.

"He *was* aware of our one o'clock appointment, Mrs. Bradshaw?"

"Yes, of course, Mr. Kenny. Perhaps ..."

"Mrs. Bradshaw, please advise Mr. Welch that I've made up my mind."

"Excuse me, Mr. Kenny?"

"Go into his office and tell him. Can you do that for me?"

"I can't interrupt him. He's on an important business call."

"Very well." I walked directly to the door and then out. I never looked back. I hurried down the stairs to my truck. A part of me didn't want him to come chasing after me. A part of me wanted him to pay for his lackadaisical manners. I was the owner, so to speak, and how dare he? Of course, then I realized I had gained nothing, nothing at all. I started my truck with an eye to the office stairs. I would give him a minute longer.

Sure enough, the door opened and Mr. Welch came hurrying down the stairs, his tie flapping over his shoulder. He was a short, rotund man and looked rather comical, but to be honest, I was relieved that he made such an effort. But I wouldn't let him off so easily. I rolled down my window.

"Sorry, Mr. Kenny," he said, gushing his regret with a gravelly voice. "I just couldn't get off the damn line. Sons of bitches. You know how some people are. Come on in!"

I got out the truck, and he shot out his hand. "Dennis Welch."

"Well, it's not a good start, Mr. Welch," I said, taking his hand. "But I believe in second chances."

"Second chances? That seems rather intimidating, Mr. Kenny."

I took him for a man that didn't do well when made wrong. I needed to adjust somewhat. "Every hitch is an opportunity, Mr. Welch, an opportunity to change one's course. You see, I am giving myself a second chance."

His eyes narrowed suspiciously. "I see," he said, which seemed neither an agreement nor an argument. And then he gestured for me to lead the way back into the office. Inside, the synchronized turning of heads.

I followed him into his office. It was spacious and nicely furnished but had a cluttered feeling. And then I noticed that his window overlooked the yard. He had a great view of his operation and the Coast Mountains across Georgia Strait. It was much like an eagle's eyrie. And then a closer look. There was paper everywhere, stacks on his desk, overflowing onto a chair, onto a table.

It had no rhyme nor reason, just paper everywhere. He took his seat behind his desk.

"Please sit."

I looked down at the chair with its sheets of paper. I picked them up and held them rather awkwardly.

"Oh, give me those," he said. "I've been trying to reorganize the office. Make it more streamlined. Mrs. Bradshaw's been having fits. She likes everything just so. But I tell her that it's hard to keep up with all the demands. I suppose you know all about that." He took the papers and placed them on top of a stack on his desk.

I sat with the folder. I opened it and leafed through it until I came up with the most relevant facts. I would begin there. "Mr. Welch, I suppose you know why I called this meeting."

"Judging by your tone this morning, you want me to tell you how we're doing. It's like an inspection. Am I right?"

"Not exactly. You see, your operation hasn't been profitable for some time now. I thought we needed to discuss it."

"What's to discuss? It's a goddamn lumber mill."

"Mr. Welch ..."

"Call me Dennis, for Christ's sake. Too damn formal for me. This is a sawmill, Mr. Kenny. I take it you have a first name?"

That man was as difficult as they come. He had the manner of a blunt tool. I wasn't interested in loosening formalities. "Dennis, I would like you to account for the mill's poor performance. It may be quite obvious to you. It would help if we could determine the cause without delay. Then ..."

He raised a finger at me, a rather bold move. "Have you ever run a mill of your own, Mr. Kenny?"

"No, I haven't."

"I didn't think so. You see, this business has its ups and downs. We're going through a stretch. That's all it is. No use losing sleep over it. There are new orders coming in all the time. We mill the best yellow cedar on the Island. Clear lumber, free of knots and imperfections. Stands up to all weather. We can't keep up with the demand. That's all it is."

"Following what you just said, shouldn't profits be up?"

"We're doing everything we can. Every goddamn worker. If you have a problem, you better come out with it!"

It was like talking to an impertinent child. "You have a yard full of raw logs, Dennis. Isn't it as simple as increasing production? You will lose your markets if your customers are unhappy. And if you lose your markets, your competitors will take them. Spencer Industries prides itself on customer satisfaction. You need to come up with a strategy to accommodate the demand."

He sat back and laced his fingers across his broad chest. He stared at me. I had clearly pissed him off. "You don't know anything, do you?" he said.

"I must be frank with you, *Mister* Welch," I said. "I must prepare a report to the company president within ten days. And if you cannot tell me why your production has fallen, then my report may not be in your favour. You don't want to hear this. I get that. You don't seem like an accommodating man. You are part of a team, but you're not acting like it. You are the captain of the ship, as they say. The men work the sails and you steer the course. You're floundering, Mr. Welch. I suggest you prepare a plan of action at once. It looks like I will be staying the night in Courtenay. I look forward to the receipt of your report tomorrow morning on my way back to Fawn Hill. Does that sit well with you?" I got up from my chair and stood before him.

"You think you know me, don't you?"

"You have a need to defend yourself, Mr. Welch. And why is that?"

"Don't be crazy."

"I must say that you fail to appreciate the tenuous state of affairs for your mill. It is not your mill, Mr. Welch. You must understand that." I turned and went to the door. The rustling of his chair behind me. A great exhalation.

"Mr. Kenny," he said, "I will look into the matter."

I turned to face him. His demeanor had dulled somewhat. He looked more normal, maybe a bit worried. "Thank you, Dennis."

At the front office, I asked Mrs. Bradshaw where I might find a good hotel. She wrote it down on a piece of paper for me. The women looked on rather sheepishly, distraught even. I was sure they overheard what was said. I was aware of my responsibility. It felt heavy and was getting heavier by the moment. I had to get some fresh air. I was glad to see the sanctuary of my truck. I wasn't feeling very well. It was if I had overperformed. But then I realized that it wasn't all a performance, a show for the obstinate, but something of myself. I was upholding Ted's core principles and values, but more than that, they were my own.

I started my truck and noticed a slip of paper tucked under the windshield wiper. I got out and removed it. There was a name written on it, and it gave me chills to read it. *Roland Lantz* and an address. I looked around. There between the office and the mill, that same fellow I had seen earlier. He stared at me for a moment, across the parking lot, as if his message was desperate to reach me, and then he was gone.

16

I drove into Courtenay, along Cliffe Avenue until I saw the Arbutus Hotel down a side street. It was a two-storey affair and had a café. I looked forward to something to eat and a cup of coffee. I needed to think about what had happened back at the mill. I thought I could deal with Dennis Welch. He had been a bit obtuse, not wanting to look at the circumstance of his operation. But numbers don't lie, as they say. And I wasn't going to try to convince him that he had a problem. He had a problem. I just hoped that he would come up with something. But more than that, and more than his grating manner, was the millworker who left the note on my truck.

I parked and went into the lobby. I checked in with the woman at the reception desk. She gave me a key to "a nice room over-looking the street." I didn't mind as I wanted to be able to see my surroundings. Old habits followed me, I suppose. I called the manor from the lobby and told Birdie that I would be staying the night. Nothing more than that. The café was just off the lobby, and I went inside and got a table by a window. I faced the door. I had my file with me and set it down on the table. It wasn't crowded in the mid-afternoon. I lit a cigarette and waited for the waitress. It seemed like a long time. Finally she came to my table with a pot of coffee swinging in her hand.

"What'll it be?" she said. A young woman perhaps twenty-five years old wearing more lipstick than she needed. But pretty. She poured coffee in my cup without asking.

"What's your special today?"

"Salisbury steak if you can wait an hour for the dinner menu."

"Yes, I can wait. The coffee will be fine for now."

"All right," she said, but didn't leave right away. "Are you here on business?"

"Yes, business."

"There was a fellow just asking about you. He seemed a little nervous."

I looked toward the café entrance. "Where is he?"

"He's standing in the lobby. He's a friend of yours?"

Someone poked their head into the café just then. I got a glance at him before he pulled back. "Go ask him if he wants to join me," I said. I thought I knew who it was.

"Sure, I can do that."

I waited as she disappeared. When she came back into the café, he followed her. I could see that he was nervous. His whole body looked jumpy. He didn't look at me, but still he came and sat down across from me. He looked out the window.

"Can I close the blinds?" he asked.

"Go ahead."

He closed the blinds, then slowly turned to me. The poor guy was worried about something. It was difficult to judge his age. I thought he might be in his forties. He had a stocky build. I noticed that his fingers were thick and cracked, a man who worked long hours with his hands. He had something to tell me, and I could sense that it was big.

"I'm taking a chance being here."

"Shouldn't you be at work?"

"This is on my time. I'm working the afternoon shift."

"You're worried about something."

"This could get me fired."

"What could get you fired?"

"I need to trust you."

"I represent the owner of the mill. Do you know that?"

"Yes, I know that. That's why I'm here. You need to know what's going on."

"What's going on?"

"You can't say anything to Welch."

"You belong to the union?"

"Yeah, IWA. Why, do you have a problem with that?"

"It's unusual, isn't it?"

"I couldn't get anywhere with Welch. I tried all the avenues. And nothing."

I reached into my pocket and pulled out the slip of paper. "Why did you leave this on my truck?"

"Do you know who he is?" He whispered now.

"As a matter of fact, I do. He drowned in the harbour. He worked at the mill at one time. What's this all about?"

"This is the part that will get me in trouble."

"Look, I'm not supposed to meet with anyone from the union. We have a process for that. But if this has something to do with my visit to the mill today, then I would like to hear it. I'm not interested in any spats you might have with Welch. I want to be clear. I'm here to find out why this mill is not doing as well as it should. That's all. And I'm giving you too much information. If you get fired over this, then that's on you. All right?"

"You don't understand."

"What don't I understand?"

"He killed Roland Lantz."

"What?"

"Maybe not directly, like sticking a knife in him. But Welch surely killed him. And his prick son-in-law."

"What's your name?"

"Tom."

"Hold on, Tom," I said. I got the waitress' attention. She brought the coffee pot and poured Tom a cup of coffee. I offered him a cigarette.

"I could use one, Mr. Kenny." He took it, and I pushed my lighter across the table. He lit his cigarette and pushed the lighter back.

"You know my name," I said. He took a long drag on his cigarette, then a longer exhalation like a relief valve. He sat back momentarily, seeming to relax. I watched the cigarette smoke curl from his fingers.

"Yeah, I know who you are."

"That's quite an accusation, Tom," I said. "You've been holding that in for a while?"

"Yeah, but I have no proof."

"So Mr. Lantz fell out of a boat or something?"

"It was no boat. He just went out one night for a swim. He didn't tell anyone. Someone had seen him along the beach. He had all his clothes on and heavy boots. He went out and drowned himself. It was no accident. Washed up two days later."

"You think that he killed himself."

"It's called suicide. That's what it was. They drove him to it."

"What do you want me to do?"

"Go see Rollie's widow. She'll tell you."

"What's this got to do with my visit?"

"Everything. Look, the owner came to the mill a few times. Mostly to see Welch. One time, Mr. Spencer came into the lunchroom and sat at our table. He started talking to us. Just like a regular guy. I offered him a smoke and he took it. And when we heard that Mr. Spencer had passed on, it was truly a sad day at the mill. I've been waiting for someone to talk to ever since, before that bastard Welch ruins the mill for good. Can't you see?"

"Tom, you speak about some kind of trouble without specifics. That's not much to go on. I would like to help you, but ..."

"The union raised a fuss with Welch. That made it worse. Things are hard to prove. I know they are. I suppose I could quit. But I can't do that. I have a family to feed. We make decent money. Talk to Rollie's wife. Go see her. Then you'll know."

"Well, I don't know if I can do that."

He looked at me in an odd way. It may have been disbelief, or perhaps it was discouragement. He sat there as if I had snatched hope from him, grabbed it from his unsuspecting hands. A card trick he wasn't prepared for. Then his head began to shake from side to side.

"About a year ago, Jim Skinner retired. He was a good foreman. Everyone liked him. The guys would go through a wall for Jim. He kept Welch away from them. As it turned out, Welch hired his son-in-law after Jim left, made him foreman. Gary Slater. Well, we all knew him to be an asshole right away. He thought he had all this power. He picked on Rollie. There was no need for it. Rollie always did his job well, on the green chain, sorting and grading. Rollie was a bit slow sometimes, but he was good with his hands. A kind sort of guy. He wouldn't hurt anyone. That prick Slater found out soon enough that he could bully Rollie. Ride him for no reason. Some kind of sick pleasure. We all told Rollie to go to the union. And he did, but they said they couldn't do a damn thing. So Gary rode him harder. He is a sick son of a bitch. One day he caught Rollie taking some scrap wood. Wood ends. They just end up in the burner. Jim Skinner let the boys take some home for stoves and such. Welch fired Rollie for theft. He backed his son-in-law all the way. Rollie took it bad, really bad."

"Bad enough to kill himself?"

"Yeah."

"So morale is pretty low?"

"It's so fucking bad, it's pathetic."

"That could have an effect on production."

"At least you're smart. Welch doesn't get it."

"You know, I could get fired for talking to you like this. And I could get you fired. Didn't you think about that?"

"Yeah, I thought about that. But I watched you when you came into the mill. I suppose I thought you were our last hope."

"How did you know I was coming?"

"I've got a friend on the inside."

"I see." I thought of Mrs. Bradshaw just then, her ear pressed against Welch's door.

"You'll see guys leaving soon, Mr. Kenny. Those two jackasses are driving the mill into the ground. There's going to be nothing left to sell, if that's what you've been thinking."

"I'm here to see why production is down."

"Now you know."

"It sounds complicated."

"Go see Mrs. Lantz. Her address is on the slip of paper. She's got something, but she's afraid of that prick Slater."

"I can't promise."

"Rollie was one of your employees. Don't you care about that?" He stood up but didn't leave right away. He seemed to be waiting for an answer.

I looked up at him. I could see that he was under a great deal of strain. He seemed like an honest fellow. Risking it all. "This meeting never happened," I said.

"All right, it never happened. But give me something, Mr. Kenny. For the guys."

Something touched me deeply just then, the inference of my power that was nothing at all. I was at Lady Spencer's disposal, nothing more. I couldn't promise anything. It was a risky venture for me, to be so moved, inspired. But it rolled off my tongue like salvation.

"I won't tolerate a bully, Tom. And if I can see it for myself, intimidation of any kind, then I'll do what I can for you."

"It's for your benefit, too, Mr. Kenny."

"I understand."

Tom left and it seemed as if he had never been there at all. It had been some kind of dream. And it lingered, the faint cry

of a woman and a body floating in the harbour. The day was
nothing like I had expected. But it wasn't so bad. Some things
that I knew, like how to handle myself at a meeting, and dis-
cussions that were ambiguous, calculated. It seemed long ago
now when I had been empowered by the federal government to
negotiate trade agreements. I had been on a team of negotiators
facing tough American counterparts who always threatened to
leave the meetings in order to achieve their goals. Winning at
the table. Yes, a game where they always seemed to have the
upper hand. One of them, I remember, had the sole purpose
of glaring at you and then making notes. It was distracting. It
gave you the impression that you missed something, that you
were perhaps unprepared, even incompetent. He was there to
intimidate. I hated that guy.

And later I hated the RCMP for what they did to me. I had
no stomach for tormentors or tyrants. I had seen it all. And as
much as I wanted to help Tom, and perhaps Mrs. Lantz, I had no
directive to do anything other than assess the production decline
at the mill. And yet it all seemed to be connected to two men.
The very answer to my question, the explanation, was delivered
unsolicited, and perhaps inelegantly, by the compelling account
of a courageous man. I wondered what I should do.

I opened the blinds and looked outside. It was getting dark.
The parking lot was filling up. Men strolled past the hotel lobby
and into the beer parlour. A beer would go down nicely, I mused.
It would help me think. My old, well-worn millworks were turning, moving me away from my resolve. No one would know. And
then two RCMP officers walked into the café for their dinner. It
brought me to attention. My whole body became rigid. I watched
them discreetly, carefully. They removed their hats and sat at a
booth. One of them looked right at me as if to mark me as an
outsider. Damn their suspicion. I had held my breath the whole
time. Then the waitress appeared.

"Your Salisbury steak special, sir," she said.

"Thank you," I said. I had forgotten about dinner. She set down a large plate of ground steak and onions, gravy, mashed potatoes, kernel corn. A bun with a square of butter. The girl stood a moment.

"I thought that I knew him," she said.

I looked up at her, momentarily confused. "Tom?"

"Yeah, Tom Lantz. His brother drowned last summer. Sad, don't you think?"

17

I made some notes before I went to bed that night, trying to sort out what Tom had told me. The brother of the victim, perhaps not the best candidate to indict the mill management. But it wasn't that complicated, not like I had let on. I had a fairly good feel for what Dennis Welch brought to the table. How one handles a work force is a challenge for many employers, but to Ted it was simple. Care about the people who work for you, who can affect your bottom line. It is a symbiotic relationship, much like what I was taught at university. The forest thrives on interdependent relationships in the same environment and enjoys mutual benefits of growth and good health. The employer and employee have similar goals: productivity and prosperity. When that relationship breaks down, by one party or the other, chaos ensues ... "the centre cannot hold," as Irish poet W.B. Yeats said.

The morning was cold and clear, a sharp frost in the night. I was just beginning to warm up when I pulled into the Aldercreek parking lot. I left my notes in the truck. I didn't need them and walked up the stairs purposefully, through the office door without hesitation. Welch's door was open. The ladies looked on, frozen, alert as deer. I smiled affably, respectfully with my day-old beard.

The drama was at a feverish pitch, and although muted, it was one that I would quickly douse.

"Good morning, Mr. Welch," I said. He stood up to greet me.

"Yes, Mr. Kenny," he said. "I hope your stay in Courtenay was satisfactory."

"It was fine." I sat in the vacant chair and he sat at his desk. I couldn't tell if he had a prepared statement or not. The stacks of paper like snow. He had an odd look all at once, as if he were waiting for something. I settled it with a question. "What do you have for me?"

"I made some notes."

"Can I see them?"

"They're rough," he said apologetically. "I needed more time."

"Well, I have to be on my way, so you better give me something." He handed over a sheet of paper. Scribbled notes. "This could have been typed by Mrs. Bradshaw, don't you think?" I folded the paper and stuffed it into my coat pocket without looking at it.

"Aren't you going to read it?"

"Yes, of course."

"That's it?" His agitation was rising.

"Yes, that's it. I will conclude my assessment of the mill back at Spencerwood, and you will be duly notified."

"This all seems a bit hasty to me," he said, clearly aggrieved. "Unnecessary, even. I don't like to be treated like this. Not at all. I would say that you're not an expert on anything. You haven't looked at the mill. How in the hell can you make an assessment without looking at the damn mill?"

His face was flushed, inflamed, looking rather damp. "I don't need to look at the mill, Mr. Welch. I've seen what I needed to see." I stood up to leave.

"What did you see?"

I looked at him, his face of bewilderment. He was truly chagrined. "Your previous mill foreman, he was a good man?"

"Jim Skinner. He was a traditional kind of guy. Why are you asking?"

"You had good production with Jim Skinner. Are you aware of that?" I was playing with him now. I wanted him to come to a realization on his own.

"What about it?" he said, his eyes narrowing, almost menacingly.

"And the current foreman, what kind of guy is he?"

"He's fine!"

"Hand picked by you, Mr. Welch?"

"What are you getting at, Mr. Kenny?"

"I gave you a bit of a road map, Mr. Welch. A clue, perhaps. Now I must go. I thank you for making yourself available on such short notice." I walked out of his office, past the captivated clerks. And then his loud appeal as I went out the door.

"Jesus Christ, Mr. Kenny, you can't leave me hanging like this!"

As I drove away, I could see him in my side mirror standing at the top of the stairs. He was having a tantrum. I didn't mean to be insensitive, but he was a hard man to like. I was more than happy to be back in my truck. The freedom of the open road appealed to me once again. Nothing but my own thoughts. I left the mill, and Courtenay, and headed south. It wasn't long before something occurred to me. My sense of alienation had diminished somewhat. I hadn't been that far away from Fawn Hill in five years, and yet there I was, in the world. Even the police officers in the café had left me alone. I was once again in an undiscovered country. I began to feel a future, and yes, possibilities. I suppose it was the welling-up of pride, or the forgotten sense of myself, that I was capable and competent. There were no agents hiding behind trees. I was pleased how I handled my first assignment, how I had managed the mulish Dennis Welch. I must confess, that the appeal of the hotel beer parlour was another matter altogether, but I did not regress. And when I saw the sign at Royston pointing to Cumberland, I impulsively turned off the highway.

I had remembered that Roland Lantz's widow lived near Cumberland. I flipped open the file on the seat. The slip of paper with her address. It didn't seem far and I had plenty of time. I was curious, perhaps more than that. It was clear to me that Tom

Lantz was devastated by his brother's suicide, and perhaps spoke with a certain bias, which was reasonable, of course. I thought I would take him up on his repeated suggestion to see Mrs. Lantz. It would be prudent to get the clearest picture that I could while I was up-island. My assessment would only benefit from a thorough review. I would never admit it to anyone, but I wanted Lady Spencer to see that I was competent. It sounded pathetic even absurd. For all I knew, if I believed Reverend Le Fleur, she was having me investigated at that very moment.

The many farms and woodlots were swaddled in frost that erupted like white fur from the shrubbery and bracken along the rural roadway. Horses stood smouldering in the sunlight. It was quite lovely, and my mood was strange, but in a good way. I read the names on the passing mailboxes. I slowed when I came up to a name painted white on the side of it. *Lantz*. It was a small farm with thick woods beyond it. A truck and a car were parked in the driveway, and there was someone chopping wood at the side of the two-storey house. I could see his breath in the chill. Chimney smoke rose without deviation on a windless morning. I turned down the driveway and continued on to the house. The man with the axe looked up as I approached. It was Tom. I wasn't overly surprised, but still, I hadn't expected to see him there. I got out of the truck, and he walked over to me.

"I wasn't sure if you would come," he said. He pulled out a pack of cigarettes and offered me one, and I took it.

"I wasn't sure myself," I said. He lit my smoke with his lighter before lighting his own. Tom had qualities I liked.

"What made you come?"

"After I learned that Roland was your brother, I thought I might need another point of view."

"I should have told you."

"Why didn't you, Tom?"

"I was worried that you would just brush me off as an angry and bitter man."

"Are you?"

"Yeah, I suppose I am."

"Hard not to be."

"He built all this, you know."

"Roland."

"He was good with anything made of wood. He built the house, the barn, and the garage there. He was a good father. He was a good brother. I helped him when I could."

"Are you helping now?"

"It takes a lot to run a farm, even a small one like this. He had five kids. He hardly had the time. I bring in firewood for Betty, split it for the stove."

"What about your family, Tom?"

"I don't have one, Mr. Kenny. I had a wife, but she died of cancer before we could start a family. That was a while ago now."

"I'm sorry. You said you had a family to feed. This is it."

"Yeah, it's something I can do."

"You've had some losses."

"I didn't want you to come out here to talk about me. Come on, I'll introduce you to Betty. She might come across as odd, but try to keep an open mind." .

"All right, I'll do that."

"I'm glad you came, Mr. Kenny. I truly am. I promised her that I would ask you to come by. I have to be honest with you, it's not about Rollie. I'm sorry."

"What are you sorry about?"

"Come on in," he said.

Tom opened the front door and he held it open for me. "Betty," he called out, "Mr. Kenny is here to see you."

"Yes, Tom," a voice answered faintly.

I followed Tom through the house, my regret sinking my mood. I was confused. He hadn't told me everything, and I was worried that I was about to be privy to something I didn't want to know. He led me into the kitchen where a woman sat at a table cradling a cup of coffee.

"This is Betty," Tom said.

"Hello, Mr. Kenny," she said. "I'm so pleased to meet you." She offered her slight, pale hand.

"Hello, Betty." I shook her hand. "I'm not sure what I can do for you," I said.

"Please sit," she said. "And Tom, get Mr. Kenny a cup of coffee."

"Cream and sugar, Mr. Kenny?"

"That will be fine." Tom poured my coffee. He added cream, the clink of porcelain as he stirred. There were no other sounds in the house. No children. Tom set my coffee in front of me.

"I'll be outside," he said. "I don't need to hear it all over again."

"All right, Tom," Betty said.

Tom left the kitchen and she turned her head as if to follow him, as if listening for the door to open and close. I looked around the kitchen. There was a photograph on the wall. A family portrait. Betty had changed since then, was hardly recognizable. And Roland, much like Tom. "Where are your children?" I asked.

"At school, in Cumberland."

"Yes, of course," I said. The awkwardness between us was difficult. I felt at a loss. I couldn't recall why I was sitting with this middle-aged woman, her braided hair as grey as a well-travelled asphalt. She wore a blue sweater over a plain dress with a faded, nondescript pattern. But it was her thinness that struck me, her drawn cheeks and hollow eyes that had no colour, no life. They had a haunted aspect, like doors to a deep and private sorrow. I felt unwell with her. I thought I better say something because I was at the point of getting up from that table and leaving. I had enough to go on for my report, even without learning more about Rollie's death. It was a tragic affair, and I felt bad for her, but I didn't need to hear it all again, as Tom had said.

"Tom told me about your husband Rollie's death," I said as sensitively as one could say such a thing. "I'm very sorry for your loss. I know it must be hard for you and the children."

"Yes, it is, Mr. Kenny," she said. "And Tom has been so good to us. I'm thankful for him. But it is not why I wanted to see you."

Tom had warned me. "I don't understand."

"Well, when I heard that you were coming, I just had to see you. It was a rare opportunity, you might say. I've been waiting. You came from Spencerwood." Her voice eked out of her mouth like a flimsy wire.

"I'm not following you, Mrs. Lantz."

"Please, call me Betty."

"Betty, if you could just tell me why I'm here, then perhaps I won't be wasting my time." I was getting annoyed with our conversation, and the reference to Spencerwood made no sense at all.

"I know that Mr. Spencer was a good man. At least I heard that he was. I never met him. I sent a letter of condolences to Spencerwood, but the envelope was returned unopened. So I sent another. I suppose it was expected."

"Expected?"

"Katey and I haven't spoken for nearly twenty years. Can you imagine that?"

"Please, Betty, could you please just come out with it? Tell me what it is so important. I need to go. I'm sorry."

"Oh, Mr. Kenny, I'm the one who should be sorry. You see, Mrs. Spencer is my sister. She calls herself Katherine now, but she will always be ..."

"You are Lady Spencer's sister. Is that what you are telling me?" My brain felt numb all at once. It wouldn't register. It was as if she had been unborn, without a family, without a history.

"Yes, that is exactly what I am telling you. I've been desperately trying to speak with her. Our father is dying. I know she won't care. She discarded the family. Disowned us. The last time I saw her was at an art event in Ladysmith. I saw a photograph of her in the newspaper. I was so proud of her. The name, of course, said Katherine Spencer. Well, I knew her differently. She was born Katey Krom. We grew up in the shadows of the coal mines, not so well off in our company house. I suppose that is what she remembered when I came to see her at the gallery. Do you know, she pretended not to know me, treated me like a stranger? The pain of losing a sister like that. It is such a cruel thing. She took it out on me, and yet she protected me from him.

"She took the slings and arrows, Mr. Kenny, took his urges to shield me. In the night he would come. Our mother never did a thing to keep us safe. Katey was so afraid. She would tell me not to say a word. 'Betty, everything is going to be all right,' she would say, but it wasn't all right, Mr. Kenny. We were young girls. She's my big sister, and she kept him from me. I won't forget. And it saddens me nearly to death that she just let me go, as if I no longer existed, as if I were something to be forgotten. She started a new life. I don't blame her for that. What she had to endure. The pain was too much for her, I suppose. It's the kind that would have surely killed her had she stayed. Still, she left me. And the old man will die soon. The doctor said he had less than a year to live. He's been asking for her. Can a man come to his senses when his death is so close? He's got the coal dust in his lungs. He won't last through the winter. He calls for Katey. Does he want forgiveness? I don't think forgiveness is the proper thing to give. Perhaps just to bear witness to the final breath of the wicked.

"You must know, Mr. Kenny, that I showed up at the Spencerwood gate after our mother died, but I was turned away. So when you get back, I want you to tell her that you came to see me. I want you to tell her about our dying father. I need her, Mr. Kenny, more than any other time in my life. That's the truth of it. And you just arrived at the mill like an answered prayer. Someone sent you. I truly believe that." She sat back and sipped her coffee.

My coffee was cold, perhaps chilled by the litany of her suffering words. "That's an awful story, Mrs. Lantz," I said, "and I can see it is not one made for any reason other than your dire circumstance. I've never heard such a sad account of one's life, and I am stunned beyond belief by the news of your sister. But you must know that I do not know your sister that well. And I must say that we are not on good terms. So what I can do for you may be little or nothing at all."

"Do what you can, Mr. Kenny," she said, then leaned forward and raised a thin finger, "but know this. If my sister does not come to her peace, does not face what has come before her, no matter the hell of it, it will haunt her the rest of her days."

"I understand, Mrs. Lantz. I'll do what I can."

"Very well, and for my dear Roland, there's nothing to be done. He suffered with dark moods, melancholy and such. Tom grieves for his brother. He wants justice where none can be found. The mill means a lot to him. Do what you can for a good man. You will know what to do. I have a good feeling about you. And I apologize if you came today by way of my scheming. I meant no disrespect. I'm not well myself. Some say the past lives in the bones. I need my sister to help me regain my strength. I have children to raise. I'll take a cigarette if you don't mind."

"Yes, of course." I removed a cigarette from my pack and handed it to her. She lit it with a wooden match from a box on the table. The scratch and flare of sulphur. "Can I ask you a question, Mrs. Lantz?"

"Yes, anything you want."

"Do you remember who turned you away at the gate at Spencerwood?"

"Why yes, I'll never forget it. It was a Black man. He was very grave. I remember that."

I pushed my package of cigarettes toward her and then left the table. It had been an extraordinary experience to listen to her, to listen to her story. I was certain that I had heard only an abbreviated version, a brief sketch of a horrific life. Outside Tom was standing by my truck. He seemed uneasy, perhaps regretting the way he had brought me to see his sister-in-law. It didn't bother me so much.

"Tom," I said, "you did the right thing."

He nodded, then offered his hand. "Thank you, Mr. Kenny."

"Call me Finn."

"I appreciate anything you can do for her, Finn," he said. "It's not so simple. Life's not so simple."

"You're right about that," I said.

I got into my truck and backed out of the driveway and onto the road. I looked back at the farm as I pulled away, to the chimney smoke and Tom standing like a man who wanted to be useful in his life, and to the woman inside who only wanted her sister. I drove back down toward Royston and soon began to feel unwell. I needed to stop before I got to the Island Highway, so pulled over near a pond. I thought I was going to be sick. The story I had just heard seemed to be lodged in my throat. I had swallowed something evil, unimaginable. I got out and walked around the truck to the edge of a ditch. I felt dizzy and leaned back against the fender. I took several deep breaths. I tried to find something reassuring to tell myself, something to calm me. There was nothing. There was only the saddest thing I'd ever heard.

18

I was relieved to be back in Fawn Hill. It was a nice little town, familiar and neighbourly. As I turned down Fawn Lily Lane, a couple at Charlie's Garage got out of their car. They seemed to wave to me, like *Welcome home, Finn*. It made me feel good. But it had been a long two days and I was exhausted. As I neared the estate, I realized that everything had changed. Lady Spencer wasn't the same. More accurately, I wasn't the same. I now knew what she was hiding from, why she wore such armour disguised as an outrageous personality. We were much the same in that regard, protecting what was so terribly hurt inside us. But what she had endured at the hands of her own father was beyond shocking or repulsive. It was sickening. How could I hate her now?

I stopped at the back of the manor. I wanted to ask Bishop a question before I retired to my cabin. I didn't know how to ask it. I didn't even know if it mattered. But hearing that Bishop sent Mrs. Lantz away from her own sister's house didn't fit the man I knew. He was a man who thought social justice was about the most important thing one could partake in for the greater good. And I was hungry for Birdie's cooking.

I went into the kitchen and Bishop and Birdie were sitting at the nook table. They both looked up—Birdie happy that I was back, Bishop with a disgruntled look on his face.

"You look rather scruffy," he said. "Did you, by chance, break a promise?"

"What kind of question is that, Percival?" Birdie interjected. "Couldn't you have asked him how his trip was?"

"A man of little faith, Bishop," I said.

"I was referring to his unshaven appearance, my dear."

"No, I didn't have a drink, if that's what's bothering you. I had work to do. And here, I brought back your thermos safe and sound." I placed it on the counter.

"Thank you."

"Can I get you a sandwich, Finn?" Birdie asked. She got up from the table.

"That would be wonderful, Birdie."

"How's corned beef on rye?"

"That's fine."

"Coffee's fresh," she said.

"Thanks." I went over to the cupboard and took a cup from the shelf. I poured a cup of coffee for myself. Bishop was watching me. "What is it?" I asked him.

"He missed you, Finn," Birdie said.

"Is that true, Bishop?"

"I do like male conversation now and then. I was outnumbered, as it were."

"Oh, I see," Birdie said, "you miss talking about what it feels like to have a fish on your lure. That's highly intellectual."

"We don't use lures. We use flies."

"Isn't that a lure?"

Bishop shook his head.

I sat down across from him. He pushed his cigarettes toward me. "So, what's new around here?" I asked. It was good to be back with my friends. I lit my smoke.

"She's out, if that's what you're asking," Bishop said. "The telephone's been ringing off the hook."

"That's curious."

"All I know is that Mayor Greenacre called three times yesterday afternoon. And Reverend Le Fleur. I don't know what it's all about. You have a telephone in your cabin, by the way."

"Yeah, who am I going to call?"

"You can call the kitchen and order your breakfast."

"It's so she doesn't have to see me. That's why I have a telephone."

"Yes, I suppose it is."

"She mentioned your name, though," Birdie said. She put a plate of sandwiches down on the table.

"She mentioned me how?"

"I just heard her say your name. Just heard it."

"Don't start something, Birdie," Bishop said, "if you don't know the details. That's called gossip."

"Oh, Percival if there was ever a man with double standards."

"That's strange, isn't it?"

"It could have been the telephone company, Finn," Birdie said. "I wouldn't read too much into it."

"Yeah, you're right."

"Tell me how your meeting went," Bishop asked. "I would like to hear it. It must have been strange in that new role of yours. I hope you kept your swagger to a minimum."

"It was different, Bishop. But I did find out a few things. The plant has a serious personnel problem. And it is not a union member."

"Good to hear," he said. "That seems rather straightforward. I'm sure your report will be well received."

"I hope so," I said. The question I wanted to ask him wouldn't budge from my reservations. I realized that it could go all wrong, and God help me, I didn't want that. I would be bringing something into the house that I now knew was forbidden. Bishop had loyalties: loyal to his principles and loyal to the master of the manor.

"Anything else?" he asked me.

"He doesn't like to miss a thing, Finn," Birdie said. "And while you two are getting reacquainted, I need to gather the bedding for the wash."

Birdie went upstairs, leaving us alone. I ate my sandwich, wondering what the master of the river was fishing for. That's what it felt like, his question a solicitation for something he already knew. That's when I truly appreciated the man. He was loyal to the manor; that was true. But he was also trying very hard to be loyal to me as his friend. He courted the razor's edge, but I had no such luxury.

"Perhaps there is," I answered.

"Tell me about it."

"How much do you know about *her*?" I asked him bravely.

"I take it you're asking about Lady Spencer. My answer is that I know enough not to inquire. I suggest the same for you."

"Does she have a family?"

"Look, my friend, what are you getting at?"

"It's a reasonable question."

"Not coming from you."

"There was someone I met this very morning, Bishop. I wasn't planning to, and I want to make that very clear. I was told to go see her. I almost didn't. But things work in strange ways, and what I'm about to tell you *is* most strange."

"Who are you talking about, Finn?"

"She claims to be Lady Spencer's sister. She told me that she came here, to Spencerwood, a few years ago after her—*their*—mother died. But she was turned away at the gate. And she claims it was you."

"Me?"

"She said it was a Black man."

"Oh, I see."

"Bishop, for crying out loud, I'm just telling you what she said. All right?"

"Well, I do recall that incident. It was my duty to carry out Lady Spencer's wishes. I don't ask questions. I don't know enough to insert my sensibilities. I do as she asks, and I did on that day."

"You never told me that before."

"Finn, you must understand that there are parts of myself that I won't divulge to anyone, not even to Birdie. My private spaces. You can call them hauntings if you want, or demons. It doesn't matter. They belong to me. And there are things about our employer that I keep to myself. She entrusted me with certain information. It's called confidentiality. Please respect that."

"I understand, Bishop. But I have been given certain information. Her sister's name is Betty Lantz. She's not well, as it turns out, and their father is dying. She's desperate to make contact with her sister. Katey, she calls her. She's asked me to speak to her."

"And how do you propose to do that?"

"I don't know."

"It's a powder keg, Finn. That sums it up. Don't be a fool."

"I'm not planning to. I just wanted to share what happened. That's all."

Bishop became quiet. He lit a cigarette, then listened for Birdie. He leaned over the table. "It seems it's out now. So yes, I knew about her. But it was made quite clear to me not to speak of her, or *their* past. Even Mr. Spencer knew how to leave well enough alone. I don't know the details, and I don't need to know. If you want my advice, just let it go. We'll carry on with our duties, and all will be tickety-boo. All right?"

"She's investigating me, Bishop. You forget that. I haven't done one goddamn thing!"

"I know what you want, Finn. You want the secrets of Spencerwood to be laid bare for the world to see. That's the truth. And I haven't forgotten. Didn't I tell you to keep your nose clean?"

"I'm trying really hard, Bishop. Believe me."

Bishop nodded his head like he truly did believe me. "Yes, I think you really are, but you're not a totally innocent party. Be honest now."

"What are you getting at?"

"That night of your dinner ..."

"What about it?"

"There's something I need to tell you, Finn. I wasn't planning on telling you and messing up your return from Courtenay. But I feel you need to know. It may be nothing."

"Say it, Bishop."

"Birdie was in town getting a few groceries yesterday, and as usual a few locals chatted her up. So far, so good. Then one of the women said something very interesting. She said, 'I hear that your gardener is a Communist.' Birdie, of course, was taken aback. But the woman continued. 'He even drives a red truck.' Birdie didn't know what to say. She was quite shocked by the whole episode."

"Jesus, Bishop."

"Well, it's not good, is it?"

"She's spreading things about me. I know she is. It's all lies, Bishop!" How swiftly my animosity returned. It took over me, filled my head with an unmitigated anger.

"I don't believe that Lady Spencer is behind this incident. I may be wrong, but I think you may have started it."

"That's a load of bullshit, Bishop, and you know it!"

"Keep calm, will you?"

"Sorry."

"Look, there were a few notables at your special dinner. And your toast, or whatever it was, must have made an impression on them. In a small town, people will talk. They want to protect their little world."

"I was drunk, for Christ's sake."

"That could make your comments more disturbing, actually. You showed them with your political rambling, no matter if it was only in jest or due to inebriation, who you are. You planted something in their little minds. This is a problem. I am sure that is why the telephone wouldn't stop ringing. And the newspaper could get hold of it, and it could race through the village like a fast-moving fire. It would be a son of a bitch to put it out."

"This is not right, Bishop."

"Most folks in the West hate Communists, fear them like the plague."

And then I remembered what had happened in town. "At Charlie Sales's garage, when I was coming through town, a couple waved to me as I passed. I didn't know them."

"It may not have been a greeting, Finn, at least not what you thought."

"What am I going to do, Bishop?"

"I'm afraid that it's up to you. You have to come up with a solution, a self-made one. A kind of countermeasure. Damn it all, I'm sorry I had to tell you."

"Yeah, I know, Bishop, but you had to."

"It's a shitty turn of events."

"I feel bad for Birdie."

"She'll be fine, Finn. She knows what's right and what's wrong."

"I'm glad someone does."

19

Whenever Bishop spoke, it was if he had a grasp on the truth and I were a mere observer. It would be easy enough for him just to tell me what I needed to do. But that wouldn't have been a self-made plan. I was at loss, and it wasn't the first time. It seemed that I was just coming out, so to speak, coming back into the community after a long hibernation. And yes, I may have planted the seed of my own failure. Spencer Industries wouldn't tolerate such a stain on their reputation for a minute. I would be gone. I had to see it with my own eyes. I had to hear whatever it was, the censure, whatever the mood was in Fawn Hill. I would go into the village. I had the chainsaw that needed sharpening. And I knew who would have his finger on the pulse of our town. Grubby Smith, at the lumberyard and hardware store.

I had a good night's sleep, more so from mental exhaustion. I had been too tired to ceiling-gaze the night through with imaginings and worries. I loaded the chainsaw into the back of the truck and left without coffee or breakfast. I thought that I would have something to eat in town. The Bramble Café would be packed with customers, and in no time at all I would surely know where I stood. The thought of it made me anxious as I left the estate.

It was a cloudy morning that threatened rain. Everything was damp and heavy. The world was slowly withdrawing, the woods shrinking back. The air had a smell of dank rot, decay, an odour of mouldy sweetness. I didn't mind it so much. It reminded me of our root-cellar in Cork, with the potatoes and carrots in crates of sand and apples cold in their boxes. Jars of floating beets, pickles, and jams from the summer berries picked along the River Lee. A smell can do that, take you away in an instant. But not for long, as I soon came up to the stop sign at Fawn Hill Road, where I turned to see Charlie pumping gas at the corner. I waited for him to look up, but he didn't. I honked my horn as I turned the corner, and finally his head came up. I waved, but I was too far along to know if he had waved back. I felt the restless need to know, to dispel what Bishop and Birdie feared, that it was all just a mistake, a misinterpretation. Nothing wrong at all.

I parked in the lumberyard parking lot. There was a small machine shop inside the hardware store. I went in the side entrance where there was a window to drop saws off for sharpening. That's where Grubby worked. I'd heard that he'd been working that window for nearly thirty years. And he worked as the projectionist at the theatre on the weekends. I put the chainsaw on the counter. I could see him at the back of the shop working a file on a long crosscut saw, the drag and rasp on metal teeth. Such a sound incites a shiver through the body. After a few minutes he looked up to see me standing there and came over rather slowly. He was getting on in age, but it was understandable. Grubby had one gear. He looked at me before he looked down at the saw.

"It's lost its edge," I said.

"I haven't seen you in a while," he said. "You been sharpening this yourself at the estate?"

"Yeah, I tried to, but I think you do a better job."

"You're right about that. Now I'll have to undo all your poor attempts. That might cost you more."

"That's all right," I said. Grubby was a tall fellow, but his back was bowed, and he had lost some height. He looked up at me as I stood there, a kind of sideways look. He was going over me pretty thoroughly. I could almost read his old mind.

"I've heard a few things about you," he said, "none of them flattering."

"What kind of things?"

"Well, people come in here and tell me a lot of things that I don't care to know. I sharpen saws, for goodness' sake. This one fellow, and I won't say his name, said to me, 'Did you hear about Finn Kenny?' 'The grounds keeper at the Spencerwood estate?' I asked. 'That's right.' 'What, did he die?' 'No, he's a Communist.' He said it just like that."

It was strange to hear it come out so easily with Grubby. I hadn't needed to go far. "It's just crazy talk," I said. "Don't listen to it."

"That's not so easily done," Grubby said. He dug into his ear with a finger. "You see, people need to tell someone. They want to tell someone who will listen. I've got no goddamn choice, now do I?"

"I suppose you get an earful," I said, with no pun intended.

"So what's it all about?"

"Something from a while ago. I guess you could call it gossip, or hearsay. There's nothing to it, really." I was trying to defend myself without explanation.

"There's no shortage of that around here."

"Yes, I suppose you're right about that."

"You keep to yourself a lot."

"I prefer it that way."

"Most people don't like people who hide. They get suspicious."

"I'm not hiding. I'm just a certain way."

"It'll stick like a nickname. I know that much."

"So how did you end up with a name like Grubby anyway?"

"My older brother Norman. I was the youngest, you know, and that's what he called me. It might have been due to the fact that I was filthy most of the time. It was a farm in Saskatchewan, for goodness' sake. Well, it stuck, and I've been Grubby Smith most of my life."

"Yeah, some things are hard to change."

"Don't let it stick," he said. "Whatever they're saying, don't let it stick. It'll be like your skin. You'll never get away from it. I don't give two shits about what people say. I just want to sharpen saws." He handed me a ticket stub for the chainsaw. "Come back in two days, and it'll be ready to cut wood again."

"Thank you," I said. And as I turned to leave, he asked me a final question.

"You don't have your eye on the mayor's chair, do you?"

I stopped and thought about the question and where it had originated. I couldn't find a reasonable answer. The absurdity of it left me mute. He looked at me as if I might reveal some detail, some evidence of my guilt. He was in a relationship, after all, one side of the counter with the other. It was an exchange that he participated in every day. I didn't blame him for it. I shook my head, not in answer to his question, but in disbelief. I was more discouraged than anything.

"You don't have to answer," he said.

I simply nodded to the old man.

"And, Mr. Kenny, do you know what's playing at the theatre this weekend?"

"No, I don't."

"*It's a Mad, Mad, Mad, Mad World*. Isn't that something?"

When I got back to my truck, I turned on the engine and sat idling until the heater warmed the cab. I didn't like the cold. I wasn't interested in the movie, although I was quietly amused by Grubby's sense of its irony. I had my own life of madness, as it turned out. I lit a cigarette to help calm my nerves, but I could feel the past threatening like a November storm. The winds were beginning to blow, the same foul wind that scoured the streets of Ottawa. Not again, dear Mother, not again.

I drove by the Bramble Café just to get a feel for it, as if to practise my nerve. It was far more difficult now that I had spoken with Grubby Smith. He had reserved his judgement despite what his customers might have said, but the café was the hub of Fawn Hill mornings. It was where people gathered to talk about community news—a death, a birth—and most usually to air their grievances with all levels of government. On my third pass, I knew it was time to face them all, go in among them and see how it really was. I pulled over and parked. The rain was spattering on my windshield. I listened to the sound on the roof, a soothing percussion. It was simple music without scale or progression and calmed me enough to have second thoughts. I wondered if I was making too much of it all. Bishop, as I had come know, erred on the side of caution, perhaps to prepare me for the worst. And I would feel a sense of relief if it turned out to be only a minor inconvenience, a bit of name calling, the way children do. But enough negotiating.

I got out of my truck and went up the sidewalk with my head down against the wind. A police car drove through town very slowly. It came from the RCMP detachment in Duncan. The police usually just drove through, but I turned against the wet slap of weather to watch him leave. And as I came up to the café, I could see a familiar face in the window. I went in and the bell sounded above the door, and immediately I felt the collective silence, the turning of heads. The restlessness of the room was palpable. I took quick notice of who was at the tables before I took a seat at the coffee bar at the back. The Willett sisters moved back and forth in a kind of caterer's dance with the orders and dirty plates. The sisters were identical twins and I had never taken the time to get their names right. Ruby and Pearl. Luckily, Pearl was wearing her name tag.

"What will it be, Mr. Kenny?" she said.

It seemed that it was business as usual. I had lost my appetite, but I ordered anyway. "Ham and eggs, Pearl," I said, to be pleasant, "and a cup of coffee, of course."

"How would you like your eggs?"

"Over easy." She wrote it on an order pad.

"Would you like toast with that, Mr. Kenny?"

"No, not today." As she reached for the coffee pot, I became aware of a murmur coming from behind me. It was strange. There was no laughter from a well-timed joke, no punctuated voices from a disagreement, not a rant. It seemed the breakfast conversation had been curtailed. It was the sound of discontent. And as Pearl Willett poured my coffee, she muttered under her breath.

"They're hostile this morning," she said. "Ruby said so, too. She keeps an eye and an ear on things." Then she turned away with my order.

I wanted to turn around, but I didn't need to. I had memorized the room the moment I walked in the door. Mayor Greenacre was sitting by a window. He was with one of the aldermen. And there were others sitting over their pancakes and eggs: Mr. Portman from the train station and Mr. Raggett, the pharmacist wearing his white smock. There was Tony the Italian barber. He would have put his sign up on his barbershop door that said he would be back in fifteen minutes but rarely was. A Dutch dairy farmer and his wife, but I didn't know their names. There were a few unfamiliar faces, but that was not so unusual for me. But I was certain they knew who I was.

I lit a cigarette as I waited for my breakfast. I smoked and sipped my coffee with an uneasy anticipation. I would be happy if nothing happened at all. But the murmurs began to swell, as if it were the bloom of madness. Perhaps turning my back to them was a mistake. I had set myself apart from them, and it would likely invite trouble. I thought better of it and decided I should leave. It was a bad idea. And then a shout at my back like a tossed stone.

"Go back to Moscow!"

It was followed by laughter from the others that gave rise to their latent bravado. And then another brazen diner, and then another, each giving licence to the next, each granting his fellow permission to hurl their contempt my way. It was the fevered domain of men.

"We don't want your kind around here!"

"Burn his *Red* truck!"

"Go back to your own country!"

"Yeah!"

"No good Commie!"

"Son of a bitch!"

"Traitor bastard!"

"Fawn Hill doesn't want you!"

"Stop it!" the mayor suddenly cried out above the insults. "We're better than this. This is no way to behave."

"Well, you're the mayor," a voice answered him, "and you should bloody well do something about it!"

The swell of affirmation silenced the ineffectual mayor, who Grubby intimated had started such discontent. I felt corralled like beef being led to slaughter, yet the worst might be yet to come. I wasn't so much afraid as I was disturbed. It quickly turned to anger. I could feel the rage rising in me, the way it did when I couldn't stop it. But I was sober, and I got up from the stool. It was all I could do to restrain myself. It seemed my whole life depended on it, that moment, that decision. I took out my wallet and left a two-dollar bill on the counter. Pearl Willett looked on with her hand over her mouth. I slowly turned around to face the ugliness of a town, a town that I had so much wanted to be a part of. I tried to look at each one of them, but I couldn't. I couldn't bear to see fear burning in their eyes, the effects of their menacing transformation. I started for the door. They were quieter now, momentarily hushed as if parting to make way for the danger they were so convinced walked with me. I wanted to say something.

I wanted to quell their outrage, extinguish the hatred burning inside them. It seemed to have taken on an entity of its own, and it overpowered the café, filled it with something impure and vile, a contagion passed from one mouth to the next. But I would give them nothing more.

20

I went back to my cabin. I never stopped at the manor kitchen. I didn't want to go through it all again with Bishop. I would tell him soon enough. I just wanted to be alone, retreat to my cave like I had always done. I would lick my wounds. That was the value of a bottle of Jameson whiskey. It had a way, albeit temporary, to restore one's beaten self-image,. I wanted a drink in the worst way. It seemed that I hadn't the strength to be the man that Bishop thought that I could be. Perhaps I couldn't manage without liquor. I had great doubts now. And then the telephone rang, scaring the hell out of me. I answered it.

"Hello."

"Mr. Kenny, I would like to see you in my studio right away."

"Your studio?"

"Yes, that is correct."

"Now?"

"Yes, I have something to tell you."

She was the last person on the planet that I wanted to see just then. And how many times had that very thought crossed my mind? I held the telephone against my chest. I didn't know what to do. I could hear her on the other end, her voice down a well.

"Mr. Kenny!"

"All right," I conceded. "I'll be right there."

"Fine." She hung up the telephone.

My temperament was all wrong. I wasn't settled enough to see her, if that were even possible. Everything was happening too fast. I needed to gather my thoughts while I was still rational. I needed to make sense of the morning—of life, for that matter. I went in through the kitchen and Birdie seemed to be waiting for me. Bishop had been mopping the floor and leaned on the mop handle. I couldn't stop to chat, so continued on through the kitchen, and as I passed Birdie, she gently touched my arm. I caught the sympathetic tilt of her head. Bishop was silent. There would be no moral support, no last-minute preparation like a trainer shoring up the confidence of his bleeding prize fighter. In the ring, the blows would surely come. And what would he say? *Don't run away, my friend. This is it. Face what frightens you the most.*

It was not so profound, but simple and direct. There could be no confusion. Still, it was all I could do to move my feet down the hall, then warily approach the door to her studio. It was open. But I couldn't step inside. I stood there, immobile and uncertain. She had her back to me. There was a painting in progress on an easel in front of her. She wore a flower-patterned smock and held a paintbrush in her hand. She held it up, gently stabbing the air as if in practice. I recognized the subject of the painting. It was the white trellis in the summer garden, scarlet roses climbing the latticework, and at its base, incomplete, was a cat.

"Come in, Mr. Kenny," she said all at once. Eyes in the back of her head.

Still I didn't move, and then she turned partially until I could see the outline of her cheek. She waited, holding her breath.

"Well, Mr. Kenny?" she said finally.

I moved to the side of her easel, wondering what she wanted to tell me. I had a feeling what it might be, but I hoped that it wasn't.

Then she pointed to a chair where Darby O'Gill was sleeping, curled up and oblivious. It was something that I wanted to do on occasion, to be unaware of the world.

"Pick up the cat," she said. "I want you to hold it. Darby O'Gill has been most uncooperative."

"Hold the cat?"

"Yes, hold the cat. Do you think that you can manage that, Mr. Kenny?"

Her sarcasm was interesting if not tiresome. I picked Darby O'Gill up from the chair, all limp and sleepy, then stood there rather foolishly.

"I just want you to hold him," she said. She glanced my way now and then, but her eyes never really landed on me. "You see, I have to get his eyes just right," she went on. "A certain look that I want. It's the eyes, really. His eyes are a cold blue. Cats are filled with mystery, don't you think so, Mr. Kenny?"

"I suppose." It was something that I hadn't given much thought.

"And his colour. Is he an orange cat or is he a ginger cat?"

"I don't know, really. Perhaps orange."

"It's not quite orange, is it? It's more like your hair, an Irish red, but a little lighter. They call it strawberry blond. Yes, I think that's it. They say that redheads can tolerate more pain. Do you think so?" She looked at Darby O'Gill, then to my hair.

"I guess so," I said. It was all so uncomfortable that I ached all over. She painted while I stood holding Darby O'Gill. And still she hadn't looked directly at me, just averted her attention as if the easel were something placed between us, impeding her view, keeping us apart. She seemed to employ devices that helped her, that protected her. I had a few myself, but I wasn't suddenly a sympathetic man. It was there, of course, as my mother instilled in me some sensitivity. But Lady Spencer was far too complex to rouse my unquestioned tolerance. I wasn't ready to see her in the full light of understanding.

"You don't seem so sure, Mr. Kenny," she said.

"What do you mean?"

"'I suppose.' 'I guess so.' It's not the self-assured tone of an advisor, now, is it?"

"I suppose not, but ..."

"Really, Mr. Kenny?"

"I don't feel quite right speaking with you just now," I said in a moment's honesty. "I'm a little out of sorts. I had a strange morning."

"It seems things are getting uncomfortable, Mr. Kenny. The mayor called. He wants a meeting."

"What kind of meeting?"

"He wants to head things off at the pass, if you know what I mean. The town is not happy with you, Mr. Kenny."

"And why is that?" I asked without thinking. Always her conversation pressing me down with a derisive thumb. Darby O'Gill began to squirm in my arms, perhaps sensing my growing agitation. He jumped down to the floor, then went back to his chair.

"You know why," she said.

"And *you* know why," I countered.

"What on earth are you talking about?"

It came rushing out, unstoppable now. "But you do, Lady Spencer, lady of the manor, who feels it her right to go into a man's private affairs. I know you were in my cabin. It seems you read things not meant for your eyes. Those are my personal papers. It was a trespass that turned into your advantage. I know that you want to be rid of me. And you're using it to that end, drumming up hate against me. I know it was you, and you cannot deny it!"

She turned to face me squarely with eyes like brands of fire, her paintbrush raised like a censure to the very air I breathed. "You think I'm some evil hag, don't you, Mr. Kenny?"

"I only know what I see."

"That does not answer my question."

"You investigated me. You looked into my past in order to ruin me. Tell me it's not true!"

"You have your proof, do you?"

"And very reliable."

"Oh, the good Reverend Le Fleur. You must think yourself very clever, Mr. Kenny."

"I suppose I'm as clever as you are."

"All right then, if honesty is what you want, I did have you investigated. It was in the best interests of Spencer Industries. As far as my alleged trespass, I was doing my duty. I did read your book, or whatever it is, Mr. Kenny. I've always had suspicions, you see. I asked one of Diefenbaker's cronies to look into your time in Ottawa. He found nothing. And that fact was both disappointing and a relief."

"Why would you be relieved?"

"Do you think that I am so removed from charity?"

"I see no charity in a witch hunt."

"The witch left no trace. It seems that you were erased, Mr. Kenny."

"I'm not surprised, really," I said. Then I considered a simple but relevant question. "Did you read about Ted, then?"

"It wasn't news to me, I'm afraid. It doesn't matter so much anymore."

I nodded. "So why the falling out with the reverend?"

"He had other, let me say, holy solutions for you."

"You wanted to investigate me. You went to a lot of trouble. You just could have asked me."

"And you would have answered civilly?"

"Perhaps not."

"Mr. Kenny, I did not set the town against you, as you so hotly expressed. I believe you are the author of your own disgrace. What I did didn't cause or enflame your position. You brought that about all on your own."

"But *why* were you disappointed that you didn't find something? Tell me that."

My question seemed to catch her off guard. She stroked Darby O'Gill. "There's a villain in every story, Mr. Kenny," she said.

We stared at each other for a long time in a haze of ambiguity. The words lingered, drifted, as if they didn't know where to land. For the first time, she had revealed herself to me. She made no attempt to look away or delve into some topic, some diversion. I saw the hardness of her mouth. It was grim, fastened with a kind of resolve that she couldn't undo. She looked older. Perhaps it wore on her, the constant turning away of the past. She wore make-up to hide the imperfections of a woman. How unfair it must have seemed, while men greet the day with nothing but the stark baggage of their lives. It could have been that she was tired, as I was tired. Looking for happiness that always seemed out of reach, like an illicit pleasure.

The truth of the matter seemed to vacillate between our stories. And still she seemed to have the upper hand, always one step ahead of me. I knew at that very moment that I could slam her with her own past. I could crush her with the things I knew, what I had been asked by her sister. I could rip open the terrible wound buried so deep inside her. My sweet revenge. But I couldn't just then, or perhaps ever. It was not the time nor the circumstance. It might come, surely, but it would be measured and humane.

"So here we are," I said.

"Yes, here we are." She put down her paintbrush.

I couldn't maintain my anger because she was right. Although it was hard to admit, I had not been so innocent, as old Bishop had reminded me. I wanted someone to blame, and I wanted it to be her. Strangely, we both found ourselves without anything further to say, nothing more to attack, nothing more to defend. And there was something inside me, a shift in my perception, what I thought of her. It was if Betty Lantz had left me with a curse that exposes one's prejudices and reveals the depth of one's hatred. It's the awareness that changes everything.

"What now?" I asked. She left the easel and lifted Darby O'Gill from the chair, pressing her nose into his fur in a rare show of affection. She had many shades, some predictable, some impulsive.

"We seem to be at a crossroads, Mr. Kenny," she said. "I'm not sure what to make of it."

"I'm tired of the discord, the constant tension."

"It seems to follow you, Mr. Kenny."

"I'm aware of that fact. And the trouble in the village this morning was hard to stomach. So, is a meeting going to resolve the rage I heard?"

"I cannot predict what will happen, but Mayor Greenacre is anxious to calm the inflamed mood of the town. You can say whatever you want at the town hall tonight. It will be a closed meeting for information gathering. I believe the mayor has reached a consensus with the aldermen."

"Then you must know what he will say?"

"No, I do not."

"I'm finished here, then?"

"Yes," she said.

"You haven't asked me about my trip. I think that I may have ..."

"You've only just come back, Mr. Kenny," she interrupted. "You have time to prepare a report. I will see it then." She walked out of her studio with Darby O'Gill.

I regretted saying anything about my trip. It was ill-timed. It was far too close to the abyss of her childhood. I left the manor feeling somewhat disoriented, yet at the same time encouraged. What was resolved between us? It was a strange question to consider. There had been plenty of suspicion, blame, threats, accusations, and sheer tension that felt like a claw ripping my insides. She had been a convenient reason to drink, to drown my sorrow, a remedy for the irreconcilable. But something had happened between us. It was the truth, the simple expression of honesty, at least as much as we could give. It seemed like a fresh breeze in the foul air, but I had to wonder if it could be sustained. When things are new, there is no telling their fortune. And understanding does not come all at once. I could only glimpse the innocence in her, the hurt child. It wasn't so easy to know her—or anyone for that matter.

How strange that a passage will visit you, will demonstrate that a lesson must be learned for one's life to be truly meaningful. My mother said that very thing, perhaps not in so many words, but in that way of hers. And to think that I had written about it, how the most difficult challenges can be a blessing. How quickly I had forgotten.

There was a miserable old man who lived near the dike outside of Cork. The River Lee ran by his little cottage, which wasn't much, thatch and stone, a few trees. When out along the river, I would see him, cane in hand, walking with his slow dog in the moors. He had cut a trail there and would go for an hour, then return on the same trail. So worn it was. His name, or what the local children called him, was Mad McGee. Mad McGee lived alone with his old dog. He was said to be a cranky sort of man, given to fits when fishermen walked his dike without permission. He snarled more than he spoke. I always gave him a wide berth when I tried to sneak past his house to find the sea trout thick in the emerald pools. He had swung his cane more than once.

He walked in the moors every day. It was his habit. I had come to know habits, not so much from my own, but by watching people, the dairyman who came every morning at six o'clock, the postman ringing the bell on his bicycle soon after. School was much the same, but a habit of a different sort, where children shared the same routine. But Mad McGee had no one to care one way or the other why he chose to leave his little house at the same time each morning.

One year when school began in the autumn, I began to think how I might regain the favour of my mother. I was "no good," after all. It was a fine day indeed, a Saturday, and Mad McGee would be out in the moors for his walk. He had an apple tree. It always seemed to me an old craggy sort of tree. It had looked half-dead all winter long, but in the spring it would come to life for the bees and in the fall it would be heavy with glorious apples. I snitched one on occasion, when out for the day, always timing my arrival after his departure. He had never caught on to me.

I had an idea for a good deed. He wouldn't miss a few of his apples, surely, he wouldn't. After he left for his walk through the moors, I took a gunny sack and climbed his apple tree, up the crooked limbs, and filled my sack. I managed to lower it to the ground, but as I began to carry it home, it was all I could do to move it along. It was like a sack of rocks. I had to drag it through the grass now and then. Once home, I left my burgeoning good deed by the shed. I didn't want my mother to find it and ruin my surprise for her.

The following Monday, I carried that bag of apples through the streets of Cork to school. I immediately told the school master that I had brought apples for all the children. He was so pleased. He thought me a grand sort of boy. I had hoped that might sing my praises to my mother for my effort. But how strange that my mother's pride would never see the light of day. It seemed that the old man had been on to me, saw me from a distance, a boy spending too long in the tree. Word got out of what I had done. It was still a good deed, was it not?

That is what I had tearfully asked my mother when the school master arrived at our house with, much to my dismay, Mad McGee. I was in a terrible fix. They made a whole lot of fuss out of a few apples. I couldn't understand it at all. "There'll be more apples next year," I reasoned, but it had no effect on their crumpled chins. Before the day was through, the adults had agreed that I should hear the story of Mr. McGee's apple tree. I was about to be bored to more tears; I just knew it. Yet I would know soon enough that there was more to an apple tree than I had ever imagined.

They sat me down with him. He wasn't angry but sad. I supposed that he was fond of his apples. He must have liked them a great deal. But it wasn't even that. He told me that his wife had died when I was just a little boy. When they were first married, they had received a gift from her father in Scotland. It was an apple tree, but not just any old apple tree. It was a Galloway Pippin, an old Scot variety. He told me they took great delight when the first blossoms came, and then the ripened fruit in September, green with a red blush, firm and crisp with a good rich flavour. His wife's name was Margaret, and she made pies from the apples and sold them on the market street in Cork. Ever since her passing, he'd been making the pies himself and selling them at the market. The money for the pies helped him get by. It seemed that along with the apples, I stole his memories, his income, and the things that he looked forward to. A small thing like that gave him a purpose, gave him the strength to live another day. He was much like the old tree, crooked and bent. I felt bad for my good deed. I felt bad for Mr. McGee as I learned how a man could come to grieve for his apples, how there was more to almost anything. It was a heartbreaking day.

Later my mother took me aside and acknowledged my good deed, saying that although my intentions were good, I hadn't thought it through. "We just never know what a neighbour, or even a stranger, is carrying with them. There can be a great weight we cannot see. So keep that in mind before you make your judgements, before you think you know the whole story. Mr. McGee has lived a long life and knows a thing or two about loss and loneliness. This day has been a gift for you, Finn. Do well with it."

She was a clever mother, and I didn't doubt for a minute that she knew my true motivation for stealing the apples. It hadn't come from generosity, but from craving her love, of course.

21

The moon blinked in and out through the drift of thinning clouds. It was seven o'clock and all was dark and cold in Fawn Hill, but the lights were on in the town hall. The Red Ensign hadn't been lowered for the day and hung limp and wet, giving a formality to the evening. I couldn't imagine what the mayor would say. Perhaps he would explain the rude behaviour of more than a few of Fawn Hill's citizens at the Bramble Café. Perhaps he would reassure me, even apologize on behalf of the town. Mayor Greenacre was a laughable man at times, although I must give him some credit for trying to contain the unruly breakfast mob. There were cars parked along the curb, one a gold Cadillac. I supposed that Lady Spencer must attend because she was my employer and would bring a certain insight to the meeting. But that was hardly reliable.

I had a cigarette on the front step of the town hall before going in. That's when I noticed the reverend coming up the street, passing under a streetlight like a spectre. His dark robe billowed and pooled and made him appear to float above the ground. I was mesmerized by the illusion he projected. It was unsettling.

"Good evening, Reverend," I said as he came up to the hall. "I'm glad you brought your feet."

"Ah, yes, Mr. Kenny," he said. "It is a phantasm of sorts, what the mind prescribes to what it cannot understand."

"All that?"

"You seem to be in good spirits, in spite of the town's bad behaviour."

"Nerves, to be honest."

"I'm sure it is. Shall we go in?"

I flicked my cigarette out onto the cold-stiff grass, then followed Reverend Le Fleur inside. I had never attended a meeting of the town council, so I felt a little lost. The reverend went down a hall past what appeared to be the council chambers, then to a meeting room. The door was open, and we went inside. Mayor Greenacre stood up immediately.

"Thank you for coming, Mr. Kenny," he said. "Please have a seat."

We sat at a long table. Reverend Le Fleur sat on my side of the table, while Lady Spencer, the mayor, and an alderman were seated on the other side. Lady Spencer was well dressed as usual in a steel-grey coat with a black collar. Her hair was neatly done up. She looked smart, like the president of a well-respected company. I recognized the alderman, but I didn't know the man. His combed-back grey hair had a white stripe down the middle like a highway. At once I identified a certain disdain on his upper lip.

In that official setting, there were no pens and paper, no notebooks, nothing to keep record of the proceedings. I guessed that is what Lady Spencer meant by a closed meeting. I had the odd sense that I was the accused, the reverend in his robes my attorney.

"I think you know everyone here, Mr. Kenny," the mayor continued.

"Yes, I think so," I said, "although Alderman Hutton and I have never spoken. But I know *who he is*." My emphasis let him know that I was on to him. He worked for the regional district and was a strange addition to the group. He had his mind made up before I entered the room.

"Very well," the mayor said. "This is an informal meeting to review recent and troubling events in our town. It is not something we are used to. We are an accommodating town, but a moral town. We need to look at the root cause and stamp it our before something regrettable happens. I cannot lose control of our—"

I interrupted him. I had to. I had a strong feeling that I was being accused of some wrongdoing. "If I could say something, Mayor Greenacre," I said.

"Yes, go ahead."

"I must say that it is most inappropriate for an elected official to request my attendance at a meeting that can only be described as scandalous."

"Scandalous, how so?"

"Well, I will turn the question back to you. Why am I here? Tell me that."

"Let's all take a pause for a moment," he said. "I don't want this meeting to be derailed before it even begins. So let me explain. As you know, there is a lot of talk in Fawn Hill at the present time, and it involves *you*, Mr. Kenny. You have made certain statements that are now well known. It has made the citizens of Fawn Hill uneasy in your presence. You represent something counter to all that they know. And I've been hearing about it, and it seems to be growing. I don't want this to turn into some sort of lynch mob, where citizens take matters into their own hands. So I want to hear it from you. Tell me what your associations are, your contacts, if you will."

Each looked at me, save for Lady Spencer, who stared uncharacteristically down at her folded hands on the table. It wasn't like her. She liked attention, whatever the situation. She liked to be heard, but she was quiet on that night. It all seemed a travesty as if the past were repeating itself. I was stunned

"I don't have to answer your questions, Mayor Greenacre," I said. "I have done nothing to warrant such questions, or my attendance at this meeting for that matter."

"So you do not deny it?"

"Deny what?"

"That you are affiliated with the Communist movement. There are such enclaves of dissention in this country. And there is the matter of your history."

"My history?"

"Yes, your liaison with a certain Russian sympathizer. Do you also deny that?"

Lady Spencer had said that she had found nothing with her investigation, but still she had read my manuscript, in part at least. She was the only one who knew about Ivanov, other than Bishop. And Bishop I trusted with my life. "Tell me, Mayor, where did you get such information?"

"I'm not privy to tell you my source. Please answer my question."

I heard the rustle of his robes beside me, the quiet Reverend Le Fleur. He had some knowledge, although how much I didn't know. He seemed to think that he need only answer to God. Everything was black and white to him. He answered to what he believed to be the greater good. But he was human after all.

"Answer the question!" Alderman Hutton suddenly exploded. His mean eyes were full of suspicion.

"I don't need to do anything," I said. I would not validate or explain my past to satisfy them.

"You need to answer the question, Mr. Kenny. You don't seem to appreciate the seriousness of this matter. And there is suspicion that you are a homosexual. Answer, Mr. Kenny!"

I shot up from my chair. "You can shut your goddamn mouth, Mr. Hutton. I don't answer to you, you son of a bitch!" I felt the dig of the reverend's hand. He took my arm and finally said something.

"Finn, perhaps we should let the mayor get to the point of the meeting."

"It has a point, does it?" I roared angrily. I glared at the alderman, who looked pale and contrite.

"Please sit," the reverend said.

"Yes, calm yourself, Mr. Kenny," the mayor said. "There is no need for hostility in this hall."

I sat back down, then looked at him. He wouldn't meet my eyes, but I addressed him anyway. "Mayor Greenacre," I said as calmly as I could, "I came here thinking that perhaps you had a plan, or something to settle the talk of the town, talk that you, perhaps, precipitated. Rumours breed contempt. I agree, it certainly has to stop. But you are full of suspicion and fear. And the alderman with his ignorance. If he says one more lie, I will reach down his throat with my bare hands and pull it out. Now, what is it that you want to say to me? I'm listening."

"Very well," Mayor Greenacre said. He looked unwell, and I regretted taxing his tired heart, but he had brought it on himself. He took a long draught of air as if he were about to plunge into deep, murky water. "We feel that perhaps Fawn Hill is not a good place for you. It may be in your best interest to move on, Mr. Kenny." Air ran out of him like a deflated balloon.

"You think I should leave?" I was dazed by what I had just heard, as if he had reached across the table and struck me with the back of his pudgy hand.

"Yes, I do, and so do many others."

"All of you here?" I looked around the table. None of them had the courage to look at me. I wanted Lady Spencer to lift her head. I wanted her to say something in my favour, in support of me. She was my employer, but she said nothing. Even absent was her haughty manner, her sarcasm, her derision. She had every opportunity to pile on top of me, to validate the hateful sentiments of the gathering. She could have pulled the Spencer Industries card. It wouldn't have been difficult to inform the board of directors of the recent events, and I would be gone just like that. But she said nothing. Something bothered her, and it puzzled me.

I decided that I would not defend myself. It would only mean that I had done something that needed defending. I would not plead my case or beg for forgiveness for my inane toast at my special dinner. I would restrain myself from lashing out at their frightened self-interest. They *were* afraid, and fear can make people crazy. How the accusers can slip into the very thing they despise. I had seen it before. Where was Bishop when I needed him?

We sat a long uncomfortable moment. Mayor Greenacre was sweating profusely. He kept looking shiftily to Lady Spencer, as if there was unfinished business. At last he tuned to her.

"Do you have anything to add, Lady Spencer?"

All heads turned to her. She had the power, the very thing I feared. It began to feel like a ruse, a poorly acted play. It all had come down to that last question. I was certain now that she had even known of it when I held Darby O'Gill in her studio. She had played me well. They were going through a lot of trouble to cast me off like garbage. But she wouldn't budge. How strange. Her mouth wasn't so hard and stiff. Her lips parted, as if to speak, but she said nothing. It seemed she had forgotten her lines.

"Lady Spencer?"

"No, Mayor," she said evenly.

I got up from the table without saying another word and walked out into the cold night. I lit a cigarette, then hurried down the street. I got into my truck and started it. It didn't take long for the cab to warm. I sat a moment, angry and puzzled. They all remained in the building. The mayor wouldn't have been happy with Lady Spencer. I suppose he thought he knew her, as did I, yet she behaved so unexpectedly. There was part of me that wanted to wait for her to come out. I wanted to know why. My mind was in a fragmented mess. I wanted to make sense of it all. Finally I got tired and pulled away from the curb to head back to Spencerwood.

But at once I noticed that the government liquor store was still open. My own impulses commandeered the steering wheel and I quickly found myself in the parking lot, then heading through the door. I had no real thoughts, just a reactive thirst propelling me down an aisle and taking a bottle of whiskey to the counter. I flipped some cash to the clerk and left.

It seemed like the finale, the end of anything more that I could do. In my life and experience, I had heard enough from those in authority, from the power-crazed police to the fat-necked local politician. If I was bitter, then I had a good reason. I drove to Spencerwood, and when I passed Bishop's cottage, I saw him in the porchlight as if he had expected me to stop and tell all. But I kept going. What would be the point in another session with him? I was deeply grateful for all that Bishop had tried to do for me, but I was done. I had nothing more to give.

I went inside my cabin and lit a fire. I had placed the bottle of whiskey in the middle of the kitchen table. I set a glass beside it and kept looking at its emptiness, its temptation. I lit a smoke and sat by the fire, gazing into the primal mystery, then looking back to the bottle and its promise. We had a history, a relationship that wanted nothing from me but my attention. Oh, I knew the game well enough, a game that never ended well. Still, I wanted to play, to worm out the demons, let them dance across the walls like hell's companions. And then like some otherworldly moment, lights swept across the inside walls of my cabin. I got up as if I had invited some ungodly punishment for my probable sins. I looked outside and there was the gold Cadillac, revealed in the window light like the emissary of my destiny.

I unlocked the door and stood before it waiting for the knock, but it didn't come. She was preparing herself, of course, choosing the right words for whatever it was that she needed to tell me. And she needed to tell me something. It was no casual visit, checking in to see how I was faring, how I was managing my unorthodox dismissal as a citizen of Fawn Hill. It had been a long day. And then a tentative knock.

"Come in," I said through the door. I went back to my chair by the fire. I didn't greet her, not even an acknowledgement. The door opened and then closed. She came up beside me and stood facing the fireplace. I could see her skirt in my peripheral vision, her bare lower leg, the smooth arc of her calf in the firelight. I felt an urge to see more of her, but I fought against it.

"Can I sit?" she asked.

"Go ahead," I said. She got a chair from the kitchen table and set it down beside me. I didn't look at her. I couldn't.

"Well, that didn't go well tonight," she said taking a seat.

I said nothing.

"Are you planning to have a drink, Mr. Kenny?"

"I've been thinking about it."

"Is that wise?"

"No."

"Are you sulking?"

"What?"

"You can hardly speak a sentence."

"Well, I don't have too much to say."

"I can see that."

"All right, I do have something to say."

"Go ahead."

"You seemed to have forgotten your lines tonight. It was quite a show. I'm sorry that I couldn't stay until the end, but I hate tragic endings."

"I didn't forget my lines, Mr. Kenny. I just changed my mind."

"Why? All you had to do was put the last nail in my coffin. The mayor gave you a slow pitch, but you didn't even swing at it."

"Yes, he did, but he is a small man who is afraid. He is more concerned with his re-election next year than with your welfare."

I pulled out my cigarettes and offered her one, and much to my surprise she took it. I lit it for her. "So, why did you come here tonight?"

"Did you know that your Irish accent gets stronger the angrier you get?"

"That's what you wanted to tell me?"

"No, it isn't, but let me say something. I don't know how to say it, but you must hear it. I've never liked you. I'm not so sure why that is. And yet you have given me some answers that have been bothering me for a long time. It is about Ted, yes, my husband, and your friendship that I could never accept. And yes, it was your memoirs, or whatever you call them. They explained so much, all of the things he couldn't tell me. And if you cannot tell your wife your deepest secrets, then how can you be a friend? And yet you were *his* friend. I hated you for that."

"I wasn't trying to come between you in any way," I said. "I was just trying to get by. I was happy to be here."

"I know that now. And I believe that all this talk about Communism and hatred and fear is just misplaced nonsense. I realized that tonight, listening to those big mouths around the table. They sounded so absurd. They based their argument on nothing but a drunken Irishman's rant."

"That's rather harsh."

"It's true."

I leaned forward, past her, and looked at the bottle. It was so eager to drown me. "I don't know why I bought that tonight. I promised Bishop that I quit for good. He'd be disappointed."

She turned to the bottle. "Then don't disappoint him. Give it to him. Say it's a gift."

I nodded. The fire danced, and we sat in a moment's silence, an interlude that wasn't uncomfortable but was unusual. I was too tired to care one way or the other, but still I wanted to come back to my question. "What did you come to tell me?"

"Nothing, really," she said, then she turned to me. "I suppose I always wondered why you are alone. I'm sorry your fiancée, Susan, or whatever her name was, left you. It seems unfair. And I see the way you look at me at times, when you aren't angry with me. More so lately. Ted never looked at me like that."

I had never thought that I would hear a civil word come out of her mouth, but there it was. Even more: a kind of flirtation. I was astounded and could only look at her disbelievingly. Then she tossed her cigarette into the fire and got up from the chair.

She moved away from the fireplace. An abrupt departure. But she stopped at the door. I got up because I was so confused.

"Did I do something?" I asked.

She just looked at me, stumped for words, perhaps flustered. How extraordinary that she was unable to answer. I thought perhaps I had offended her. Then she said something that seemed so improbable.

"I don't want you to leave, Mr. Kenny."

"Excuse me?"

"Don't let them chase you away."

"I don't understand. Why this all of a sudden?"

"I don't know." She shook her head slightly, then turned and went out the door.

I followed her outside. I wanted more information. "Hold on," I said. But she got in her car and drove away. I watched the headlights search across the frosted lawn as she turned toward the manor.

I stood there as perplexed as a man could be. I looked out over the estate, gleaming blades of grass all around me. Moonlight bathed everything in a diffused and enchanted light. And then I looked up into the clear sky of muted stars. The eye of the moon burned through the trees, and branches and limbs, blackened, seemed fastened to it. I was in a state of bewilderment, ecstatic in a way I couldn't understand. The world shifted slightly, my perceptions at least, perhaps because I had forgotten something so simple: how much life was willing to show you.

22

There was still a tree that I needed to check on. It had come down the same stormy night that snapped the cedar in two. It was at the back of the property, and seeing the gap in the woodlot reminded me to pay it a visit. I told Bishop about it over bacon and eggs, how it was one of the old ones, perhaps several hundred years old. It had survived the intense logging of the early part of the century only to come down in the wind. He was interested, perhaps too much so. He wanted to go with me to check on it. That started Birdie.

"Now you leave the trees to Finn," she said. "You have much to do around here with Christmas coming in a few weeks. And don't you have a meeting with your downtown decorating committee? What are you thinking?"

"I just want to have a look at a tree, for crying out loud. What's got into you?"

"I don't want you around saws and such, that's all."

"Birdie's got a point, Bishop."

"You're not helping."

"All right," I said. "I promise you, Birdie, I won't let him touch anything sharp."

"Did I suddenly become feeble? What is it with you two this morning?"

"You're sixty years old, Percival. Must I remind you?"

"I just want some fresh air. Is that asking too much? A man has to get out once in a while. Commune with nature. Finn, you know what I'm talking about."

"I'll watch him, Birdie, don't worry."

"You promise me."

"Yes, I promise."

I finished my coffee and went over to the side counter. There were several new file folders in my tray. I looked at them briefly then tucked them under my arm. "Thanks for breakfast, Birdie," I said. I started for the door. "I'll wait for you in my truck, Bishop."

"I just need to get my boots."

"It's cold this morning," I reminded him.

He pawed at the air. "I noticed," he said.

"You'll need your thick wool coat," Birdie added.

While I waited for Bishop, I had a closer look at one of the files. It was a requisition for new equipment purchases, and other installations, including conveyer belts and drying kilns. It totalled over a million dollars. Lady Spencer seemed to trust me now, but strangely, I wasn't sure what I had done to gain her confidence. I had only begun my report on the Aldercreek Sawmill file. I had made good progress but hadn't finished. Still, her trust felt good.

The door opened and Bishop climbed in. He looked at my files. "Look at that, my friend. Work is coming your way. That's just wonderful, Finn."

"What are you so happy about?"

"First I get to go out into the woods. And second you can tell me what the hell happened last night. Lady Spencer told us that it was a kangaroo court. They want you to leave town. My God, they made you out to be some kind of a gunslinger."

"Yeah, but I'm pretty certain that she wanted me to go at some point."

"People change."

"*She* changed her mind, Bishop. She wants me to stay. She told me so. I couldn't believe it. I still can't."

"See, you don't have to quit this place, Finn. The hell with them!"

"It's not over, you know? There'll likely be more coming my way. And I haven't quite come up with my self-made plan that you talked about."

"Unless you do something about it."

"That's what I'm telling you, Bishop."

"Come to church on Sunday. Let them know that you are a God-fearing man."

"Well, that's a lie now, isn't it?"

"All right, but we better move before Birdie finds something for me to do. She's been acting strange lately."

I started the truck and began down the road that would take us to the back of the estate. "What kind of strange?"

"Well, I had a check-up, and the doctor said that my blood pressure was a little high. I made the mistake of telling Birdie."

"You had to tell her, Bishop."

"Yeah, I know."

"Are you feeling all right?"

"Don't you start, Finn. I'm fine. I just need more time on the river, things like that."

"Give up smokes?"

"Hell no, and take away all my fun?"

I pulled out my cigarettes and offered him one. He hesitated, then took it. "My father died at my age," he said, "and he was never partial to tobacco. So who knows for sure?"

"And Birdie knows that?"

"She surely does."

I drove to the back of the estate as far as I could, and parked. We got out and walked toward the woodlot. There was ice on the grass swales in some places, a kind of clouded-thin ice, brittle, that was frozen down to the ground. We stomped on it like children. Hollow crunches, and we laughed and went on.

"See that gap in the woods," I said, "like a missing picket in a fence? That's where it came down."

"Yeah, I see it. It's surely one of the big ones."

We walked to the edge of the woodlot, past the bracken and salal where sparrows scratched in the leaf litter, and saw the trunk, roots and all. It must have been ten feet tall. We walked around it, looking down the length of the fallen tree.

"It's a Douglas fir," I said, "a good hundred and fifty-footer."

"It didn't break off," Bishop said. "It just went over in the wind."

"It's the ground here," I said. "It's wet most of the time now. The creek's been overflowing in the fall rains. It takes the soil away from the roots."

"Shall we buck it up for firewood?" Bishop asked eagerly.

I turned to him in his toque and red-checkered wool coat, thick gloves. "You do look like a lumberjack, Bishop, but I think we might want to leave it."

"I suppose," Bishop said. "What would nature want?" He looked around him at the mouldy dampness and decay of late fall. He inhaled deeply. It seemed to invigorate him.

"I know that Ted wanted this forest preserved," I said. "This fallen tree will feed the woods for a hundred years. The clearing it created will grow huckleberries, and maybe a hardwood tree like cascara or alder. Deer will come in the summer evenings when it's cool."

"Yeah, just leave it," Bishop agreed. "Oh, we humans cannot just let things be. We need to control our world. Make it into two-by-fours. It's our limited minds. We can't see the perfection that's already around us." He shook his head, lamenting that fact.

"That was an easy decision."

And then Bishop raised his hands and spoke as if to the forest. "For in the true nature of things, if we rightly consider, every green

tree is far more glorious than if it were made of gold and silver.'
Martin Luther King, Jr."

"I think he's right," I said. The moment seemed perfect. It was
cold, but we each drew warmth from the other. I thought it would
be a good time to give him the bottle of whiskey. "I bought you a
bottle of Jameson," I said.

"You don't say."

"Really, Bishop."

His eyes fell briefly, as if considering that it was a breach of
my word. "Unopened?"

"Yes, unopened."

"All right."

"After the meeting last night, I had it sitting in the middle of
my kitchen table. I don't know why I did that. I suppose it was a
challenge, to see if I could really resist it. To be honest, I was close
to giving in to it, but Lady Spencer knocked on the door. I think
I wanted to prove to her that I wasn't a drunk."

"I guess it doesn't matter how you arrive at sobriety, as long
as you get there."

"You don't have one of your Sportsmen, do you?"

He reached into his coat pocket and pulled out a pack, removed
a cigarette and handed it to me, then took one for himself. "So
something's changed between you two."

I lit our cigarettes with my lighter, and Bishop gestured toward
a log. We sat and continued our conversation. "Yes," I said, "but
I'm not quite sure what it is yet."

"You have changed, Finn. You don't see her in the same way
anymore. How could you? And it could be that she sees you differently. The mind will create a whole world of fiction in place of truth."

"I haven't spoken to her about her sister, Bishop."

"I didn't think so."

"How the hell am I going to tell her now?"

"I don't know. Maybe you don't have to tell her. Maybe it has
nothing to do with you. Think of that."

"I feel a responsibility to tell her, Bishop. I really do. I sat with her sister. I told Mrs. Lantz that I would tell her. It was like a promise. I didn't know what else to do."

"Then I don't know what to tell you, Finn." He threw a hand up. "It's going to be trouble, and you can be sure of it. What it will look like is anybody's guess."

"I don't think she's even grieved for Ted. At least, I haven't seen it."

"It's different for everybody. Birdie tells me she sees her in her studio just looking out the window. There's nothing to see there now, no flowers, no summer sun to invite her out, but she stares. She doesn't move for the longest time, as if hypnotized, or lost in some other time. Birdie stands there with a tea tray but has to turn away because Lady Spencer can't hear her. That's the kind of grief she knows. I wouldn't suggest that she doesn't grieve, Finn. Birdie's been unsettled by it more than once."

"Who does she see?"

"I don't think we'll ever know what goes on in her mind. Don't dwell on it now."

I saw what she was looking at, the family she ran away from. And what horrors had her father inhabited her with? "I'm fighting a bear that I cannot see, Bishop."

"You need to look at that goddamn thing in the village," he said, suddenly annoyed with me. "That's one thing in the way, your bear, and when that's all put aside, then you go face the other bear. You have to do one at a time. And I'll say it again: come to church on Sunday. Show them who you are. They're making up stories about you, Finn. Give them a new and honest version of Finn Kenny. Repent or something, goddamn it!"

I looked at him. His eyes were throbbing in their orbits. He was mad as hell. "Why are you so upset, Bishop?"

"Because I had to face that church. That's right. It wasn't long after we began to work at Spencerwood. We weren't received with open arms, you know. The people of our town were suspicious.

They had their minds made up. The prejudice up here is different than it is the States, but it's here. There's a certain tolerance in Canada, but don't let that fool you. They ignore you like you don't even exist, like you're from some far-away country and shouldn't be here. I'm more Canadian than most of the people in Fawn Hill. I would never say so because they wouldn't believe me. It doesn't register. It was our colour, pure and simple. We had to show people who we were. I didn't want to at first, but Ted kept on encouraging us. I think he campaigned for us over and over. It took a while, but the town eventually realized that there was nothing to fear. And if we can face that group, so can you, Finn. There's no other way!"

"Do you feel better?"

"Don't you get angry sometimes, when you get frustrated?"

"Yeah, I do."

"I love Birdie, don't get me wrong. But we live together, sleep together, and work together. We're never apart. How do you think I resolve my frustrations?"

"I don't know, go fishing?"

"That's one way, but sometimes I just want to scream. It builds up, but I have nowhere to put it. So I disappear inside myself. The silent treatment. Men are very good at it. It drives Birdie crazy. And eventually we have to deal with it. We just talk it out. We deal with it, Finn. That's the only way through. I feel better, and it does Birdie a world of good too."

"Nothing like being out in the woods." I laughed.

"Your troubles follow you wherever you go. Sometimes it's the woods that calm your mind enough to help you sort through the rubble of your days."

"Do you need to go back?"

"No, not yet. I like being out here among these wise and placid trees. I don't have memories here like the children would, you know. They created memories with every touch of stump and limb. Not like that. I have good memories on Salt Spring, but the smells here, now that reminds me of *my* river. You can taste the woods at this time of year. It's the smell, like a mouthful of leaves and moss. I know the Cowichan River from Skutz Falls to Cowichan Bay. It's a thing entire, and it too has memories. That's what a smell can do to you. It creates a longing."

We sat on that log for nearly an hour, until our backsides grew numb with cold. We smoked his cigarettes and we laughed, and then at times we were quiet. The sun crept over the estate lawn, and the shadows were long and dark. The sun found us on the edge of the woodlot finally and warmed us for a while. The trees sheltered us from the world. We heard winter wrens singing their tinkling winter songs, and I felt safe. I always felt safe with Bishop.

23

Sunday, and the church bells at the Anglican church in Fawn Hill chimed mutedly but undeniably as I stood before the mirror in my bathroom adjusting my tie. I was more than nervous. It was a torment to imagine my reception, to run the whole event through my head one more time. And when I managed to stop the incessant worrying, it would cease for but a moment only to begin again. I put on my sports coat and thumbed an unidentifiable smudge from the lapel. I ran a comb through my hair, then bared my teeth, futile gestures rather than the show of courage I had prayed for. I was ready.

The others had gone before me. I didn't want to arrive at the church with a crowd of worshippers milling about who hadn't received their weekly allotment of guilt. Hearing those words in myself made me realize that I had no real faith, that I was cynical of any good that it might bring. But I had to believe in something now. I suppose I had been torn between bitterness and hope for much too long. The festering rents had left an indelible mark on my hide. I had learned one thing, though, that of all the things to believe in, it was the belief in ourselves that was the hardest. At best it was fleeting, but in the end it was the only worthy cause.

As I drove away from my cabin, I wasn't feeling very confident—perhaps more desperate than anything else. Still I moved
forward in the only way that I knew how. And when I came up to
the gate, and then passed through it, I saw the very reason that I
at times loathed the world. My heart broke into pieces. There was
a splash of red paint on the articulated iron lettering, a stain, an
indictment on Spencerwood. I got out of my truck to look at it,
the drips onto the driveway, the spray pattern beyond, as if from a
projectile. As horrid as blood. I got back into my truck and left the
desecration behind. Apprehension crept into my bones like rust.
The enemy was at the door, so to speak. I feared that my limbs
would seize and I would be no more. It seemed foolish to go to
the church now, to show my face and prove that I was worthy to
be among them. "Damn it!" I shouted aloud, willing forth some
defiant bone in me. And then I prayed as a boy about to face the
nightmare that wouldn't leave him alone. *Oh, dear Mother, keep me
safe among those who would harm me. And if I must leave this place
forever, take my hand and lead me away.*

Cars were parked well down the street, and that was fine
with me. I needed the time to prepare myself, for what I didn't
know; the very fact that I was about to reacquaint myself with
the church was enough on its own. That I knew. I had seen what
religion can do to a country and had no investment in its tenets.
As for the other, I couldn't prepare. I could only hope, and it
had nothing to do with faith. I walked briskly up the sidewalk,
hunched up, cold in my thin tweed jacket, because one cannot
walk any other way in a chill. A cigarette dangled loosely from
lips, my hands jammed into my pockets.

At the foot of the stairs I could hear the strain of the organ
and the rising voices of dreadful canticles. The Willett sisters, a
fixture of the benign in Fawn Hill, simple and honest ladies whose
hymnal offerings were eagerly lapped up. It was never music to me.
It was more a dirge, the sound that accompanied the death of a
neighbour or the terrible truth of a burned-out British sympathizer.

Widows upon widows. I dropped my cigarette and pressed my heel into it, then made my way to the top of the stairs. The sound was feverish, even joyous, yet only gave the impression of it. And then I recognized what had fastened to me like a burr, the cynical and the bitter, two sabotaging agents that had no purpose other than anarchy. I had to spit them out before I opened the door, lest I be lost for good.

I pulled the big iron door and it yawned terribly behind me as I went inside. The hymns lifted up into the rafters and floated there, a sound that didn't seem quite human, a sound manufactured from religious fervour itself. It was a strange moment to behold, looking into the backs of people I knew, and some that I didn't. At the front of the church, Lady Spencer sat by herself, as if in mourning, Birdie and Bishop behind her. I looked for a place to sit. I didn't want to walk up and sit with the Bishops. Oh, I would have liked that very much, but I didn't dare to be so bold. I looked around the back of the church and noticed an empty seat in the pew next to where I stood. But before I could move, a person next to the empty seat read my mind and slid over and occupied the space. I turned my attention to another empty seat, but the same thing played out, the shifting of bottoms—a language for the unwanted.

There was nothing for me to do but stand as the service continued. I was anonymous save for the few near me who sang and watched me narrowly as if seeking approval of their ardent voices. I looked straight ahead, my chin slightly elevated to shore up my courage, or more rightly to disguise my fear. Reverend Le Fleur was standing near his pulpit, slightly turned to the organ and the Willett sisters. Ruby willed a yowl of strangled notes from the organ as Pearl stood beside her singing and encouraging the congregation with gestures of cadence and pitch. Then Pearl Willett lifted her eyes from the assembly for a moment and found me standing alone at the back of the church, centre aisle. I looked as through a wall of voices, a haze that seemed to have taken on a three-dimensional existence, heat waves on hot asphalt. And then Ruby noticed her sister's distraction and she too turned, and then stopped playing. The chorus fell flat all at once, deflated, fell from the ceiling like something shot from the sky.

I felt handcuffed by the sudden cessation of music. One by one the congregation turned, from slouched backs to pink faces. A collective gasp and then the familiar murmurs did nothing for my flagging courage. That was how it began at the Bramble Café. But there in the House of God, I was on sanctified ground. Surely, they would all recognize what I was trying to do and it would speak to the best of them, inspire a certain tolerance, even forgiveness. I had made myself guilty by my very presence. I was beholden, asking for their acceptance. And then Bishop's bright face. He was moved, that old man. I suppose he had his doubts, but there I was. And how disappointing that the talk began, unfavourable comments, and poor Bishop looking around at his brothers and sisters with defeat written all over his face. A man called out now.

"This is no place for you," he said. The swivel of heads. I recognized him as one of the schoolteachers.

"Surely it is," I said, but my voice fell flat, unconvincing.

"You're not wanted!" said a woman raising her bible as if to cast out a sin.

"A deviant in our church!" said another.

Then a chorus of that sentiment. "Leave, leave, leave!"

I did not turn away. I looked at each one of them. They feared me, what I represented. I had come to steal their good lives, rob them of their identity, as if I had such a power. I was the Antichrist among them. I quickly realized the folly of my presence, my self-made plan. My heart sank when I saw Bishop's slumped head, Birdie consoling him. Even Lady Spencer seemed to reach out to him, her arm over the back of the pew. It was so difficult to watch that I hadn't noticed Reverend Le Fleur step up to his pulpit to address his congregation. He began to speak, barely audible against the discontent.

"Please," he said. He repeated his appeal until the talk died down. "On this holy day," he continued, "we must seek something more than our anger, more than our fear."

"No, Reverend, not for him," an emboldened woman said. It was Mrs. Neaves, the banker's wife. She had been so sweet at my dinner, but that seemed long ago now. I wondered what had prompted her to speak in such a way. Some monetary threat, perhaps. I supposed that one never knows what lies inside the other. That was something I was learning over and over again. We all go to great lengths to protect the self-made parts of ourselves, the good and the bad.

"Yes, for him," Reverend Le Fleur said. "If not for him, then who?"

"You're forgetting yourself, Reverend," a voice called out.

"Listen to your congregation," said another.

"It's an evil in our midst!"

"Yes."

"Yes!"

And on it went around the church, from pew to pew. I knew who my friends were, but they were silent, not once coming to my defence, except the reverend, of course. He had access to the standard Christian responses that he hoped would still the bleat of protests from his flock. I was reassured but felt a heaviness in my chest. Silence was the cruel absence of courage. And as I had those thoughts of resignation, even defeat, a man stood to face the malcontent. His earnest and beautiful glower.

"Hear me," Bishop said, but his words were impotent against the murmur and grumble. "Hear me!" He raised his big hands.

And then Reverend Le Fleur joined in. The calming flap of his arms. "Let Mr. Bishop speak," he said. "Please, hear what he has to say."

"I want you all to hear the story of Finn Kenny," Bishop said.

"We don't want to hear it," a voice answered.

"You must hear it," Bishop forged on. "You are making judgements based solely on what you have accepted as true. Rumours from one mouth to the other do not guarantee the truth of the matter. He hasn't defended himself. Did you notice? Have you seen for yourself anything that he has done wrong? Or only what you *think* he has done? Listen to him. Let Finn speak. Please!"

The congregation turned and looked at me doubtfully. It seemed they were deliberating the merit of Bishop's request. The thud of silence. Then Reverend Le Fleur stepped aside from his pulpit and gestured with his hand. It was a frightening moment to realize that what I was about to say was in fact my self-made plan. Bishop had forced it out of hiding, but I was not prepared. I hadn't one measured or careful thought, no compelling argument to save myself. I found myself walking up the aisle to the front of the church. I looked straight ahead, and as I reached the front, I turned to Bishop and looked reverently into his dark and charitable eyes, and to Birdie, too, my sanctuary. Lady Spencer did not avert her attention from me. I met her briefly. Her lips pursed, as if captivated. It seemed that she wanted to hear what I had to say, or perhaps it was only her trepidation of what my words might reveal to the world. But of all the people in the room I wanted to convince of my worth, it was her acceptance I wanted the most, and I didn't know why.

I stepped up to the pulpit, and it was surely stage fright that made my stomach roll over. It was as if I had poisoned myself with my willingness to stand before those who would banish me from their town. Reverend Le Fleur did not seem worried, but he did look mildly concerned. I doubted that he knew how it would all play out, but he was open to something different, and I had to respect him for that. He was the mediator, a man to broker a civil transaction on that morning. I would speak to the congregation, but I wanted to find the core of hate, that someone before me. The person I wanted to speak to, perhaps, had a spot of red paint on his shoes. That's who needed to hear me. I stood at the pulpit and looked out upon the doubting faces, to pick out the one I would speak to, a face painted red with anger. He held the rage of the times inside him. And I found him, his head shaking ever so slightly, a steel-hard mouth, clenched. The menace of his intolerant eyes. I knew him, and as he shook his head, I nodded back to him, and as words began to form, I began the eulogy of me.

"On October ninth, 1942," I said loudly enough to startle myself. The sound of my own voice threw me off. I cleared my throat over a ripple of grumbling, then continued. "There was a young seaman aboard the SC *Carolus*, a merchant ship among a convoy of ships bound for Montreal from St. John's. As the *Carolus* entered the Gulf of St. Lawrence, a German wolf pack was waiting. A U-boat from that pack fired on the convoy and after several minutes there was a loud detonation. A second torpedo struck the *Carolus*. There was a fire, and before the crew could muster defensive measures the ship began to sink. There were men in the water amidst a sea of oil and fire. The ship sank. So close was the enemy, so lethal his actions. The young seaman found himself in the water with his shipmates and watched as their ship went down. He pulled a sailor up onto the debris from the wreckage. He knew him well. The sailor had just become a father. But his body was lifeless, as well as ten other seamen. Survivors were rescued by another Canadian ship.

"The young seaman was awarded the Marine War medal for his service in the Battle of the Atlantic. It wasn't for his bravery on that day, as he wasn't a brave man, but still he was prepared to die for his country. After the war, he went to university and graduated with a degree in forestry. He was soon employed by the Canadian government. He was proud to represent Canada at high-level meetings with his contemporaries from the United States, but all was not well inside him. He had his demons, perhaps from the war, or his childhood. He drank to battle the things he couldn't manage. He was an alcoholic, but concealed his drinking, even from his fiancée. He went to a hotel bar every noon hour.

It was his safe place. It was known as a place where homosexuals congregated, but he didn't care because he was only there to drink. But unknown to him were the eyes that were watching. They were looking for government employees who they had reason to believe were homosexuals. They were feared because they were thought to associate with Communists, and Communists wanted Canadian secrets. So began the civil service purge.

"He was interrogated by the RCMP for three days. They wanted names, associates—Communist or homosexual. He found himself in a situation that he couldn't get out of, no matter how hard he tried. He was guilty by association, not for something that he did but for something decided for him. He was fired from his government position along with six hundred other employees. His career was over. His relationship with his fiancée was over. He was blackballed. He was on a no-hire list. His life seemed over. But there was one man who believed in him. That man was Ted Spencer, whom he had assisted in securing markets for his lumber. Ted made no judgements but offered him a job at his estate in British Columbia."

I looked out over the congregation, let what I had just revealed settle into their minds before I continued. A few turned to those next to them, looks, then whispers. And after a moment, I carried on. "I am guilty of keeping a secret. Hidden away, it could not harm me, or others for that matter. It's just my awful past. And if you walk through the cemetery on these very grounds, you will doubtless pass over secrets that are long dead. We all have concealed something from our past, and it will not let us go, will not allow us to have our peace." I stopped there and turned briefly to the reverend, to his bowed head and folded hands, and then to Lady Spencer with the same pose, as if my words had come too close. There was one last thing that I wanted to say. I took my time. They were listening now.

"To be rejected is like a death," I said unhurriedly. "There is no greater punishment than to deny someone their innate worth based solely on things they don't understand. In this life, if we take the time to understand our differences, then perhaps we can see how we are united by our common humanity. We can accept. We can forgive. I want that peace."

I was finished, but all was silent. I suddenly felt a wave of panic at what I had just said. The words were not my own. How could they be? I bolted down the aisle between the hushed congregation. Not a murmur, not a breath. I went out the door and down the stairs in two giant leaps, then ran all the way to my truck.

24

Golden sunlight threw down on the cabin floor, repeating the geometric pattern of the window. The day was trying hard to be promising. I lit a cigarette and took a cup of coffee and stood at the window as I had done a thousand times before. It seemed a good way to begin the day, to assess the weather, what I needed to do, what the day might bring. No one bothered me, thinking that I needed to regain my composure, I surmised. But it wasn't so much that I needed to sort out what I had said at the church, but more of wondering if it had done any good.

After a while I would go on up to the manor for breakfast. Bishop would be encouraging no matter what, so I looked forward to his take on my defining moment, good or otherwise. And I needed to hand in my Aldercreek report. I had only to add my signature.

I had recommended most notably that Spencer Industries personnel department inform Mill Superintendent Dennis Welch that he must immediately remove his plant foreman, Gary Slater, and that a new mill foreman be appointed. The vetting of that position should be conducted under my oversight. That was a bold insertion, but I connected the poor mill performance with poor morale as a result of Mr. Slater's inadequate and unacceptable supervision skills. The high rate of plant accidents during his tenure supported that connection. I further noted that Mr. Slater was Dennis Welch's son-in-law, a potential conflict of interest that could not be ignored, and that a review of personnel recruitment policies should be undertaken. It was all typed on Spencerwood Industries letterhead. I signed the document and attached it to the file.

As I looked out over the grounds, I noticed someone at the gate. Bishop stood with his arms folded across his chest, Charlie Sales standing before him. I could also see Charlie's tow truck, his name on the door below the big B/A decal. I quickly finished my coffee and threw on a coat.

The grass was damp and here and there puddles mirrored the sky. I picked my way across the lawn toward the entrance gate. I could see that Charlie knew I was coming. I suppose he expected it. He stood back as I approached, a paint brush in one hand and a can of paint in the other. I had no need to say anything, as it seemed that Charlie would do the talking. I noticed at once a certain embarrassment in the way he stood, round-shouldered and contrite. Bishop, on the other hand, seemed only to want the gate restored to its former black gloss. His posture hadn't changed.

"Charlie," I said simply.

"Finn," he replied. His black fingernails were imbedded with the grease of every Fawn Hill automobile. Vapours vented off his coveralls.

"Go on, Charlie," Bishop said.

"Well," he said, "the fact is ..." He shrugged sheepishly.

"Charlie," Bishop said, "tell him what you told me. Do that."

"I did this," Charlie finally said. He pointed at the gate with his paintbrush. The red paint was all but gone. "I waited until Lady Spencer left for church. I was mad as hell at you. That's the truth. You hear things, and then you believe them. I had a brother die in the war. He just landed on Juno Beach. Killed that first day, June sixth, 1944. I just couldn't stomach someone wanting to turn against his own country. I thought then perhaps it wasn't your country. You can go back to where you come from. It brought up a lot of sad feelings for me. And I suppose I spread a good deal of your troubles. People come in for gas and they want to know things, mainly my opinion. Well, I give it and then some. Then you spoke at the church. I didn't want you there. It got me even more riled. I couldn't listen to you, but a part of me must have been listening when you spoke of the merchant marines. Sailors dying in the water and your war medal. It changed my mind."

"I see."

"I don't know what got into me."

"I'm sorry about your brother," I said. "He must have been young."

He nodded. "Too young to die at eighteen. It changes your life. It leaves a hole that never gets filled. It's always there. But thank you."

"It looks like you're all done, Charlie," Bishop said.

He looked over his work, touched up a few places, then stuffed the brush into the can of paint. He turned away and started walking back to his truck. He stopped halfway and turned back to us. He shrugged one last time. "I'm sorry."

We watched Charlie drive away. When he disappeared, Bishop looked at me.

"He *is* sorry," he said.

"I think he is, too."

"Charlie had been pumping more than just gas. It just goes to show you."

"He had everyone's ear," I said.

"He surely did. And it's a shock to realize that you've been kidnapped. There was a church full of people who identified with his version of *your* life, Finn. As strange as it may seem, it's prejudice. It may not be the racial kind, but it distorts they way you see just the same."

"Is it over, Bishop?"

"I think it is."

"Goddamn."

"I think you need a good breakfast. Come on, I'm buying."

We walked toward the manor. I was feeling relieved, vindicated, and then I thought I saw movement in the upstairs window. I looked up, but there was no one there. Maybe a curtain catching the breeze. But I doubted it was something so simple and unremarkable. It was Lady Spencer's bedroom, after all. And all I could think about was how to tell her about Betty Lantz. Things were going too well to sink it all with a promise to a woman I had never set eyes on before *that* day.

"She's joining us for breakfast," Bishop said.

"Who?"

"Don't give me that. I saw you looking up there."

"You don't miss a thing."

"That's my job."

"And thanks for what you said at church, for standing up for me."

"Something I could do."

"I imagine you couldn't wait much longer for my self-made plan."

"That's the truth of it, Finn. But it worked out just fine."

We walked around to the kitchen. "She never has breakfast with us," I said, "or any meal, for that matter."

"It's sad really, the way she eats alone. Birdie keeps asking her. I think Birdie needs a woman to talk to, just the way we talk about men stuff. She's no different. And I think Lady Spencer has come to appreciate Birdie. She's done little things for her lately, thoughtful things. It surprises me, I must say."

When I walked into the kitchen the first thing Birdie did was give me big hug. I was moved that she knew what I needed, that an unwanted human being was in danger of falling into the cracks of alienation, perhaps never to return.

"That was a most eloquent speech that you gave," she said, standing back as she held my arms. "I don't think Reverend Le Fleur could have done better."

"Thank you, Birdie, but I owe a lot to this man here."

"Oh, he's so full of himself, I wouldn't want to put that in his head." She went over to the stove and picked up the coffee pot.

I sat with Bishop at the table with places set for four. He was looking over a copy of the *Fawn Hill Gazette*.

"Not a word about any of it," Bishop said. "I'm proud of that fact."

"That's because Carl Lieberman is a friend of yours, Percival," Birdie quipped.

"You promised to take him fishing," I added.

"No, not that, Finn," Bishop said. "Listen, he knows better. He likes a community paper, nothing sensational or controversial. Nothing like that."

"So you went to see him?"

"Not exactly."

"Then what?"

Bishop paused before he answered. "Yes, I went to see him. I just reminded him what hate can do to a town, or even a country. He had seen its malignancy on an inhuman scale. I didn't need to tell him anything really. I just didn't want that grassfire to take hold."

Birdie brought over the coffee pot and poured our coffee. The rich warm steam. "Spencer Industries advertises in his paper every week," Birdie pointed out. "A half page, sometimes a full page. The hardware store sells a lot of Spencerwood lumber, you know."

"That's true, Birdie," I affirmed

"All right, it was leverage," Bishop said. "But it was only implied." She came into the kitchen just then.

"I see that we're all here," Lady Spencer said.

"Yes, Lady Spencer," Bishop said, "and how are you on this new day?"

"It is a new day, Mr. Bishop, and I did notice you out at the gate with Charlie Sales. I suppose he was apologetic?"

"Yes, he was, Lady Spencer."

And then, much to my surprise, she sat in the nook beside me. I inched toward the window as much as I could, but still her arm brushed up against me. I squeezed my arm into my side to separate our bodies, sitting as if my arm were in a sling. I was afraid to reach for my coffee cup.

"How are you this morning, Mr. Kenny?" she said. "No doubt, you're feeling better." She turned to me only slightly, as we were too close for her do otherwise.

"Yes, I'm feeling better," I said brilliantly, anxiously. "I'm glad it's over."

"We all are," Birdie said. She poured coffee into Lady Spencer's cup. "And if you ask me, Fawn Hill is better for it." She went back to the stove, the pop and spit of frying bacon.

I didn't know what to say. I had normal conversations with the Bishops, with their generous sprinkling of gossip, sarcasm, and plain fun, but with Lady Spencer so close to me I found myself tongue-tied. I couldn't find one sensible word, not one articulate thought. My mind was a wasteland of the unintelligible. She had that effect on me. It was unnerving when her shoulder pressed into mine now and then. And my god, I could smell her perfume. It wasn't disagreeable, but it belonged to her, a signature. I managed to catch an expression on her face, her profile more than anything, one of satisfaction. She looked around the kitchen, her kitchen, as if taking in new surroundings. And Bishop sitting across from me, his eyes jumping from her to me and back again, as if my rather bold and unbridled examination had been expressed in words.

"It's good to have you at breakfast, Lady Spencer," Bishop said. He noticed everything, read faces, looks, like scripture.

"Thank you, Mr. Bishop, but it does feel rather strange. I'm not used to sharing a table. Don't take me wrong. I don't mean to disparage you all, but it was always me, Ted, and the girls. Then it was Ted and me, and now it is only me. What is the point of sitting alone in the dinning room staring up at his portrait?"

"Then that settles it," Bishop said.

"Yes, we can talk about the weather, politics, and perhaps a bit of business."

"Yes," Bishop said, "I'm always eager to discuss politics."

"Don't encourage him," Birdie said, "or you might regret it."

"And you, Finn?" Lady Spencer said.

A question, and for the first time she addressed me by my first name. It sounded a bit odd, as if by virtue of her proximity she could acknowledge me personally. She seemed to have stepped over the wall that had come between us, an obstacle of our own making. I was trying to understand what was happening. I wanted to ask her, but, of course, it was far too complex, treacherous to look deeper. The riptide of untried waters.

"I suppose a bit of business would suit me," I said agreeably. "And I like to talk about trees."

"And he's been known to talk *to* them," Bishop lampooned.

But she seemed to accept that well enough. "All right then."

Birdie put down heaping plates of bacon and eggs, hash-brown potatoes. A stack of toast a foot high. A jar of strawberry jam, marmalade, and peanut butter for me. A bottle of ketchup was passed around, each of us tapping the bottom in turn. We ate our breakfast and talked about the weather, and of course Christmas, which was fast approaching. Lady Spencer gave specific instructions to the Bishops.

"You know how I feel about Christmas, Mr. Bishop," she said. "It's not a happy time for me. No fuss. Don't get carried away. Birdie, there's no need for all the baking. I know you like to bake. Please just leave me out of it." She stopped there. Her mouth hardened as she struggled with things we didn't know. Then she raised her chin and continued. "I want to get through it. I'm sorry to say that it depresses me. It always has. I could endure it when the girls were small, but now I don't have the heart. They'll be coming for the holidays. You'll be fine with them. I don't mean to be a spoiler, I'll do my best, but just the same I'll be glad when it's over."

The Bishops with their glances, as if they had never heard it before. Christmas was supposed to be a happy time, but I was much like Lady Spencer, averse to expectations of happiness, especially at the most anticipated time of the year when joy would surely erupt from the most cynical of hearts, but never did. She was quiet now, subdued by the thought of Christmas. I was so aware of her moods that it disturbed me, and like her I became uncommunicative and distant as well. Where did I go? Where did she go?

After we finished our breakfast, I took my dirty plate over to the sink. I followed Lady Spencer, of course. We thanked Birdie for another wonderful breakfast, and before Lady Spencer left the kitchen, she touched my arm. It sent a shiver through me.

"Could you see me in my office before you leave?" she said. "In five minutes or so?"

"Yes, of course."

She left the kitchen, and I lit a cigarette. I thought I would sit a moment, finish my coffee before I went into see her. Bishop sat staring at me. His hand was cupped over something, and then he slid his hand across the table. He looked over his shoulder, then lifted his hand from a piece of paper. There was a telephone number scratched across it. He leaned over the table.

"She called twice this morning," he whispered.

"Who?" I met his discretion.

"You know who. Betty Lantz."

"I can't do this now, Bishop."

"I've been keeping her away from Lady Spencer. You need to call her."

"All right." I picked up the piece of paper and stuffed it into my shirt pocket. My fingers began to tap on the table. The tune of the tentative.

"Are you all right, Finn?"

"You know, I thought I was. But now I don't know."

"Sorry, my friend. The other bear awaits."

"Thanks for reminding me."

Bishop lifted the palms of his hand, his gesture of empowerment. "You'll think of something."

The man with too much faith in me. I got up from the table, drained my coffee cup, then butted out my cigarette. "Thank you for breakfast, Birdie," I said once again, a delaying tactic that was futile. She smiled anyway. And then I drew a deep breath, inviting the faculty of resilience that I had often prayed for, and left the kitchen.

25

She was sitting behind Ted's desk when I walked into the office. It still seemed like his office, although the sweet–rank aroma of cigars and leather had been supplanted by the suggestion of her own fragrance.

"Sit down," she invited.

I took a seat, and at once sensed that she was about to inquire about the Aldercreek file. My report was due shortly, and before I could reassure her of its timely delivery by the end of the day, she said something totally irrelevant to business.

"I must say that you surprised me."

"How so, Lady Spencer?"

She sat forward with her hands clasped on the desk. "It was your speech, if that's the correct word. It wasn't a sermon, or even a defence for that matter. It was a kind of self-disclosure. It was very brave, and you did quite well in front of a collection of excitable Christians. Not many could have done that."

"Well, thank you. I appreciate your support."

"It wasn't always there, was it?"

"I suppose it wasn't."

"But that's not what surprised me. Perhaps I shouldn't have been surprised. Perhaps it only revealed the person you are, and not the person I thought you were. I don't often have these insights. That's surprising in itself."

"I don't know if I'm following you, Lady Spencer."

"You had an opportunity to say what you wanted to say, and you did. But it's what you didn't say that was most striking."

I nodded, not because I understood her, but because I wanted her to say more.

"You could have said something about Ted. It would have shocked them all, no doubt. Some may have been disappointed, and some outraged, betrayed. But you said nothing when you so easily could have. And the reverend, yes, Reverend Le Fleur—you spared him, and in doing so, spared me, and ..."

She stopped. She couldn't finish the sentence. But the word seemed to materialize on its own, perhaps out of something unknown and essential. "Michael?" I asked.

Her eyes suddenly flared, as if the sound of his name had never been spoken in that room, in that house, so sad the terrible and shattering circumstance. "Yes, Michael."

There was space now in our conversation. I waited. "I just wanted peace," I said. "The world seems to burn at times, and it scorches our communities, our homes. I just wanted decency and kindness. I was tired of hiding, curling up in the corner like some wounded thing."

"Yes."

"I want the same as everyone else."

"Those are worthy goals."

"You must know ..."

Her eyes drifted down to her folded hands. I could see the flutter of her eyelashes, perhaps blinking back tears. I regretted my assumptions, my casual conversation as if with a friend. She was no friend, but the talk had turned candid, perhaps too personal for our undefined relationship.

"You see," she continued, "I always thought it was me, that I was to blame. He never told me what bothered him. He confided in you. Did you have pity on me?"

"I didn't really allow myself to feel that way. He fathered children, after all. So perhaps ..."

"No, sex is not a remedy when you know something is wrong. It soon divides."

"Yes, it was difficult for him ... and for you. I'm so sorry."

"He lived his life as a lie."

"Yes, but he made out all right."

"Two tortured souls and not a lick of truth between them. Is that 'all right'?"

"No, I suppose it's not."

"Knowing the truth does not make it any easier. It only explains it."

"He was loved."

"Yes, he was loved. I admired him for that, but resented him for it in the end. I wanted his love. Do you know what I'm talking about?"

"I think I do."

"You're so accommodating when you don't drink."

The conversation was bold now, honest, but still she jabbed me with her bitterness. "I'm trying to understand just as you are," I said.

"You seem to hold the answers to the riddle of my life. You know far more than I had ever dared given you credit for. Did he tell you about Michael's father?"

"No, he did not."

"So ...?"

"When I was at the library preparing for my trip to Courtenay, I saw you visit the cemetery. It wasn't Ted's grave you stood over. It was the child you lost. How strange that Ted wasn't buried by his son. And then later that day, someone else had left flowers on

Michael's grave. It was the anniversary of his death. That someone was Reverend Le Fleur. I sort of figured it out."

"The secrets you alluded to."

"That's all I was ever going to say. I know what pain feels like."

"I was punished, you see."

"Don't judge yourself."

"And you haven't judged yourself, Mr. Kenny?"

"I poured it into a glass."

We sat in what was not precisely an awkward silence—it felt like relief. The fervid resentments that we harboured were freed like doves. I could see it in her cheek and the line of her jaw, all hard edges softened, smoothed over, as if by a painter's brush had changed the mood, altered her appearance and what I thought of her. I had never imagined that she could have possessed human qualities of sensitivity and reflection. I had only just come to understand why they had been absent.

"I'll have the report ready this afternoon," I said, returning to more formal—less revealing—talk.

"That would be fine, Mr. Kenny."

"I don't mind if you call me Finn, Lady Spencer."

"Then you should call me Katherine, don't you think?"

"That might take a while to get used to."

"We have our habits, Finn."

"Yes, we do."

I felt new hope. It was a good feeling, something that had evaded me for a long time. But inside I felt already the tremors of unstable ground. I knew my newfound optimism wouldn't last because in my pocket was the means for its dissolution, a sister wanting, a sister desperate for my courage.

I left the office, and when I walked through the kitchen, Bishop and Birdie turned to me, always that question on their faces, always their concern, but they said nothing, not words at least. Bishop pointed to the telephone hanging on the wall, and then placed his closed hand against his cheek in pantomime, mouthing, *Phone her.* I could only nod my head in response, although my scowl might have suggested the contrary. It got me out of the manor without further insistence from him. I swear that at times Bishop was more mother than a father figure to me.

On my way back to my cabin all I could think about was how Betty Lantz would make her plea that was so reasonable, yet it remained nearly impossible to carry out. I tried to remember what I had said to her. Had I promised her or merely said I would do my best? Oh, I wanted it to be the latter. And it could be that the old man had died. Surely there would be nothing to do then. And Katherine's sister was not well herself and needed her. And just like that, I was back with Bishop and his dramatics. *Phone her.*

The telephone sat on the counter in my cramped kitchen, the cord just long enough to reach the table. I set it down, removed Bishop's note from my pocket, and pushed it to the side. Next I arranged my pack of cigarettes, lighter, and ashtray close to the telephone. I wanted everything to be just so before I called her. I sat back in my chair and drummed my fingers on the table. They seemed to be unsure, uncertain whether they would dial the number. The power of the universe in my deliberating hand. Then the drumming stopped, and my hand drew the note back to me. I removed a cigarette, took up my lighter and lit it, all in a ceremonial moment. And then at last, with nothing but my will, I inserted my index finger into the dial and called her.

The telephone rang five times before she answered. "Hello." The listless voice that I remembered.

"Mrs. Lantz, this is Finn Kenny returning your call."

"Oh, my goodness, thank you for calling me back, Finn. I was wondering if you'd been able to speak to Katey."

The voice of the despairing, so direct and urgent, but still very rational. "I'm working on that at this very moment, Mrs. Lantz." It would have been a lie if she had known how impotent it made feel even thinking about it.

"Betty. Please."

"Yes. Betty," I said. "You have made a challenging request, and although I sympathize with you, it's not as simple as it would seem."

"Heavens, Finn, I'm very aware of the challenges that you face. The unapproachable Katey Krom has held me at bay for more years than I care to know. Of course, it's not simple or easy, but our father may not last the week. He's taken a turn for the worse but calls out for her still. It's a harrowing thing to hear. It seems that he is not prepared to meet his maker until he has been forgiven. He won't go to the hospital. I tend to him every day. Tom helps when he's not working at the mill. Poor Tom will be burying the two of us, I'm afraid, if I don't get some rest."

"With all due respect, Betty, I don't think your sister will be forgiving her father. It doesn't seem reasonable under the circumstances."

She went silent. "Well then," she said after a moment, "that is that. I thought you would help me. You seemed like a nice man, a caring man, but you have jumped to a conclusion. How would know what she will or will not do? You haven't spoken to her."

It was the worst thing she could have said, like a petition to the gods where my mother assuredly listened in on the party line for the good intentions of her son. I had to answer. I had to do something. "Betty, I'll do what I can," I said with a secret grimace.

"Yes, of course you will. You said that before." Her thin fractured voice.

I closed my eyes and held the phone against my chest briefly. I couldn't get away from that sad woman. "I'll do it today," I said without much enthusiasm. "I promise, but I cannot guarantee anything. She's not easily persuaded."

"Don't I know it?"

"So please leave it with me."

"Thank you, Finn. I realize that you cannot will my sister to do anything that she does not want to do. I suppose I rely on prayer. I don't have much else. Please, just ask her to come home."

"I understand."

"I believe you do."

"All right, Betty, I must go now."

"Thank you, goodbye."

I hung up the telephone. Her voice had a lingering quality, warning of impending doom, perhaps her own. Such an immobilizing situation, no right way to turn. Someone was going to get hurt all over again. I sat wondering what to do, how I could possibly tell Lady Spencer, Katherine, about her dying father and ailing sister. It was unfair really to be the bearer of bad news, bad memories. It had nothing to do with me. But why did I feel so responsible and duty bound, accountable to a promise? Oh, mediator of a bad dream. There was no way out now.

I felt so much like a coward as I stared at the solution on the kitchen table. I inserted a blank sheet of paper into the typewriter, searching for the words that would absolve me from the crime of inserting the key into her vault of memories. Damn my bloodletting grammar. And then I positioned my fingers over the keys, a tremble in the poised tips like aspen leaves.

Dear Katherine,

I'm sorry that I didn't have the courage to tell you in person today. Yes, I had the opportunity, but I just couldn't bring myself to jeopardize our relationship, which has seen a welcome improvement. I realize the pettiness of my fears, so please bear with me.

I must inform you that on the day I conducted my review of the Aldercreek Sawmill in Courtenay, I found a note on the windshield of my truck. It included a name and an address, the name of an employee who drowned last summer. As I later learned that his widow had important information for me that could shed light on the mill's problems, I made a visit to her home. Much to my surprise, she claimed to be your sister. Betty Lantz.

I listened to a most tragic story. She asked me to tell
you that your father is dying and may not last much longer.
Reluctantly I agreed to do what I could, which was not easy,
as it turns out. Your father has asked to see you. I am only the
messenger and make no judgements or assumptions. Betty
informed me that her previous attempts to ask you for help have
not been successful. She understands why. But she appealed to
me again today.

Katherine, your sister is not well. She wants you to come
home. Her words on the telephone just today reveal a woman
who is perhaps beyond recovery after years of caring for your
father.

It is with regret that I inform you in this way. It is my
utmost wish that you can forgive me.

Sincerely,

Finn

I read the letter over several times, then folded it, and inserted
it into an envelope. I wrote her name in pen on the outside. The
flare of my penmanship seemed far too bold, even pretentious,
as if it were just another chapter of our intimate correspondence.
Katherine, a person without a title.

As the day wore on, I watched the manor, waiting, looking for
an opportunity. And then in the late afternoon her Cadillac pulled
up to the gate and then left the estate. It seemed she had some
business to attend to. At once I grabbed the file and letter and left
my cabin. I hurried across the lawn, half-running, not knowing
how long I had before she returned. I went in through the front
entrance, a rarity for staff, but of course, Bishop was on to me.

"Front door?" he said.

"I have to put this in the tray in the kitchen," I said. I lifted
the file to show him.

"Does this look like the kitchen?"

"No."

"What's wrong?"

"Nothing's wrong."

"Why do you look like a thief?"

"Well, I suppose it's because I'm about to rob someone of their peace."

"So you waited until she left?"

"I couldn't tell her, Bishop, so I wrote her a letter. Her father's dying, and her sister maybe not be too far behind. I'm a coward, all right?"

He shook his head. "No, you're not, Finn. I don't envy you, my friend. Go on."

"She'll hate me all over again, Bishop."

"That's a possibility. But one can never know for sure."

I walked past him and into the office. I placed the envelope on her desk. She would see it right away. I looked down at it and was seized with such regret. I could have easily picked it up and done nothing, ignored it all. But no, there was something chasing my honour, something much larger than me—or more important, at least. I had made a promise and that had to mean something in this life. I turned away.

I went into the kitchen and put the Aldercreek file with my report in the tray under the telephone. As I was about to leave Bishop reached out and took hold of my arm, not in an aggressive way, but in a consoling manner.

"She knew this day would come, Finn," he said. "I'm sure of it. Every time there was a letter from her sister, or a telephone call, she knew about it. I never told her directly, but I always had that feeling that she was listening, or perhaps it was a sense she had. I don't know. But you know it yourself, the past is never too far away. It'll leap out at you sooner or later."

"Damn it, Bishop, trouble just won't leave me alone."

"You seem to be doing fine."

"I'm glad you think so."

I went out the back door and hurried to my cabin. I wanted to sit out the rest of the day. I lit a fire and made a cup of coffee. I stood at the window, watching anxiously. It nearly drove me mad, the anticipation, the fear. There was a moment when I felt like making a dash for the manor and taking back the letter. But I couldn't. I had to leave it. I had to let it all be now. There was no turning back.

As the light was beginning to fade, she returned to the estate. I watched her car disappear behind the manor and turned away from the window. As I sat before the fire, there was comfort in the flames, the warmth tumbling out from the hearth. The ancient ritual of gazing into flames was hypnotic, pacifying, but I could only stare with a kind of alert attention, something like heart-pounding vigilance. I tried to read a book, *Wild Horse Mesa* by Zane Grey. Wandering riders of the vast tableland. Something to distract me. And then Chane's dream of wild freedom must have worked its way into my tired mind. I fell asleep.

I didn't know how long I had slept slumped in the chair when a loud noise awoke me. The book had fallen onto the floor. The fire gave a weak light from the orange-red coals. I reached for the book. Then another sound. Perhaps the one that had awakened me. It seemed to be coming from outside. I got up and went to the window. The manor was dark. It was late. That sound rising, floating, an ululation.

I opened the door and stepped outside. It came again, like a wolf, or perhaps a cougar. There had been a few sightings in recent months. I listened, holding my breath so that I could get a bearing on where it was coming from. And when it came again, I followed the sound and knew at once its source. I moved out onto the narrow porch and turned toward the manor, to the upstairs window where a dim amber glow emitted from Katherine's window. It was her. Her pain cut through the black cloth of darkness, a scream inhuman and raw, and then all at once died, only to begin again as a whimper, and then the shredded bawl of her outbreath that seemed would never end but did. A tortuous rhythm. It was the worst of my fears. I backed away. Then the porch light at the Cottage came on, and Birdie emerged in her house coat, Bishop behind her. Birdie ran across the lawn, and I lost her until she reappeared under the yard light behind the manor. Bishop looked my way from his porch. I stood in the dark without an answer for the misery that infused the night air. He had suggested that I need not do anything, that it wasn't my responsibility. He had warned me. And although I was certain he couldn't see me in the shadows, I knew he was thinking of that very thing.

26

I crept up to the back door with the rain slapping my backside as if to punish me for my spineless deed. I cupped my eyes and peeked in the window. Bishop was sitting in the nook by himself. He noticed me staring at him like a peeping Tom and waved me in. I walked straight to the cupboard for a coffee cup, and then I grabbed the coffee pot from the stove and filled my cup. I'd say Bishop was watching me like a cat, except Darby O'Gill mostly slept and wasn't interested in humans. I joined him at the table.

"Why are you looking at me like that?"

"It's been three days and she hasn't left her bed," he said gruffly. "I've been wondering what the hell you wrote. And where have you been?"

"I've been afraid to come out of my cabin."

"Well, Birdie is up with her now."

"Is she all right?"

"No, to be frank, she's not. If Birdie can't get her up today, she's going to call the doctor."

"Jesus Christ, Bishop, I knew she would be upset, but ..."

"You heard her in the night?"

"Yeah, it was awful. It sounded like someone being tortured."

"I suppose it was just that."

"What's Birdie doing anyway?"

"She sits with her. She brings her soup, but Lady Spencer won't touch it. Nothing. It's a worrisome thing, Finn. She's had some kind of breakdown. Tell me, what did you say in that letter?"

"I told her that her father was dying and wants to see her. I told her that her sister wasn't well, that she had been looking after him."

"That's it?"

"Yes, and I apologized. I did that. I did what I thought was a decent thing to do."

"If it was a decent thing to do, she's not taking it well."

I thought about the old man just then, what he did to her, the things I kept from Bishop. It didn't seem like something to be shared, but I had to tell him something, perhaps only for myself. "Can I have one of your Sportsman?" I asked.

"Why don't you buy a pack for yourself? You seem to like them. Switch brands, or is it that you just like mine?"

"I like yours better."

"Here," he said, shaking his head. He slid his pack across the table.

I shook one out and lit it. "It reminds me of fishing."

"Yes, that's why I smoke them. Have you something else on your mind?"

"Does it show?"

"You've done that damn cigarette trick before. You're setting me up for something. Well, let's hear it."

"Bishop," I began, "there was something else that Betty Lantz told me that day."

"When you visited her?"

"Yeah." I took a sip of coffee. "You see, the old man was a bastard. I mean a real bastard."

"Go on."

I hesitated. I didn't know how to say it, what words to use. I wanted to be sensitive, respectful about it. "He hurt Katherine in the worst way," I said finally, "and I don't mean physically so much, though he may have. She was just a girl, and it went on for some time. Betty said that Katherine protected her from him. That's what her big sister did for her. The mother knew about it but did nothing to stop it. I didn't want to say anything to you. It seemed wrong even to think about it. But as awful as it was to hear it, that's when I began to understand her, why she kept away from her family among other things. Betty knows why, of course. Still, she needs her sister. She looked to be in a bad way. So I told Katherine in the only way I could, knowing it was going to bring up awful memories. And it hurt her all over again. I feared that would happen, but I wasn't prepared for what poured out of her window the other night. If a nightmare had a sound, then that was it."

Bishop's head slumped. Then he began to nod the way he did when processing something difficult and grave. "Damn."

"I'm glad Birdie's with her."

Bishop looked up. He took a cigarette from his pack. He lit it and inhaled deeply, then turned slightly and exhaled the blue plume. "Birdie has a part of her that can stand a lot of pain," he said thoughtfully, "and I'm not talking about her own. I'm talking about other people's pain. She has a way. I don't know where she got it from. It's like she absorbs it, takes it away. She did that very thing with Isabel when she was just a little girl. She had a fever one time, and Birdie willed it out of her, just sitting, rocking the way she does, stroking her forehead. The doctor came and said it *was* love. A strange thing to say, I thought, coming from a doctor. But I suppose it was love, and not some otherworldly power she had. It sounds so simple, and we all have it. It's free to give away, but few choose to."

Just then Birdie came into the kitchen. She went to the stove and poured herself a cup of coffee.

"Well, how is she?" Bishop asked.

"She's sitting up in bed now," Birdie said. "It's a good sign."

"Thank God," I said.

Birdie reached into the cookie jar sitting on the counter down, removed several cookies, and put them on a plate. She joined us at the nook table and set the plate of cookies. Bishop slid over for her.

"Finn," she said, "there must have been something powerful in your letter." She looked at me, a scolding squint in her eyes.

"I know, but I had to ..."

"No, that's not what I'm talking about. She wants you to get the car ready."

"What?"

"You heard me right."

"What are you talking about, Birdie?"

"Those are peanut butter cookies, by the way." She motioned at the plate in front of me.

I took one, as if it were my move in a board game. "Birdie, what's going on?"

"She wants you to take her."

"Take her where?" Bishop asked, reasonably, I thought.

She looked at him as if amused by the question, then turned back to me. "To Cumberland."

"Son of a bitch," Bishop exclaimed as if a miracle had just manifested before his disbelieving eyes.

Birdie held her index finger up to her lips. "You will need to look after her, Finn. Can you do that?"

"Yeah, I guess I can."

"I mean *look after her*. Who knows what she's going to find, and what that'll do to her?"

"I suppose I can do that."

"Look, Finn, I'm not talking about a family reunion with disgruntled relatives here. Do you know what I'm saying?"

It seemed that she was searching for what I knew. I could feel the heat of her inquiry, her attention, her rooting out of all of my apprehensions and anxieties. "Her sister," I said, "told me all about it, Birdie. Everything. I'll look after her."

"Good."

"Is there anything else that I should know, Birdie?"

"Like what?"

"How much she hates me for it?"

"I wouldn't use that word," she said.

"What else could there be?"

"I'd expect that she will be angry with you," Bishop said. "It's all in the open now."

"No, it's more like shame and sorrow," Birdie said, "and a deep grief that has never been allowed out of the cage of her misery. You'll know for yourself."

I sat in pool of strange sensations, my head buzzing with rambling thoughts. I couldn't think of anything else to say about it, not another question.

"And how are you, my dear?" Bishop said. He took her hand and held it in his.

I didn't need to look away from them and leave them to their intimate moments. They were showing me something that I never had. I envied them, the way they cared for one another. I thought that a person would be lucky to have such companionship in a lifetime. In a world where people come and go, blink in and out, and circumstances can drive you to your knees, sometimes you stay there and can't get up. The Bishops were the foundation of my meagre life. I didn't know what I would have done without their steadfastness. They possessed a loyalty that was rare and precious, and in spite of the years, they never seemed to lose themselves in the roles they played.

The next morning, I sat in the Cadillac behind the manor. It was an overcast day, cold with the threat of snow. I was warming the engine, waiting for the heater to take off the chill. I thought that there was a good chance that we'd be away for several days so had packed a duffel bag. I was feeling uneasy, which wasn't unusual when it came to Lady Spencer. Yes, the mystery of her title had been exposed as nothing but air, but I still didn't know what I was going to say to Katherine, what the conversation on the drive to Cumberland might look like. Perhaps she wouldn't even talk to me. I wouldn't blame her.

The kitchen door opened, and Bishop came out with her suitcase. I got out and opened the trunk in a cloud of exhaust, and Bishop carefully placed the case inside.

"You all set?" he asked.

"I'm nervous as hell." I closed the trunk.

"You have every reason to be, Finn."

"Thanks a lot."

He reached into his coat pocket and removed four packs of Sportsman cigarettes. "Here," he said, "a going-away gift." He handed them to me.

"You don't have to do that." I turned them over as if I had been given something rare and remarkable. The trout-fly patterns on the back.

"I know, but if you stayed, you would be bumming them off me."

"Do I do that?"

Bishop stood back all at once. That all knowing look of his. "Look, I know this is not easy for you, Finn. I admire you for it. At one time I think I even told you to stay out of it. I thought about that. Some things you just can't ignore. You have to face what frightens you most. And yes, I told you that more times than I can remember. It takes courage. And I never imagined that Lady Spencer would face what she had left behind. I would have put money on it. But I was wrong. Perhaps you gave her the courage."

"I didn't say anything to her."

"You didn't need to. You showed her."

"Why don't I feel brave, Bishop?"

"Because courage takes a certain amount of fear—fuel you might say."

"It's all so strange."

"Yeah, it's been a peculiar year," he said. "So much has happened around the world, and here. Life happens everywhere. I'd prefer a more stable state of affairs, but I suppose that wouldn't be as interesting. No, something must be going on. The world is changing. Perhaps it's growing pains. Everything is being challenged, looked at, poked at, thrown away, and resisted. People don't like change. Some will even kill a good president."

"I wish I knew what's going to happen, Bishop."

For once he didn't have one of his patented answers at the ready. "Finn," he began after a moment, "the old man had to be found out. No more hiding, even in Cumberland. Don't think on it. Let it happen on its own."

She came out of the manor just then. She was wearing sunglasses, smartly dressed as usual. A good teal coat with a fur collar. Always a sense of business. At once Bishop opened the rear door for her.

"Front," she said. Bishop corrected his assumptions and opened the front passenger door. She got in.

I moved up alongside the car and turned to Bishop standing like a father sending his children off on their own for the first time. The look on his face. I had seen it before, when he was unsure of himself, when he doubted his own wisdom. He was only a man, after all. He couldn't know everything, and if he did, he would likely be a god. *Good luck,* his expression seemed to say—a surrogate kind of reassurance. But I always knew that it was more of a prayer than anything else. That didn't matter so much. Old Bishop was such an anchor in my life, and more than ever now, I liked the sound of his voice.

"Keep the coffee on," I told him.

"Always."

27

We drove to town in silence. I felt the return of the wall between us. It kept us in different time zones. She had a lot to consider, and I knew that her attention would be absorbed by the torments of another time, perhaps not a specific moment, but the whole unsettling reel of it. I stopped at Charlie's garage for gas. He came out right away, and I rolled the window down.

"Good morning, Lady Spencer, Finn," he said, "what'll it be today?"

"Fill 'er up with the good stuff, Charlie," I said.

"Very good."

He set the nozzle and left it to fill the tank, and then sprayed the windshield with cleaner and scrubbed it with a squeegee. Once finished, he lifted the hood and checked the oil. He removed the dipstick and checked it, then wiped it clean with a rag. He replaced the dipstick and closed the hood, then came over to the window.

"Down half a quart," he said. "Get it next time." He went back to top off the gas. Several short clicks of the nozzle. He came up to the window wiping his hands clean with the rag, if that was possible. "Five bucks, Finn."

Katherine handed me a five-dollar bill from her purse. I gave it to Charlie, and we left.

"He's trying really hard," I said as we pulled out onto Fawn Hill Road. But she said nothing, and we continued on in the same walled-in silence. I thought that she might comment on Charlie's service, the way he tried to make things right. The windshield was bright and clean. But she didn't say a thing until we got to the highway at Mill Bay, and it had nothing to do with Charlie Sales.

"Your letter," she said, "was well written."

I turned to her, mildly stunned, but pleased. She looked straight ahead. Sunglasses on a dark day. "I had to write it," I said. "I knew."

"Please, don't explain yourself. I can read." An inflection like a well-placed knife. She removed a cigarette from her pack of du Mauriers and pushed in the lighter. After a minute the lighter popped, and she lit her cigarette with the red-hot coil. She turned toward the ocean.

It seemed that she couldn't look at me. A terse rebuff to shut me up. She was clearly not happy with me, and perhaps it was a simmering anger that made her so ill-disposed. I had questions, and maybe helpful answers, but she was so utterly unapproachable. I quickly forgot the progress we had made. I couldn't even recall the circumstances that had made me feel so hopeful. The letter seemed to have returned us to a previous time, as if I had been dragged back into the resentment and bitterness that once defined our relationship. But I knew I could be quiet and allow her the time she needed. And something else was *needed* of me. I was trying so hard to be empathetic and not selfishly hurt.

We travelled like strangers with not an arm's length between us, but an emotional distance that might as well have been infinite, like two random people heading north. The gold Cadillac floated heavily over the bare macadam. Snowflakes fell now and then, and the leafless trees, cryptic with their black-forked hands, appeared solemn along the verge of the highway. A mood seeped into me like oil. How was I to look after such a woman? I had been relegated to driving and nothing more. Oh, my resentment wasn't too far away, just under my thin skin, boiling away in my dark sanctuary. How quickly I judged her now. The miles were difficult, long, uneventful save for the churning monologue in my head that claimed its self-righteous duty to analyze and revile. And then outside of Nanaimo, she removed her sunglasses. She spoke once again, but nothing mocking or mean-spirited this time.

"Tell me about Susan."

"Susan?" She caught me off guard. I kept looking straight ahead.

"Your fiancée."

"What would you like to know?"

"What did she look like?"

"Well, she was pretty," I said, but it sounded rather juvenile. "I mean attractive. She had auburn hair, light skin, pale blue eyes. Not tall like ... but more Birdie's height."

Boldly, I turned to her as I waited for her response, and glimpsed the dark shadows of her eyes, swollen and purple as moles. She didn't hide from me. She had cried a thousand tears, it seemed. I turned back to the highway, astounded at the vacillation of my mood, from sullen irritability to empathy once again in a rural mile. I was at the mercy of her temperaments. It was all so confusing.

"She left you," she said after a long pause.

"She thought I was immoral," I said, "that I had committed a great sin and brought shame to her family."

"All that?"

"I brought it on myself. I was drinking in the bar of a renowned hotel. I couldn't deny it. I didn't really care who was there or why. But people fear what they don't understand. Then they can hate without knowing that it comes from inside them, not outside. She didn't even want to hear what I had to say."

"You sound like Mr. Bishop. He influences you."

"He does."

"Well, you're lucky that you found out what kind of person Susan was."

"Yeah, I suppose so." She lit another cigarette, one after the other now. The conversation was civil, almost normal, even thoughtful. But I had learned that it could change at any moment.

"I never had such luck," she said.

"He wanted to tell you," I ventured. "He knew it was difficult for you."

"Oh, well, the conversations you must have had," she said, her tone accusatory now. "The intimate details of the unfulfilled wife and all that. Man to man or ... something." Her tossed hand.

As I listened to her, it seemed at times that her language revealed the need to impart something of herself, a tentative hand reaching out to me.

"It wasn't like that," I went on. "I only wanted to help him if I could. But what did I know? I just listened mostly."

"I didn't get even that," she said bitterly.

"You had everything."

"What does that mean?" A hard turn to me.

"He gave you what he could."

"Compensation?"

"No, that's not what I mean," I said, feeding her a little more now, things that perhaps would help her understand. "Maybe it was just too hard for him. Such fear and shame followed him everywhere he went. Ted was human. We gave him perhaps an inflated version of himself. He was just a fragile man trying to get by. He couldn't speak to you about something he didn't really understand himself. He loved you. He wasn't going to hurt you. So he said nothing."

"Actually, he did in his own way," she said indignantly. "But he never broached the subject directly. He had great difficulty with the truth, as it turned out. Most people do. What a pair you were.

And you, Finn, giving up on life. I never gave up. I had a better solution. I denied the part I didn't like, erased it. But it wasn't erased completely, now, was it? My oversight. The truth haunted me, stalked me, and eventually found me. It was inevitable. I could blame you, but that would be too easy. You said it yourself. You were the messenger. And what did Ted have to do with all of this? I suppose he kept my nose above water, and yours as well. A life ring until all the evil in the world had passed. And it is evil!"

Her scorching tone, the dark reference. I could say nothing, and mercifully the conversation flagged. The cheerless hand of gloom clutching my throat. Meaning seemed to have left us, and all seemed sad, irreconcilable. A psychiatrist would have fared better. I began to fear that looking after her was more than I could manage on my own. But I had seen something beyond the wounds, the lacerations. A fierce intelligence. And surprisingly, she had more to say.

"Are you finished your book?" she asked.

"I thought I was," I said, "but I think life is not finished with me."

"And what do you call this book?"

"The title, well, I'm playing with something."

"Tell me."

I hesitated, allowing the words to form. "*The Sum of One Man's Pleasure*," I said, "something like that."

"You're certainly ambitious. Will you spare me?"

"Yes, of course."

"But how do you tell the story of your life without the truth? All of it."

"And your life?"

She turned away. My question seemed to have upset her, and I regretted flinging it in her face, as if I had any idea of what was going on inside her. As we drove along Qualicum Beach, I needed a break and pulled over at a rest area. She got out of the car without saying a word and walked away. It seemed she wanted to be left alone. I wondered if I had said too much. And yet she hadn't lashed out at me with anger and accusations as I had feared. She had been rather tolerant. She seemed to have accepted my part in orchestrating the inevitable. I sat and waited for her to return. I smoked and watched the grey sweep of sea. Time went on, and soon I became worried. She had been somewhere along the beach for nearly half an hour. She wore a warm coat, but her skirt and shoes were inadequate for a squally day. I got out of the car and went to look for her.

There was a rough trail down to the beach where the incoming tide battered beached logs. I searched one way and then the other, looking through sea spray to where the beach curved and disappeared. I couldn't see her anywhere. I felt a sudden surge of panic. I began to jog down the beach over barnacle-encrusted stones and tide debris. Logs pulsed in the seafoam, and waves swelled in their rows and crashed at my running feet. Gulls screamed as if mad with delight. My face was wet with the splashing sea. I could taste the brine on my lips. And when I came to the curve of beach, I saw beyond it, down along a little bay where a derelict boat lay on its side with a great gash in the hull. She was standing beside it with her head down, as still as something broken and forgotten. I was looking at the wreckage of her life.

I walked slowly, keeping my eye on her. She hadn't moved at all, and then I called out so as not to startle her. "Katherine, it's time to go!"

She turned lazily and watched me come toward her. She had been crying. Her mascara had run down her cheeks in ghastly rills, and her mouth was chapped and stiff. And then I glimpsed it, that something beyond her that I had only vaguely been aware of but was unable to define or understand. It was in the eyes. The little girl behind them was shining through, if only briefly. It was an impression, something so swift and yet undeniable. The hurt child.

"Are you all right?" I asked.

The languid lifting of her eyes. "What does that even mean?"

"I was worried, that's all."

"I've noticed that about you. You care. I wouldn't have believed it."

"I think you care, too." I removed a handkerchief from my coat pocket and gave it to her.

"Don't be too quick to sway me with such talk," she said, dabbing her eyes. "I know how I am sometimes. And how Birdie overlooks it. She brushes my hair every evening. I never ask her, you know."

"And yet that day it seemed that you asked the Bishops to leave."

"Do you think I don't know what I am, what I do? Sometimes there is a mercy that must be offered. How else should I have said it? I am not a good judge of my tendencies. The day Ted died, my deception began to fade. No one calls for me, no art shows, lunches, not like it was before. I am not so revered, as it turns out. But you know that was Ted, his creation, making me something that I was not. I loved him for that, for protecting me. But the imposter has been exposed. I am not a "Lady." That was a device of his making. I was cold and callous the day of his funeral. You can't deny that. Put that in your book. You thought me a terrible bitch."

"No, I didn't."

"You certainly did. It was written all over your face. I can read faces too, as well as letters from the abyss."

"Why are you so hard on yourself? You've been through ..."

"Look at this water, Finn. This deep and churning ocean. Roland drowned in this water. Yes, Betty's husband. I knew it. I knew all about it. One letter I opened, but I regretted it at once. It was full of a past I didn't want to look at. I didn't want to hear that I was needed, that I should come home. I hadn't the strength. Betty is the strong one. She truly is, but ..."

"She would say that you had all the courage."

"It wasn't courage for God's sake; it was fear," she said, shaking her fist. "It was horror. It was not knowing what else to do. I would have killed him if I had courage. I would have!" She slumped all at once, and I reached out and caught her.

I held her with a bitter wind tossing the drifting flakes of snow back against the grey sky, never to reach the ground. Seawater washed in and out through the broken hull of the boat. And the crazed gulls were indifferent to human drama and eyed us as trespassers. I drew her into me as one does a wounded soul, the way mothers can become a fortress, a sanctuary, even heaven for our terrible fears, our greatest terrors. I just held her tight, not knowing why I did so. And then she gently pushed back and looked into my worried eyes.

She reached up and touched my cheek with a finger, ran it down to my chin, never taking her eyes from me. Saying nothing. She was someone else now. She was unafraid. She was safe. It changed her whole appearance, softened the hard lines of her life. The brief flare of her beauty. A portrait of her innocence. We stayed in that moment of attention, of peace and empathy, for a long while. I was certain that a conversation was underway that was not of this world, but something else. Perhaps the deepest parts of us recognized in the other that human longing had not been expunged but was being restored.

"I used to dream of good days," she said, "but they never came, and may never come at all. I had to let go of such notions. My life at Spencerwood had the appearance of good days, but they were counterfeit. Wealth cannot purchase happiness. Such states are for someone else, not for me. I was much like Roland. I would have followed him into the sea if I was as brave, and perhaps preceded him by many years."

"I think I know how that feels. I remember how the Ottawa River invited me. We have no clarity when we are drowning in our despair. And it *is* drowning."

"So we search for something to save us."

"And the reverend offered that?" I took a chance now.

"How does one find happiness in a man sick for a week with his guilt?"

I nodded. There was nothing more to be said about Reverend Le Fleur. "You create art," I said, "beautiful paintings, portraits. There is some pleasure in that."

"I have a closet full of art not fit for the eye. Darby O'Gill once hissed at their frightening palette."

"What do cats know anyway?"

She searched my eyes, as if I had spoken with such profundity. "Mr. Kenny," she said, "after all that you know about me, you can still hold me. What is it about you that wants to remain?"

The restored formality felt playful now, and the deep water not so dangerous. I wanted to keep it going. "I don't know for sure," I answered. "Perhaps it's because no one can know the pain of another unless awakened by their own."

"Ah," she said simply, a gesture of agreement. And then, tilting her head slightly, she made a revealing observation. "You are such a mystery to me. A man in a cabin with his unlived passions. That I dreamt about."

We walked back along the beach toward the car. She held my arm. We never spoke. Enough had been said for now. Silence enveloped us, moved us along. Language seemed unnecessary. We were too fragile for words. The wrong ones could shatter us both, undo the best of words. They had such power when used carefully.

28

We headed north once again, and as we neared Courtenay it began to snow heavily, the dense drift of flakes from a fractured sky. I turned off the highway at Royston. It wasn't too far to Betty's farm now, and Katherine's hands suddenly clutched tightly, her knuckles white as the falling snow. Her head began to drop until her chin rested on her chest. She was hanging on now, it seemed.

"We'll be at Betty's in a few minutes," I said. "It will be all right."

The Cadillac handled snow-covered Royston Road well with its weight. Still, I took it slow. I kept checking on her. She was holding her stomach now, and then a faint whimper. She was trying to say something.

"What is it, Katherine?"

"Pull over," she said faintly.

"Pull over?"

"Pull the goddamn car over. I'm going to be sick!"

I moved over to the side of the road at once and stopped. I got out of the car and went around to her door to help her out. She was sheet-white in a white swirling world. I took her hand and helped her to the ditch. My feet began to slide in the accumulating snow, but I managed to hold her as she leaned over it. She gasped. Her breathing was short, rapid, and then her roiling stomach could no longer be contained, and she retched over and over, evicting the bilious tenants that oppressed her.

After it was over, I pulled her away from the ditch and turned her toward me. I cleaned her face with a handful of snow from the trunk of the car, and then wiped away the melting snow from her chin with my handkerchief. There were tears in her eyes. The burn of vomit and more. I helped her back into the car.

As I went around the car to get back in, I looked out over the farms for a moment. There were sheep in a pasture standing indifferently in woolly coats gathering snow, and the black forest beyond brightened, emerging as if coming into existence. Then a split in the sky, shards of light. The snow stopped falling. It was a new world. It all looked so beautiful, and I wondered how it was possible, how such beauty and such pain could coexist. And on that same stretch of road, I had been overwhelmed myself, but only with the knowledge of what she had lived.

We sat a moment before continuing. I lit a cigarette for her, and she took it. Then she turned to me.

"Betty doesn't know we're coming," she said, her voice weak and dry. "I didn't want to tell her. I wasn't sure if I could do it. I wasn't sure."

"Are you sure now?"

"No."

"Take your time."

"Let's go. The waiting is too hard."

It was only a short drive before the farm came into view. "That's it," I said. Woodsmoke drifted over the rooftop of the house. There was a car in the driveway, an older Pontiac that I remembered belonged to Betty. She was home at least, but Tom Lantz's truck wasn't there. I was a bit disappointed as Tom had seemed a decent fellow. I pulled up behind the car. Her hands were clutching once again.

"Do you need a few minutes?" I asked. She didn't answer, only her short breaths and a sound coming from her chest that seemed a desperate kind of language. She looked straight ahead, her head tipped down slightly, fighting for control once again. I knew that it was all up to her now. Encouragement seemed perverse.

And then the front door of the house opened all at once and Betty stepped onto the porch. She threw a sweater over her shoulders, then peered hard into the car, a look of confusion, even fear. A moment passed, and her gaunt face suddenly brightened with a certain shock. Then such doubt. She looked at me through the windshield, as if trying to account for the arrival of a gold Cadillac in her driveway. She looked again, holding onto her arms in the cold. She seemed to falter as she realized without a doubt that Katey had truly come home, and that recognition drove her to her knees. I opened the door to get out, but Katherine was out of the car before I could move. She hurried to her sister. I stayed back as witness to the awesome power of courage and blood. Katherine helped Betty to her feet, and they regarded each other not with estranged distance but with something immutable and enduring. Time had no merit, no influence, other than the span to measure their suffering. They embraced for a long time. I could see their slow rocking, a dance of reunion and restoration. Betty seemed so tiny in Katherine's arms, and I was certain that she despaired over her little sister's frailty.

I leaned against the car and lit a cigarette. I tried not to look at them directly, as I did when the Bishops were held by something beyond the grasp of the world. I began to realize that I was part of it all now. I could no longer separate myself from the life around me. But I had to look away finally as the sudden swelling of tenderness in my chest caught me by surprise. The welling of my unshed tears. It was a good feeling, though, and as such was not expected. I hadn't felt that in a long time, had long forgotten that such a state even existed. They went inside and I remained by the car watching the brightening sun melt holes in the snow.

I didn't mind being by myself. They needed time alone. It was a moment that I had hoped for, and that Betty had prayed for. I wasn't so sure of Katherine's wishes. Perhaps that would have been too optimistic. She had fought to stay away all those years, a war she had fought in isolation. And I knew she had battled still on that day, the countless demons along the Island Highway. It would have been dishonest to say that I wasn't gratified it had all turned out, so far at least.

It had been nearly an hour and the last heat from the engine was sucked up by the cold. I wanted to give them more time. They surely would have much to talk about, and I knew that it would not be all joyous like long-lost sisters reunited by an act of serendipity. But I was growing colder standing out on the driveway, so went up to the front door and slowly opened it. I waited outside and listened. I could hear the even timbre of conversation. It seemed safe to go inside and I went in, but I thought that I would let them know that I was coming into the kitchen.

"I was getting cold out there," I called out.

"There's coffee on the stove," Betty answered. "There's a cup on the counter for you, Finn."

"That sounds good," I said. I went to the stove and smiled briefly to them at the kitchen table. It was only a fleeting glance, but I saw that Betty was holding her sister's hand, cupped it as if were a child's. There were crumpled tissues on the table. Betty appeared even thinner than the last time I had seen her. I poured myself a cup of coffee and stood, uncertain where I should go with it.

"Please sit with us, Finn," Betty said.

It was an invitation I wanted to decline, but I couldn't identify a better option just then. "All right," I said, "but I don't want to intrude."

"Don't be silly," Betty said.

I sat with them. At first Katherine ignored me. Her eyes drifted down onto the table and remained there. It wasn't until I looked away that I felt her look at me. Never before had I been so near to her, to see her in all her starkness and vulnerability. She allowed it and that was the most surprising thing of all. I suppose it had taken all of her strength to uphold her identity at the estate, always in character, always in hiding. And now the simple cloth of truth.

"After the children return from school," Betty said, "we'll go to the house. Will that be all right, Finn?"

"Yes, of course."

"I need to bring him his supper."

I nodded.

"Katey's going to lie down for a while. There's a cot in my sewing room upstairs. Now Tom comes by after his shift at the mill. You remember Tom, Finn. He'll come with us. Our father can be hard to handle at times. I like to have Tom with me. How would that be?"

"That sounds fine," I said, but thought it might be too much in one day. "Perhaps it would be best for Katherine to go tomorrow."

"No!" Katherine swiftly interjected.

"She wants to go today," Betty said. "The waiting would hurt more than she can bear."

"You're right, of course," I said. I could see that Betty had a routine that had served her well for more years than I knew. I was a mere accompaniment to the enormity of what was yet to come. It wasn't too difficult to imagine that there was another level of fear that Katherine had to approach and finally face. She had come so far that day, and soon the road would end.

Betty took Katherine upstairs so that she could rest. I went out to the car to get her suitcase, and as I was removing it from the trunk, a school bus stopped out on the road in front of the house. Five children spilled out, all of different sizes. They came marching down the driveway toward me. They stopped in a gangly knot. Three girls and two boys. One boy, who seemed to be the oldest, stepped forward.

"Who are you?" he said straightaway.

"My name is Finn."

"I know that name. You were here before."

"That's right. I came to see your mom."

"Yeah, I know."

"Did you bring her?" a young teenage girl asked.

"I brought your Auntie Katey," I said.

"Auntie Katey is here?" she squealed.

"Yes, but she's upstairs resting. So you need to be very quiet. All right?"

"Uh-huh."

"Do you think you can carry her suitcase?"

"Yeah."

The excited mob of children continued on to the house. The girl struggled with the suitcase but seemed eager to carry it. They went around to the back door. I watched them before they disappeared, the way the older boy herded them along, already filling the void in their young lives. And then the orderly delivery of duty and guardianship, Tom Lantz pulled into the driveway and parked alongside the Cadillac. He got out of his truck, a surprised look on his face, even overjoyed.

"Finn," he said, "you brought her?"

"I brought her, Tom."

"Son of a bitch, you did it. I never thought that she would come!"

"It wasn't easy, but we're here." I watched Tom, how excited he was. I had never seen his smile. He looked much younger now.

"Betty never gave up hope."

"She doesn't seem the type to quit on a purpose."

"That's so true, Finn. Well, where is she?"

"Having a nap. She wants to go see the old man today."

"That's some nasty business," Tom said, shaking his head. "I don't know how Betty does it. He lives in a ... well, you'll see."

I offered him a cigarette. He took it gravely and I lit for him. We each smoked and looked out over the pasture as if it were a consoling feature that we both needed just then. The snow had all but vanished, and the sun had begun to slide behind the mountains.

"How is he?" I asked.

"He's living much too long. He didn't deserve a long life. But I can tell you it's not much of a life. It's the damnedest house I've ever seen, a kind of cave. At least it's too cold for maggots."

"A cave?"

"It surely is."

I helped Tom unload firewood from the back of his truck. We stacked it against the shed behind the house. It was alder, and the orange burnish of the wood was striking in the fading sunlight. I could see that Tom liked to work with his hands, a very physical man with the thick hands of the wood trade. Betty called us into the house once we finished.

Inside, Katherine had returned to the kitchen and the children stood around her at the table wide-eyed as a clutch of owls. Betty named them each in order of their age. They seemed mesmerized by her, as if seeing for the first time something mythological, or perhaps the embodiment of what their mother had kept alive for them. They were unsure of themselves, not knowing what to say to her. But the youngest seemed to be a curious boy. His name was David.

"Where have you been, Auntie Katey?" he said. Of course, it was a reasonable question from a nephew.

But he had no idea of the bounds of the answer, and it seemed that Betty would intervene and made a gesture to answer for her sister, but in the end, she allowed the question to stand.

"David," Katherine said after what seemed a long deliberation, "I was not well."

"You were sick?"

"Something like that."

"Are you okay now?"

"I'm trying to be."

"That's good," David reassured her. Katherine smiled and lightly shook her head as if astonished by his sweet words. Perhaps more than that, it was his innocence that moved her, a quality that had been stolen from her.

Betty ushered them away after they all had a good look at their long-lost auntie. Betty had a good sense of one's capacity, it seemed to me. She was far stronger than her frail stature would suggest. I had gained great respect for her in the short time I had known her. The complexity of family was not something new to me, but it astonished me how she was with her children, in spite of it all.

"I have a stew on for the children," she said. "I'll take a plate for him. The oldest, Curtis, will be in charge."

There was a lull all at once, somewhat uncomfortable. The air in the kitchen thickened with a palpable tension. I turned to Tom, whose mouth was stiff and resolute. His eyes met mine with a grim foreshadowing. I knew it was the prelude to what came next. Betty leaned down to Katherine finally, and she looked up at her little sister. After a time, she simply nodded. It was time to go.

29

We took the Cadillac, and I drove with Tom in the front. In the rear-view mirror I could see Katherine's head slumped against Betty's thin shoulder. Nothing was said as we passed the last of the farms and entered a forest that shut out all the remaining light of the day, but now and then Katherine groaned, a chilling account of her pain, the assaulted mind and its protests. We seemed to enter another world, one of dark legend and portent. I couldn't imagine the old man, but Tom had not spared his awful sketch of him as well as the house. I suppose one could not separate such things.

On we went until the forest thinned and again light appeared.

"Cumberland," Tom said.

"Just point the way, Tom," I said.

We came into the village, and he told me where to turn, down Dunsmuir Avenue past the hotel and post office and sundry businesses, then through the grid of streets until we came to Windermere Avenue. Soon he pointed to a house on the corner, dirty white in the remaining daylight. It looked vacant, no porch light or light within. Even the neighbouring houses stood well away, as if there were some dissociation among the dwellings. I stopped in front of the house but kept the engine running. We sat. I could hear Betty speaking softly to Katherine, reassuring words, I imagined, or perhaps just what to expect. I caught Betty in the mirror as she looked up.

"You will be shocked, Finn," she said. "You most likely haven't seen such a thing before, or even heard of it. I don't shock easily anymore. So let me do the talking. I know how to handle him. We'll take it slow. And we'll leave if it's too much for Katey. Now, if we all agree, we can go in."

There were no dissenting words. I could only wonder what Betty and Tom were talking about. It was just a small house with a dying man inside. I turned off the engine and we got out of the car. The air had cooled and faint stars were emerging above the mountains that rimmed the Comox Valley. It was a rather pretty scene, the dark forests, the blinking night sky above the ordered streets, but such thoughts clashed with Betty's forewarning. Our breath smoked as we went up to the porch, Betty guiding her sister as if she were incapacitated. I had never before witnessed such a devastating emotional collapse. But how remarkable that Katherine continued on in spite of her terror.

All at once I had a bad feeling about that house, as if it were wounded, an entity dying itself. I felt uneasy, hesitant. Tom stepped past me and rapped on the door with his fist, then slowly opened it. The others followed him in, so quiet. I was the last to enter.

I felt a presence, not of a particular thing as the light was too dim to discern what it might be. But as my eyes adjusted, the presence became tangible. The entire space was crammed with things. My mind could not grasp it. I followed the others down a narrow corridor, a trail perhaps a foot wide. The smell reached us next, most foul: rot and decay, mustiness, and the human stink of urine and excrement. I covered my mouth and nose with my hand as my stomach rolled over, then held my breath as an appalling mass—tin cans, jars, and bottles, discarded clothing, newspapers stacked to the ceiling like soda crackers, teabags and parings scattered like corrupted blessings—was revealed. In every corner, piles of garbage, food waste, and rinsings. There was no furniture visible, no tables or lamps. And then something stirred, and I heard Tom cuss ahead of me. The choking pong of rodent.

"Damn rats!" He picked up a jar and threw it into the heap. More scurrying and rustling, the mass of squalor moving as if alive.

We stopped abruptly. Someone was talking, but the sound was muted and distant. I moved up close behind the others, where I could see *him* now, sitting in a chair under a bare lightbulb hanging from the ceiling. A cadaver of a man seated on his throne of ruination. There were empty bottles of liquor piled beside him, one half-full at his feet. Tom moved aside and allowed me to come closer. I joined Betty, and together we held Katherine. She was anchored now.

"Katey has come to see you," Betty said.

"Who, you say?" the old man said.

"Katey."

"I want to see her," he said angrily. "I told you that!"

"This *is* Katey, just as you asked." Her voice was even but firm.

He leaned with a sightless glare. I had a good look at him now in his homespun hell. He was filthy in a hide of grime. His clothes were the colour of parchment, threadbare as gauze. The lightbulb above his head made him appear even more hideous, emphasizing his hollow, unseen eyes. I could not believe that life still coursed through his veins. He regarded Katherine the way a curious animal might, then with a certain repulsed scrutiny. Then his eyes turned to me.

"Who is this one?"

"A friend," Tom answered.

"He's come for me. He's no friend. Come here and I'll cut you!"

"He's not going to hurt you," Tom reassured him. "He brought Katey."

The old man waved at me, hacking at the fetid air that surrounded him. I saw no point in talking to him. There was nothing to be gained on that night. I could feel Katherine now, heavy under my arm. How did she endure? The old man continued ranting.

"I'm not going," he went on, "but I'm drunk as hell and preaching. I was a good man when the world made sense. It's all a shame that you don't want me. Out of my house. I'm a bastard. You think so, eldest daughter. I'll die early so you can sleep at night. See what I care. I got the black lung. I shit coal dust. But you want to forget that I was born. You will be sorry when the night comes. You hate the dark. You both cried like babies. I heard you. So don't tell me about the fists. I wasn't that bad. Two daughters. Useless as sin!" He reached down for his bottle and took a long drink.

I could feel Katherine try to move from under me. I let go, but Betty still held her one arm. She bent toward her father, as close as she dared. "Your life is your punishment," she said, her voice a shrill whisper, portentous. "What better sentence than a long, sad life. Forgiveness will not come from me. You will answer to that which created you. You will harm us no more."

She turned away, and the old man rose up from his chair. But he didn't get very far, as he was seized by something, perhaps his own rage. His eyes emerged from the hollow caves momentarily. The look of the stunned. He remained motionless, suspended, then fell back onto the chair He sat unmoving, his head slumped on his chest, his breath gurgling.

Betty took Katherine by the arm, and we all started back down the aisle. "I'll call for the ambulance next door," she said. "The telephone here is long disappeared."

Outside, we waited for Betty by the car as she went to the neighbour's house to use the telephone. Tom and I held Katherine, kept her warm as she stared back at the house, perhaps remembering. Soon Betty returned. She seemed unfazed by it all, perhaps conditioned to his sorry existence. We lit cigarettes and waited for the ambulance. When the ambulance came, the attendants had difficulty getting him out of the house. We could hear them pitching garbage out of the way. When they finally emerged, he was on a stretcher covered in a sheet up to his neck. Neither attendant asked any questions, just packed him up and left.

Betty gestured to the neighbour's house. "Mrs. Fairfield thinks me a fool," she said, "for looking after him all these years. I guess the old man raised a fool. He surely did. She came over to the house one time, tried to help him get rid of some of his junk. He nearly lost his mind. She never came back. I tried myself more than once. Same thing. He wouldn't part with a scrap of his garbage. It's a sickness. She'll be happy when he's dead. She said once over tea, that it would be a mercy to the town if the house burned down. Remove it from the earth once and for all. Let it burn, even if he goes with it. That's what she said. And Mrs. Fairfield is a kind woman, as gentle as a lamb."

Then Betty moved away from the car all at once and stood motionless before the house, as if realizing she had forgotten something inside. I wondered if there was anything of value that remained. She walked slowly up to the front door and pushed it open. She stood for another moment before reaching into her coat pocket. We all understood immediately.

She struck the match against the door jamb, a pop of flame. She let it burn for a few seconds, then tossed it into the house. It seemed that she might light another, but at once an amber glow appeared before her. Betty turned away.

We watched from the safety of the car as the fire grew and roared like an approaching train. It didn't take long. Soon flames were shooting through the roof and windows, a blistering con-flagration on a chilly night. I looked up at the sparks swimming among the stars. A miserable beauty. Mrs. Fairfield and the rest of the neighbourhood came out of their houses to watch. The Cumberland Volunteer Fire Department arrived, sirens and flash-ing lights, but when the firetruck pulled up alongside the house, the firemen got out only to safeguard the surrounding houses. One fireman, recognizing Betty, walked over to the car.

"It's just a matter of time for a hoarder," he said.

"Tonight was it," Betty replied.

"That means your father's gone, then?"

"Forever."

Mrs. Fairfield worked her way over to Betty once the fireman left. "You did it."

Betty didn't speak but nodded her head as if in agreement. "It was the proper thing," she said at last.

We left Cumberland as the firemen mopped up the charred remains and smoking ash. As we drove back through the forest I kept wondering if that had been Betty's plan all along, crafting a ritualistic end to their father's reign. There was no bowl of stew in the car, I realized. She had purposefully left it back at the farm. It was a grand and perhaps diabolical scheme, but Betty had the sense to recognize that freedom would come only with staring down the devil, she and her sister together, refusing to turn away. That would destroy him. On that day Katherine showed me something about what a human being can endure, how one can rise up and reclaim one's power.

We returned to the farmhouse and drank coffee until midnight. There was not much to say after such a horrendous experience, other than gentle thoughts and reassurances. The children crept down the stairs and listened. Realizing the value of restoring truth, Betty allowed them to remain just long enough to hear the essence. Then Tom left, as he had an early shift in the morning, and Katherine went up to the sewing room. There was a sheet partition in the room, and I found a spot on the floor with a blanket and pillow.

In the middle of the night, I was awakened by a voice. Perhaps it was a dream? Then the voice spoke again, and again, before I realized that it was speaking to me.

"What is it?" I whispered.

"Hold me, Finn."

I stared up at the ceiling in the dark wondering if I had heard her properly. She said it one more time. I moved up to the narrow cot and under the blanket and held her, her back to me. She trembled and I pulled her closer, breathing in her hair. Her body shook as if from the cold. But it wasn't cold. It was the trauma leaving her, his wickedness loosening from her memories bit by bit. It would take time.

"Write about it," she said. "Don't spare him."

I didn't answer but held her until she finally fell asleep. I couldn't sleep, of course. My head was full of the day, that horrible day, and the profound sanctity of her body. I poured into her all the good that lived inside me, the work of some benevolent force— God, perhaps, or even my dear mother. I had no such knowledge, but something else had occurred out of the old man's madness, out of the fire of purification. A correction in a bankrupt world.

The old man died the next day. Betty arranged that he be buried with his legacy made public for all to see, although she was certain there would be few mourners. She instructed the funeral parlour that his epitaph be a summation of his wasted life.

A LOVELESS MAN IS BURIED HERE
ALBERT KROM
1883–1963

30

I had come to the last pages of my book, the more poignant details of my life, but wanted a fitting end. I saw no need to write about Cumberland in detail, bringing life back to the heinous, what the old man did to his own daughter. I didn't know and would not create a fiction in its place. It would only add to the horror of it needlessly and irreverently. I would write as Katherine had asked me—*spare him not*. And as I searched for a concluding passage, I couldn't stop thinking about that time with her. I couldn't help myself.

The drive back had been mostly in silence. Her gaze was constant on the passing scene, the woods and the towns along the seamless highway of reflection. Driving did that, of course, the perfect time for sorting out earlier days, as if they could be sorted out. The mind will drift back to those moments, unfinished and unresolved, and attempt to make right, to place in an order that can be lived with, even understood. I wasn't sure if that was what she was doing, but I hadn't sensed unease, or even a dark mood. Both would be reasonable states, all things considered. She would tousle her hair with a finger now and then, twirl it unconsciously. She smoked but not incessantly. She had no questions for me, no idle chatter. I didn't want to spoil her meditation, so drove on with a certain repose.

It hadn't escaped me, how similar our lives were, our haunting pasts, our fears, what we did to survive. Strategies to keep an unsafe world at bay. It was not an uncommon story in a human life, but it was ours. She came to see me, and we talked about what came next. She said that I needed to leave the cabin. We had come so far—astonishing, really. I thought that Ted would have been pleased that two people could find a common wish for happiness, having known its absence for so long. In the end, I wanted to convey in words an act of grace that at one time seemed unlikely if not implausible. And how fitting that it was Bishop who delivered it to me as a rare and humbling gift.

One morning after our return to Spencerwood, I was awakened by a knock on the door of my cabin. I got out of bed and looked out the window. Bishop was blowing into his cupped hands. It was cold; a white rime of frost covered the lawns. I let him in.

"Bishop, you're up early, don't you think?"

"We've got work to do my friend," he said. "Besides, it's nearly noon."

"Can't it wait? The sun's still below the trees."

"It's winter. Come on, I'll fill you in on the way."

"On the way?"

"We're going to get a tree."

"A tree?"

"Yes, and it has to be a big one. It's going in the living room. I would say about ten feet should do it. And a fine shape to it."

"A Christmas tree?"

"Very good. Get dressed." He went back out the door.

I got dressed and grabbed a swede saw from my truck, then hurried after Bishop, who was waving me on. I caught up to him. "Well, fill me in."

"All I know is that she wants certain things."

"Who?"

"Lady—correction, Mrs. Spencer."

"Katherine."

"You may have been elevated in her esteem, but she must remain as my employer."

"She's my employer, too."

"Finn," Bishop said, stopping all at once. "She told Birdie and me a little about your trip to Cumberland. What you did. I will admit that I wasn't sold on your idea. But you went ahead and did it anyway. Proud wouldn't be the right word." He continued on toward the woodlot.

We walked into the woods, the sun throwing its rays through the limbs and thickets. There was a nursery of Douglas fir and we soon found one that fit Bishop's requirements for height and symmetry. I cut it down and we dragged it out of the woodlot to the edge of the estate lawn. And keeping with our rituals, we took time out for a smoke. I noticed that Bishop kept looking toward the manor, then at his watch. It was rather odd.

"Tell me about the 'certain' things she wants," I said.

"She asked me to do something a few days ago," he said. "I wasn't too keen on the idea. I thought that she should do it. But you know, she was giving me another chance. She really was. So I called Betty Lantz. I introduced myself and apologized for my behaviour, which had been unpalatable, to her as well as myself. She is a very understanding woman, I must say."

"So?"

"She's coming for Christmas. And Mrs. Spencer's been shopping, Finn. I mean *shopping*."

"The whole family's coming?"

"Yes, the whole family, and Tom Lantz. You know who he is. She should be here any time now. I wanted to time it just right. I told her to come around to the back of the manor. I wanted to witness it. And I wanted you with me. I wanted it to be a surprise. It's your Christmas present."

"That's awfully nice of you, Bishop, but why from back here?"

"I don't know. I like to see things from afar sometimes. Isabel will be coming later, and Phillipa and Tiffany. I'm happy to get close with family. But with Betty, I cannot underestimate what it's going to mean to her, and to Mrs. Spencer. I wanted to share it with you. The looks on the faces of the children. Such moments have a potency unmeasurable to the mind. It goes far beyond that. Birdie will tell me about it all over again, and it will take on something new. It will forever be the moment of transformation. Alchemy, the ancients called it."

We waited and smoked and talked about the smell of wood-smoke, the way it clings to the limbs of trees like angel hair, and the smell of the freshly cut tree. Then we both saw it at the same time, the old Pontiac coming around the back of the manor. It still seemed a little unbelievable, yet so right and proper. Betty got out of the car and hurried to the kitchen door, and Birdie was there to greet her. Soon Katherine was in Betty's arms, and then the children, all five, and finally Tom Lantz. The milling around the kitchen door was like a restorative dance.

And as I looked on as witness with Bishop, I wanted to see his face. I turned to him and our eyes met. He had that look of satisfaction. A fisherman's pleasure. I had seen that look on the Cowichan River as he stood solidly in the current. Oh, the mystery of rivers and the life beating beneath clear water. He just looked at me now, nodding that old head of his. I simply nodded back to him. I wasn't sure what event had caused such a profound shift at Spencerwood in just a few short months, where it all began. It may have been that day in Ottawa after all, when two police officers waited for me with their accusations, or perhaps the day I survived the fiery water when a torpedo sank my ship on the Gulf of St. Lawrence, or maybe it was stealing Mad McGee's apples in old Ireland, or farther back still when my dear mother shamed me in the mirror. It was only her fears. I knew that now.

And those moments in my life had only been my experiences. How can one point to every grain of sand under one's feet? One cannot, of course, because life can never be reduced to a single thing. And I was certain that Bishop was thinking just that. But the more I looked at him standing so grand, it occurred to me that he had taken me on. He had seen something salvageable in me, something worth saving. He had picked me up and dusted me off more than once, then always pointed the way. It was Bishop, every man's conscience, a friend, and a man to love like a father, who demonstrated what a father could be and should be. He did it without knowing that he did, and that made all the difference.

Author's Afterword

The following points are intended to provide a historical foundation for the people and places that inform Finn Kenny's story.

THE FRUIT MACHINE: A device employed by the Canadian government during the 1950s and 1960s to identify suspected LGBTQ+ employees, predominantly gay men, in public service. It was part of a campaign to eliminate gay men from government jobs, including the RCMP and the Canadian military. During the Cold War officials feared that LGBTQ+ employees would be at risk of blackmail by Russian operatives seeking government secrets; the government fired the identified employees from their jobs to reduce its risk. The machine, targeted at men, was coupled with a camera that measured pupillary response of subjects when presented with pornographic photographs of men and women. It had been determined that the eyes would dilate in response to the level of interest in the photograph. The subjects had been previously told that the purpose of the test was to measure rates of stress. The practice ended in 1967 although the actions of government's discriminatory policies against LGBTQ+ people continued into the early 1990s. The careers of more than nine thousand people were affected by the purge. On November 28, 2017 Canadian Prime Minister Justin Trudeau delivered a formal apology in the House of Commons for the historical policies and practices of the Government of Canada that led to the oppression of and discrimination against LGBTQ+ people in Canada. *The Fruit Machine* is a 2018 Canadian documentary film directed by Sarah Fodey.

SYLVIA ESTES STARK: An African American pioneer who was one of more than six hundred Black Americans who emigrated to the newly formed Colony of British Columbia in 1858 at the invitation of Governor James Douglas. After a brief stay in Saanich, Sylvia Stark, her husband Louis, and two small children were among the original settlers on Salt Spring Island, where they cleared land and farmed. She died in 1944 at the age of 105 years old. She is buried at Pioneer Cemetery, Ganges, Salt Spring Island, British Columbia.

EMILY STARK: The eldest daughter of Sylvia and Louis Stark, she was four years old when she arrived on Salt Spring Island with her family in 1860. The family moved to Cedar, BC (near Nanaimo), in 1873. After a few years her mother returned to Salt Spring Island. Emily stayed with her father and completed high school in Nanaimo. In 1874, at the age of eighteen, Emily was hired to teach in a one-room school in Cedar, becoming the first Black teacher on Vancouver Island.

EMMITT HOLMES: A British Columbia trade unionist during the 1950s, a Black activist, and a baseball player, Holmes infused his trade unionism with Black activism in Vancouver for decades. According to the BC Labour Heritage Centre, he was an IWA delegate to the Vancouver Labour Council who became chair of the Joint Labour Committee to combat racial discrimination. He held this role for fourteen years.

KUPER ISLAND: The Kuper Island Indian Residential School was a Canadian residential school located on Kuper Island, now known as Penelakut Island, near Chemainus, Vancouver Island,

British Columbia. Run by the Roman Catholic Church, the school operated from 1889 to 1975. A poll in 1896 found that 107 of the 264 students who attended the school had died. The school building was demolished in the 1980s.

Acknowledgements

It is important to recognize that this story takes place on the unceded Coast Salish traditional lands of the Cowichan Tribes, Snuneymuxw First Nation, Nanoose First Nation, Qualicum First Nation, and K'omoks First Nation.

I would like to thank the staff at NeWest Press: Matt Bowes for his trust in me, Claire Kelly for her diligence and spirit that makes the publishing process a joy, Meredith Thompson and Carolina Ortiz for their enthusiasm and clear attention to schedule and process, Leslie Vermeer for her support and unfailing editing precision, and finally, the NeWest board who believed in my story.

I would like to thank my readers of the original manuscript, Victor Seder and Rick Tough, for their friendship, enthusiasm, and constant support. I would like to thank Mitch McLellan, Rick Hansen, Ron Smith, and Kerry Grozier, for their support and enduring friendship. I especially wish to thank my family, Rod Neil, Kathy Parrish, Scott Neil, Mark Neil, Kathy Jameson-Neil, Casey Stepaniuk, and Jesse Stepaniuk, for holding up my world.

I am also indebted to my wife, Kathy Jameson-Neil, for helping me conceive this story and develop the complex character of Katherine, Lady Spencer, the driving force of the book. She is a character we may despise, but who ultimately needs to be understood. Fiction can accommodate a character's flaws and can strive to help us make sense of their world. The bad can be redeemed. But in real life, the star burned out; there was no character arc, no satisfying ending, only the irreconcilable flash of her life. I was gifted with insights, personal accounts of an excessive and bigger-than-life personality. I am grateful for the inspiration, the courageous examination, and humbled to have informed my fiction with empathy and veracity.

The title of the novel, *The Sum of One Man's Pleasure*, was developed from Roderick Haig-Brown's classic book *A River Never Sleeps*. Haig-Brown wrote of the pleasure of being present with a river and its seasonal complexity, the pleasures of companionship, fishing alone, patience, and the heavy water of November. I have a personal collection of Haig-Brown's books, and his writing is one of my greatest influences. Chapters 7 and 8 are my tribute to Roderick Haig-Brown. I wanted to create a mood along the Cowichan River, wanted readers to smell the dank earthy woods, hear the rush of fast water, and see the flash of bright fish. I wanted readers to feel Bishop's pleasure as he fished, and to know Finn Kenny's reverence as their own.

Danial Neil was born in New Westminster, British Columbia and grew up in North Delta. He began writing in his teens, journaling and writing poetry. He made a decision to be a writer in 1986 and took his first creative writing course in Langley with *Alive magazine* editor Rhody Lake. Danial worked steadily at his craft. His short story "Grace" was published in the 2003 Federation of BC Writers anthology edited by Susan Musgrave. He went on to participate in the Write Stretch Program with the Federation of BC Writers teaching free-verse poetry to children through the Delta Schoolboard. He won the poetry prize at the Surrey International Writers' Conference four times and studied Creative Writing at UBC. His poetry and fiction articulate a close relationship with the land, its felt presence in his narrative and vision. He has written twenty-two novels since beginning his writing journey. He is the author of *The Killing Jars* (Trafford 2006), *Flight of the Dragonfly* (Borealis Press 2009), *My June* (Ronsdale Press 2014), *The Trees of Calan Gray* (Oolichan Books 2015), *Dominion of Mercy* (NeWest Press 2021). *The Sum of One Man's Pleasure* is Danial's sixth published novel. In addition to having his novels celebrated for their wonderfully crafted characters, he was a contributor to poetry anthology *Worth More Standing* published by Caitlin Press in 2022. Danial lives in Nanaimo on Vancouver Island, British Columbia, Canada.